WAKING NED

FOX SEARCHLIGHT PICTURES and TOMBOY FILMS PRESENT IN ASSOCIATION WITH THE GRUBER BROTHERS MAINSTREAM SA BONAPARTE FILMS, LTD. THE ISLE OF MAN FILM COMMISSION and OVERSEAS FILMGROUP WITH THE PARTICIPATION OF CANAL+ IAN BANNEN, DAVID KELLY, FIONNULA FLANAGAN 'WAKING NED' WITH SUSAN LYNCH and JAMES NESBITT

CO-EXECUTIVE PRODUCER STEPHEN MARGOLIS
ASSOCIATE PRODUCER MIARA MARTELL
CASTING ROS AND JOHN HUBBARD
PRODUCTION DESIGNER JOHN EBDEN
EDITOR ALAN STRACHAN
COMPOSER SHAUN DAVEY
CO-PRODUCER NEIL PEPLOW
DIRECTOR OF PHOTOGRAPHY HENRY BRAHAM
EXECUTIVE PRODUCER ALEXANDRE HEYLEN
PRODUCERS GLYNIS MURRAY and RICHARD HOLMES
WRITTEN AND DIRECTED BY KIRK JONES

Wendy Holden is a journalist and author of ten
books to date. She lives in Suffolk with her
husband and two dogs.

For Sue, sister and soul-mate

WAKING NED

Wendy Holden

Based on the screenplay by
Kirk Jones

HarperCollins*Entertainment*
An Imprint of HarperCollins*Publishers*

HarperCollins*Entertainment*
An imprint of HarperCollins*Publishers*
77–85 Fulham Palace Road,
Hammersmith, London W6 8JB
www.fireandwater.com

Published by HarperCollins*Entertainment* 1999
1 3 5 7 9 8 6 4 2

Cover art and photographs courtesy of Fox Searchlight

The author and publishers are grateful to A. P. Watt Ltd on behalf of
Michael B. Yeats for permission to reproduce copyright material from
'He Wishes for the Cloths of Heaven' and 'The Second Coming', and to
the actors for permission to reproduce photographic images. Every effort
has been made to obtain permissions where appropriate.

Wendy Holden asserts the moral right to
be identified as the author of this work.

This novel is entirely a work of fiction. The names,
characters and incidents portrayed in it are the work of the
author's imagination. Any resemblance to actual persons,
living or dead, events or localities is entirely coincidental.

A catalogue record for this book is available from the British Library

ISBN 0 00 653151 2

Set in Sabon by Mick Sanders
Printed and bound in Great Britain by
Caledonian International Book Manufacturing Ltd, Glasgow

Chapter
One

*May you have the luck of the salmon – may
your current be ever swift, your belly ever full
and your lips ever wet.*

– Irish toast

Jackie O'Shea sat stock still in his battered brown-striped armchair, transfixed by the flickering images on the television screen a few feet in front of him. The room was lit by a single small lamp and was cosy, with brown and gold sixties-style geometrical patterned wallpaper, and a few pieces of well-worn furniture with soft cushions scattered around. Sixty-two years old, a great bear of a man with a shock of silver hair and a fleshy, rounded face lined from years of toiling in the fields around his coastal farm in all weathers, Jackie lifted his empty dinner tray off his lap and carefully placed it on the small table by his armchair, never once taking his eyes off the screen as the programme he had been waiting for – the live draw of the national lottery, from the RTE television studios in Montrose, Dublin – began.

It would have been of little interest to Jackie to know that in sixty-three countries around the world, millions of people prepare themselves similarly for a weekly event which had also become an integral part of their lives. Dozens of lottery machines spin hundreds of lottery balls day in, day out, as anxious ticket holders watch and wait. An event which is generally over in minutes – it takes seconds for the numbers to be selected, seconds for the losers to realise that they have lost – but for the winners it is an event which will undoubtedly change their lives for ever.

Jackie O'Shea was a man among millions, a man who shared the hopes of so many around the globe, who allowed themselves to be intoxicated for a brief moment by the excitement, the drama and the pure escapism. It was a little bit of magic, a chance to fantasise about one day waking up rich. But as Jackie sat in his own living room on the west coast of Ireland, listening to the familiar theme tune and watching the opening credits, he could also allow himself to feel that this was strictly personal – between him and Fate – and if he happened to defy the overwhelming odds and become a winner then in just a few seconds all his wildest dreams could be realised.

Through a doorway behind him, sitting at a kitchen table reading a magazine under the overhead light and finishing her own supper was Annie, his wife of thirty-three years. Oblivious to the shivers running up and down her husband's spine, she read her horoscope and absent-mindedly spooned another mouthful of dessert into her mouth.

On the television screen, the cameras closed in on dozens of brightly coloured, numbered balls sitting one above the other in the seven vertical rows of the lottery numbers selector machine. The veteran commentator, Ronan Collins, accompanied by the ubiquitous independent observer, was welcoming viewers and reiterating the rules of the game. A later round-up programme would, Collins said, give the jackpot amount. True to Irish style, there was no glitz or glamour, the show would be over almost as soon as it began – three minutes precisely – with none of the nonsense of celebrity guests or interviews with past winners. It was just as well, because one minute longer and Jackie O'Shea could not have lived through the tension.

'If you can match six numbers on the one line in any order you could win or share in tonight's jackpot which, as always, is tax free,' Ronan Collins was saying, as Jackie's grip tightened on the arm of his chair. The shiny patina on the threadbare patch beneath his hand bore testimony to the years of slapping and hammering its owner had given it as he eulogised to the long-suffering Annie on some major national issue or other, ever the one to rant and rave about matters which were absolutely none of his business.

His ancient television set was of the same era and just as abused. One of the first colour sets ever to be sold in western Ireland in the late sixties, it was – for once – behaving itself. Its teak-effect veneer chassis bore the scars of many a battle with its impatient owner, after it had been battered and beaten, punched and kicked while the eighteen-inch screen had temperamentally flickered in and out of life in the last thirty years.

'Annie, where's me ticket?' Jackie called over his shoulder, not daring to take his eyes off the screen, as his wife carried on reading.

'In your trousers,' she replied, flatly. His ticket was always in the back pocket of his trousers and yet he always asked. For twelve years, ever since the National Lottery had first started in 1987, all activity in their tiny two-storey white stone farmhouse overlooking the rugged Seal Bay had ceased for three minutes twice weekly, on Wednesday and Saturday nights, at precisely eight o'clock. Meals had to be completed beforehand, guests kept away and all business suspended as

7

Jackie O'Shea eagerly awaited the news he was convinced would one day come – that he had won the jackpot.

He had, of course, decried the scheme at first as nothing less than a 'descent into gambling and debauchery'; an immoral game 'devised by the devil himself to entrap good Catholics' (spitting at the mention of the word devil to avoid misfortune). But within a month, Annie had discovered his one pound lottery ticket secreted in the inside pocket of his Connemara cloth jacket. He had long ago given up the pretence of not agreeing with the game and – claiming that it at least did some good for charity – had since become its most avid fan, joining the sixty per cent of the three and a half million population of Ireland who played every week.

When the price of a ticket was increased to £1.50, Annie had not heard the end of it. Jackie poured forth for weeks about the outrageous increased cost and how unjustified it was that 'only' ninety-six new millionaires had been created in over a decade. Never mind the £700 million doled out to charities, or the seventeen thousand smaller winners each week. 'It's a scam, that's what it is,' Jackie would say indignantly. 'Rich city folk making money out of poor people's dreams.'

Yet still he played on, changing his numbers each week for a greater chance, buying his ticket from the tiny local post office at the last minute, precisely five o'clock – just as Mrs Kennedy was closing up. 'There's no point paying the buggers any earlier – they'll only earn interest on me money,' he would growl as he painstakingly selected his numbers and begrudgingly handed over his cash.

Humming softly to herself in the kitchen, and musing on her husband's many moods and eccentricities, Annie O'Shea couldn't help but smile. Younger than he, but just as silver-haired, wearing a soft red-brown woollen cardigan, white cotton top and skirt, her thick hair was feathered gently to the neck and casually swept back, setting off her high cheekbones and large blue eyes. At the age of fifty, she was still a striking looking woman. Glancing across at her husband's familiar profile in the living room, she sighed. That large nose, the proud chin, those steel grey eyes. His deeply lined jowls didn't disguise the face of the young man she had fallen in love with thirty-five years ago at the Tullymore Christmas *ceilidh*.

One of the many bachelor farmers who put on their Sunday best, complete with cloth cap and wellington boots, and came down from the hills to attend the regular village evenings of singing and dancing in an undisguised quest to find themselves a wife, he had twirled and spun her around the straw-strewn floor of the village barn that night until her head swam and her polka-dot skirt flared out at her waist.

As three stout musicians sat on stools with their fiddles, tin whistles, uillean pipes, accordions and drums, playing age-old Irish tunes and exile songs with a steady foot-tapping beat, she had felt the pounding in her heart and knew it wasn't just the rhythm of the ballads. Laughing louder than any man she had ever heard, his head thrown back, his eyes twinkling with mischief, Jackie O'Shea had captured her heart with his charm. He, in turn, had set his cap at the young Annie Daly and would not be diverted from his course.

It was the start of a clandestine courtship which was to last a full two years, during which Annie regularly rode pillion on the back of Jackie's pride and joy, his black 1959 Triumph Bonneville motorcycle, a wildly extravagant purchase brought with some of the money his father had left him when he died, along with his smallholding on the very edge of Tullymore. Clinging to Jackie round the twisting country boreens of the County More cliff tops, the wind in her chestnut hair, his leather jacket creaking under her grasp, the young Annie would press her face close into his back and tingle at the sheer bulk of the manly body next to hers. If only her father, Eamonn, would give his consent to their getting married, then she could stop resisting Jackie's advances and feel his bulk in a more intimate way, she daydreamed.

But her daddy was a righteous man, a fearless fisherman and a widower of ten years with nine children to care for. A devout Catholic, he repeatedly refused the boisterous suitor's pleas to marry Annie on the grounds that his youngest daughter could surely do better than an impecunious and Godless farmer with a flashy motorbike. It was only when Eamonn was swept overboard and lost for ever from his fishing trawler during a terrible February storm which claimed the lives of two others, that Annie was finally free.

She walked down the flag-stoned aisle of the little St Anthony's Church a month later on Jackie O'Shea's arm, carrying a posy of wild flowers and wearing a beaming smile. She had captured the man who had stolen her heart and was blissfully happy. But their marriage hadn't all been a bed of roses. Falling pregnant almost straight away, she had suffered two miscarriages before finally carrying a baby to full term. The child – Joseph, they christened him – was born dead, the umbilical cord wrapped tight around his neck. He was buried in the tiny windswept churchyard next to her father's grave. If Annie had been married to a lesser man, she would have lost her mind at the death of her infant. When Dr Moran told her she could bear no more children, she wanted to throw herself off the sheer cliffs of Killian Point, but gently, oh so gently, Jackie had brought her back, with his promises of the happy life they had yet to share, and the comfort they could find in each other.

Her grief had made her strong and, over the years, shy young Annie with the sad eyes had blossomed into feisty Annie, the resilient farmer's wife Jackie always knew she could be. It was a tough way of life and she bore up to it well; up at dawn with him to milk the cows; bringing in the sheep during the raging thunderstorms which threatened to blow them over the cliff, encouraging him when yet another crop failed in the howling gales. With their bittersweet banter and companionable silences, the couple had grown old together, devoted to each other during three decades of affectionate contentment.

Jackie's eyes could still light up in the same way as they had that first night they met, and each time they did, Annie's heart was lost to him once more. Watching him from the kitchen table now, she smiled as she saw his eyes sparkling at the television screen. He was like an excited little boy as he watched how, on the press of a button, the lottery balls dropped out of the selection machine and down the chute as if in slow motion. Entering the drum, they exploded into life, ricocheting and cracking into the glass case with a tremendous clatter. Spinning round and round, faster and faster, they mesmerised Jackie O'Shea, and he sat hypnotised in his armchair, his lips moving quickly and silently as he willed the numbered balls he had chosen to win for him tonight. It was the only time Annie ever saw him truly pray.

Never one to forget his food, even at such a crucial moment, and remembering her delicious pudding, Jackie called out to his wife from his armchair without even turning his head: 'Annie, bring me me apple tart, will you?' There was a familiar pleading tone in his voice.

Annie, who often berated her husband for his laziness around the home, knew that tone only too well. 'Fetch it yourself,' she called back defiantly, taking another mouthful herself and deliberately ignoring her husband's thick wedge of apple tart topped with custard sitting in a blue china dessert bowl in the middle of the kitchen table a few inches from her.

Jackie's lined face creased further with dismay. 'Annie,' he pleaded, pointing at the television screen, a pen in his hand, 'the Lotto's starting!' She knew that he was in a hurry and couldn't possibly leave his chair at such a moment; he had promised to meet Michael O'Sullivan, his childhood friend, at Fitzgerald's bar at a quarter past eight for a drink and he needed to line his stomach in preparation for a few pints of Guinness.

As Jackie watched and listened the presenter said: 'There's all your numbers – numbers one to forty-two, poised and ready over the draw drum. And we're ready now for a weekend Lotto. Now, we'll start the selection.' Jackie followed the first lottery ball as it dropped through the slot at the bottom of the chute and rolled satisfyingly along the rack at the base. His excitement started to build and he felt an even greater need for some warming pudding to fill his already ample girth. The presenter announced: 'And our first number is nineteen. Nineteen.' Jackie glanced at his ticket hastily and smiled.

'Oh yes,' he called animatedly, 'there she goes. Number nineteen.' Leaning the ticket on the arm of his chair, he duly ticked off the number with his pen. Talking back over his shoulder once more, he instructed: 'Annie, come in. Bring me me tart, we've got the first one.'

Still ignoring him and deeply engrossed in her magazine, Annie kicked off her shoes and toasted her feet by the little oil-burning stove to her left, on which she had cooked all their marital meals. It was as ancient and temperamental as the television set, second or even third-hand by the time it was shunted unceremoniously through the front door and into her home all those years ago, but she loved it all the same, especially as it had been an unexpected wedding present, wheeled in on a wooden cart by the big man who had made her his bride. It provided the only heating in their house, and even though it was August, the weather recently had been decidedly unseasonable with several inches of rain falling in between the brighter days, sudden cold spells at night and raging thunderstorms. She was glad for the little stove's warmth right now, as a chill wind was coming straight in off the sea.

Jackie's eyes flicked to his wife with irritation and then back to the screen as the second ball rolled down the chute. 'And the second number,' the presenter announced. 'It's number forty. Number forty.'

Jackie's expression was one of increasing vexation. 'Jeepers, Annie, will you believe it? – I've got the second,' he said, shaking the ticket in his hand as the presenter announced that the second ball was number forty. When his wife still failed to materialise at his side with the desired platter, his face fell.

'Our third number is number four,' the presenter announced, his smile fixed.

Jackie sat bolt upright in his seat and stared at the television in disbelief. 'Will you look at that, girl,' he called, as his wife – her spoon poised mid air – put it down at last and pulled herself up from the table.

'Here's our fourth number – seven!' the presenter called out.

Glancing round to check that he had her attention, Jackie allowed the pitch and volume of his voice to rise still further as he shouted: 'Can you believe it, Annie – number seven – will you come in out of that? We've got the first four!'

Her husband's plate of apple tart in one hand, Annie hurried into the sitting room, her eyes glued to the television screen. 'You're having me on,' she chided, standing beside him in the doorway, hardly daring to look.

Her husband flapped his hands at her, signalling her to hush and edged further and further forward in his seat. 'Now our fifth number,' Ronan was saying, 'is twenty-five. Twenty-five.'

Jackie thrust the ticket aloft and tapped at it speechlessly. 'Annie, we've got it!' he finally gasped.

13

His wife couldn't look, she was as transfixed as he was by the flickering screen and the dancing balls spinning wildly in the machine. 'Jesus, Jackie, that's five,' she said softly, her heart pounding in her chest. Jackie had only ever got three numbers and a bonus number in a row before, and had charged down to the village post office like a priest on a mission of mercy, banging on the door to raise Mrs Kennedy and get her to hand over his cash prize. He was crestfallen to discover that three numbers only netted him fifteen pounds; he had already spent thousands in his mind. He ranted for weeks afterwards about how unfair the system was, banging his armchair and complaining that the jackpot ought to have been shared more equally between the winners.

When he heard that old Mr O'Riley's nephew down in Cork had won £100 a week later by getting four numbers, just one more than him, he was apoplectic with rage. 'And he doesn't even go to Mass,' was how Jackie had concluded his tirade. And that, coming from a man who only went to church each Sunday because Annie dragged him there and to qualify for the free sip of communion wine.

Now, as Annie clutched the edge of the bowl with both hands and watched the shimmering television screen alongside her husband, she hardly dared breathe. As long as it was all just a fanciful dream, it was fine by her, but the idea of actually winning scared the living daylights out of her devout Catholic soul. It was a bit of fun, that's all it was, a fanciful dream. A chance to pretend for a minute what it would be like to have money, to joke about the gifts she would buy, the places she would go, the things she would do. She never really believed that it would come true, that they might actually win. What on earth would they do with the cash if they really won?

Jackie studied her aghast expression and murmured a prayer for them both: 'Oh God help us, God help us,' he whispered. Annie nodded with a gulp and silently made the sign of the cross.

'And now here's the sixth number – twenty-nine; that's twenty-nine,' Ronan Collins announced, his voice rising to a crescendo as a trumpet fanfare sounded. But his final words went unheard by Annie as her husband hunched his great body and thrust his arms upwards into the air, kicking his feet out as if they were dancing a merry jig.

'Yes! Yes! Yes!' he hissed triumphantly, his face florid, his eyes gleaming in the glow of the television.

Clasping her hand to her chest, for fear her heart would burst out of it, Annie watched in astonishment as, grinning from ear to ear, Jackie flapped the ticket at her meaningfully. His eyes streaming with tears of mirth and, in time to further cries of 'Yes! Yes! Yes!' he tore the ticket into three pieces and tossed them casually onto the carpet, before grabbing the bowl of apple tart from her trembling hand and settling back into his armchair.

Shakily standing over her husband, her mouth open in wonderment, her eyes wide, Annie looked down at him and asked, hoarsely, 'Have we won?'

Jackie looked up at her with a wicked smile, tears of laughter still in his eyes. 'No, but it got me apple tart brought in, now, didn't it?' he said, stuffing a spoonful into his mouth while he laughed.

Holding her breath for a moment, taking in what Jackie had done, how he had led her on and risked killing her stone dead with the shock, the colour flooded to Annie's cheeks. With a perfect trajectory, she slapped him full in the face before retreating to the kitchen in a great flurry of indignation. His cheek still smarting from the force of the blow, Jackie giggled like a naughty schoolboy, rocking himself backwards and forwards with glee, and crammed another huge spoonful of apple tart into his mouth.

It was rather less palatable humble, not apple, pie that Jackie O'Shea had to eat for the next forty-eight hours as his sharp-tongued wife punished him ruthlessly for the joke he had made at her expense. Between bursts of fiery temper, she maintained an atmosphere of stony silence in their home, setting him extra chores and calling in favours. Even a pretty bouquet of wild grasses picked from the moors failed to bring the smile back to her lovely face and all he saw of her was her stiffened back in their old wooden bed that night and the next.

It was only after a suspension of hostilities two mornings later, and with a mission in mind, Jackie felt confident enough to escape the house for a while. Wheeling his old Triumph motorbike out of the dilapidated cow shed adjacent to his farmhouse, he sat astride its lovingly polished chrome body and wished that women were as easy to handle. Adjusting his old-fashioned red helmet and fixing the broad leather strap beneath his chin, he placed his goggles over his eyes, zipped up his favourite brown and white striped anorak and kick-started the engine. Revving up, he sped off across the stone-flagged farmyard and headed along the coast road towards his regular rendezvous. Only on this morning, with the sun in his face and the summer breeze whipping around his brown trouser legs, there was a peculiar glint on his eye.

Heading out of Tullymore, past the village sign with the Gaelic spelling Tulaigh Mhór on it, past heather-coated cliffs that formed the edge of the rugged coastline, his trusty steed sped him past fields criss-crossed by dry stone walls, and through gorse hills which eventually gave way to wild mountains with great boulders tumbled about. He crossed a swollen river by a small stone humpbacked bridge. On a winding lane he passed a grotto hewn out of the rock in which a figure of the Virgin Mary stood vigil over a spluttering candle. The lane eventually carried him down from the

16

highlands towards a shallow cove lined with bracken, woodland and smaller granite rocks. The day was crisp and bright, the sea shone silver in the sunlight and the craggy Blue Stack Mountains in the distance formed a hazy purple backdrop.

Skidding to a halt at the end of a track leading to a shingle beach that marked the start of Glenskellig Bay, Jackie dismounted, tore off his helmet and immediately started to march across the pebbles towards the sparkling water, his feet making a crunching noise as he went. A few yards beyond him, sitting in the lee of a cradle of jagged dark rocks, his old friend Michael O'Sullivan was getting dressed after his regular morning swim.

Had he arrived five minutes earlier, he would have seen the sight that greeted him most mornings. Stark naked and splashing around in the water, Michael's skin was so startling translucent, his legs and arms so scrawny and bony that he looked like a skeleton under the water as he paddled awkwardly, trying to keep his head above the waves. A thin apology for a man, he had an impish face, with a long jaw, large nose and deep creases like ravines. He had lived his sixty-three years without so much as an inch of excess fat on him, unlike his childhood companion who – now running across the beach waving something at him – carried the profile of a man who regularly enjoyed a pie and a pint.

The two men had been coming to Glenskellig Bay for an early morning swim for as long as they could remember. In their youth, they had been joined by several from the village – Fergal, Cormac, Padraig, Niall and Dermot, now all long gone. There were girls too; Jessy, Michael's lovely sweetheart, Kitty Moore – always angling for a kiss, even then – and Annie and her three sisters. In the autumn months, when the people of the village were busy cutting peat and gathering the late heather all around the cove, the hidden beach had become a meeting place and a venue for happy family gatherings – but as the years had passed and most had died or moved away from the tiny rural community that was all these two men had ever known, they were the only ones left to tread the chill water when Annie cried off coming, claiming it did nothing for her health.

It was here that Jackie had first taught Michael – a fisherman's son who was afraid of the sea – how to swim; here that freckle-faced Padraig had informed them that he and his flame-haired brothers were – like so many before them – selling up and moving to Dublin to look for work. In the bay one freezing cold morning, Jackie had learned of Eamonn Daly's death in the great storm and knew that Annie would now be free; it was here that Michael came to be alone and shed his tears after Jessy, by then his wife of twenty years, died of cancer. It was at this sacred place that Jackie had finally proposed to Annie during a midnight skinny dip; and it was here now that he was about to tell his old friend something quite momentous.

'Michael!' Jackie called, his face even more animated than usual, 'Michael O'Sullivan! Are you a millionaire?' In his left hand he was waving a greasy piece of newspaper, crumpled and torn at the edges.

Michael glanced up at his friend bearing down on him and raised his bushy grey eyebrows to the heavens. 'Now, Jackie, would I spent me time sitting on this old beach if I was a millionaire?' he called back, pulling on his brown trousers and thin white cotton top after towelling out his grey hair.

Jackie nodded after a moment. 'And I believe you would,' he replied honestly, approaching briskly. 'Hold on there now, I've some mighty news.'

Michael lit a cigarette and puffed on it as he watched his old pal come skipping across the rocks towards him. There had been many a time in their sixty-year friendship when Michael thought Jackie quite mad with his antics and practical jokes, but ever since he had retired completely from the farm he seemed to have reverted to his childhood and Michael genuinely wondered if his friend was going crazy. There had been the fireworks incident last Guy Fawkes night, when he had tied some Chinese firecrackers to tin cans in old Lizzy Quinn's back yard and nearly killed her and her many cats stone dead with the shock. It was generally felt to be a pity he had not killed off the old witch. There was the time – before Annie – that he had disappeared for three days, claiming he was going across to Dublin to get a spare part for his motorbike, and had come home instead with a hangover he could have sold to science and wild stories of having got drunk with a girl in a pub in Temple Bar. Now, here he was, bearing down on Michael with what looked little more than a tatty old scrap of newspaper.

'Are you going in for a dip?' Michael asked, pulling on his shoes as his friend arrived breathlessly next to him. Michael couldn't see a towel and was surprised. He knew Jackie always loved a swim, especially on a glorious August morning like today.

'I've more important things to do,' Jackie said gleefully. Shaking out the folded newspaper, he cried, 'Now look and see what I found in the small print of *The Irish Times* last night.' He eyed Michael mischievously, before handing it to him. 'Look at it, the front page, down at the bottom, winking at you. Lotto results. Winner from County More West.' The last sentence was spoken with great aplomb, as if he were up on a stage announcing the name of the winner himself.

Michael drew on his cigarette and studied the newspaper cautiously, covered as it was in tomato ketchup stains, grease and vinegar from what looked like a recent encounter with a portion of fish and chips. With astute detective work, he surmised that Jackie and Annie must have had a row the previous evening – the only time Jackie ever parted with money for a meal was when Annie refused to cook him one – and he was far too mean to buy his own copy of the newspaper. Nonetheless, Michael was reasonably impressed with the news bulletin, although not as impressed as Jackie clearly expected him to be.

'A local winner, God, that's a thing,' he nodded in appreciation. There had been a woman from Ballyneath, their nearest big town, fifty miles away in the next county, who had won a few thousand once, but this sounded like it might be a much more substantial win. As far as Michael knew, there was a guaranteed jackpot of half a million pounds these days for anyone who got all six numbers in a row.

Jackie was far from finished. An impatient expression furrowing his brow, he knew he would have to spell it out to his less than quick-witted comrade. 'Jeepers, Michael, it's more than local!' he exclaimed, his eyes ablaze. Turning to the sea as if it was an auditorium, his arms outstretched, he added: 'County More West is big, but there's only one village in it.' He spoke the words with a slow deliberation, to give Michael the maximum time for the halfpenny to drop. The lottery terminals were few and far between in this part of southern Ireland – there had been none at all to start with – but finally their little village had qualified and the machine had arrived amid tremendous pomp and ceremony. It had even warranted a visit from a strikingly good-looking young woman, a lottery representative from Dublin.

Michael scratched his head for a moment as he allowed the information gradually to filter through. 'Tullymore?' he finally asked, his eyes like saucers.

'Tullymore!' Jackie echoed sarcastically.

'Is it a fact, Jackie?' Michael asked, his mouth agape as the implication of what Jackie was saying only just sinking in. It was not beyond the man to be 'taking the Michael' as he liked to call it. 'A winner in the village?' But Jackie was deadly serious and nodded, his eyes bright. Michael gasped at the idea of their tiny community, where everyone knew everybody else and had all grown old together, being affected by such a remarkable event. The winner had to be local. It was a rare day that there was a stranger in Tullymore; even the tourists avoided it because of the poor roads and the fact that on many maps it simply did not exist. The last outsiders to visit were an American couple called Quinn in July, who had come looking for the birthplace of their ancestors, only to be told that they were in the wrong place, the Quinns of Tullymore had all perished in a house fire in 1934. It was the Quins of Johnston Castle they wanted – a hundred miles further north.

'In Tullymore itself ... yes,' Jackie confirmed, still stunned himself by the twist of Fate that had selected someone from their midst as the recipient of what could be a prize jackpot worth several thousand pounds.

'And, er, how many are living there now?' Michael asked, his mind still working away furiously to take it in as he finished his cigarette and put on his jacket. In their childhood, there had been over three hundred souls in Tullymore, in the days when it boasted a church, three bars, five shops, a smithy, a weaving shed, a turner's workshop, a bank and a small tweed factory. That was before the advent of the television and the motor car killed the old Ireland that they knew. Now, in these days of high unemployment and a dwindling local population, the number was considerably less. Their small county was on the westernmost fringes of Europe, considered by the EC as a poor and distant relation. The young all whispered dreams of emigration and the old were left behind with only their memories. Tullymore was now a shadow of its former self; most of its amenities were

21

closed, the tweed mill had shut long ago and there was only one bar, Fitzgerald's.

Jackie had already done his homework on the demographics of the area and answered with the confidence of a man who knew exactly what he was talking about. 'Well, there's fifty-two precisely, Michael,' he said. It still seemed an awful high number to him, but not to Michael. Jackie wasn't finished: 'Now if you've not won, I've not won and Annie's not won, that leaves a total of – er – forty-nine.'

Michael was even more astounded. 'Jesus, forty-nine, and one is a winner!' He still couldn't quite believe it. A thought clouded his face. 'Has the news reached Tullymore?' he asked, ominously. His mind raced ahead of itself and flashed up an image of free drinks being served at Fitzgerald's as he spoke. He hoped to God he wasn't missing anything right now, but Jackie shook his head vehemently as the two of them picked up Michael's few belongings and headed back up the beach.

'Nobody's figured it out yet, so nobody knows but the winner.' Jackie grinned impishly, assured that he would have been amongst the first to know had the news got out. It was sheer luck that his fish supper had been wrapped in that particular page by young Mary at the mobile fish and chip van. He had nearly choked on a piece of cod when he lifted a chip and spotted the lottery announcement. Annie, who had been in the kitchen pretending to ignore his noisy, grumpy attack on his take-away supper, had to fetch him a glass of water and slap him heavily on the back before his lips turned blue.

'God, it's mighty, Jackie,' Michael acknowledged as the two men reached Jackie's motorbike. 'Does Annie know?'

Jackie smiled again, the smile of the righteous, as he put on his red helmet once more and handed Michael his white one. 'She does,' he said, with feeling, remembering the look of

22

astonishment and then forgiveness on his wife's face when he had finally got his breath back and read her the amazing news. 'She's looking for the winner now.'

All was quiet in Tullymore, but for a few dogs barking, a cockerel crowing and a distant female voice singing. The cluster of small whitewashed houses set awkwardly on the side of the hill comprised a few old stone buildings, including the village barn, some thatched cottages and several 150-year-old thick-walled bothies. They were surrounded by a handful of small farm buildings. There was one main street and a winding lane that curved lazily around the village before heading north to the hills and then east.

The tiny stone-built Tullymore post office which doubled as a newsagent and general store, selling everything from broom handles and fire grates to postcards, stamps and soda bread, was distinguishable only by the 150-year-old green-painted pillar box with its distinctive intertwined Queen Victoria insignia built into the wall outside. It was from within the cluttered building that Maeve Kennedy, the redoubtable postmistress, was singing.

Nobody knew how old Mrs Kennedy really was. If asked, she professed to be in her late forties, but most suspected she was nearer seventy. Skeletal of face, her huge eye sockets adorning sculptural cheekbones, she had dyed platinum blonde hair, so fine and straight that it had to be carefully combed to one side and lacquered into position each morning. Her only claim to fame was that – as Maeve Mahoney – she had once toured Ireland with a small theatrical company as an actress and singer, treading the boards and basking in the footlights for two years, before returning alone and quite unexpectedly to Tullymore, bearing the name 'Mrs Kennedy' and holding an infant daughter.

Having never lost her taste for the theatrical, she still maintained the air of a fading star, and had a wardrobe of unusually dramatic clothes and moth-eaten feather boas that she paraded through the village in every Sunday on her way to church. Her face was permanently plastered with makeup – thick streaks of beige foundation, bright blue eye shadow, black mascara and glossy crimson lipstick. Her vividly coloured clothes added to the false impression of youthfulness.

Dressed this morning in her purple floral polyester housecoat over a pink dress worn with red stiletto shoes, she tidied and restacked the little shelves piled high around her as her thin voice warbled an old nursery rhyme: 'When the first little bird comes knocking at the door, I'll send her away and ask for more. When the second little bird walks up my path, I'll bake her a pie with straw and grass. If a goose comes along to sing her song, I'll light a fire with a big pot on ...'

Annie O'Shea, her eyes sparkling, her hair freshly groomed, stood in the open doorway, watching and listening. 'Well, you're blessed with a grand voice, Mrs Kennedy,' she complimented warmly, before stepping inside.

Someone who normally had the hearing of a bat – an asset she used to great advantage when eavesdropping on conversations in her shop, before spreading the gossip around the whole village – Maeve Kennedy had simply not heard Annie creep in and was quite taken aback. Annie apologised for frightening her and wandered further into the shop, past the incongruously modern lottery terminal, which she tapped lightly with her fingers as she passed.

Positioning herself directly opposite the old woman and staring her straight in the eye, Annie, her face shining with expectation, told the postmistress that her song was just the sort of tune to sing when good news comes along. Mrs Kennedy sighed and smiled, a sparkle in her own eye. Suddenly, spontaneously, the two women broke into song together, to finish the song she had begun. 'But no one knew if it was true, if the goose always paid, with the eggs she'd laid.' Bonded in a moment of friendship, the two women, who had known each other most of their lives but who still always addressed each other formally, fell towards each other, laughing conspiratorially.

Three miles away, on the road from Glenskellig Bay, Jackie and Michael, both in large black motorbike goggles, sat one behind the other on the old Triumph as it flew along at breakneck speed. So accustomed were they to the breath-taking seascapes and stunning scenery that flew past them, so oblivious to the sweeping landscape which was all they had ever known, that they barely looked up from the road. Besides, they had other things on their minds. They were discussing their plan of action.

As always, it was up to Jackie to come up with an idea while, almost certainly, Michael would have to do the dirty work. A gentle, rather nervous character, with his own unique brand of dry humour, Michael had spent much of his life following Jackie O'Shea around like a devoted old dog. Different in so many ways, they were nonetheless like two sides of the same coin – Jackie tough and bossy, always up to some mischief; Michael timid and neurotic, acting as Jackie's conscience. Denied a childhood in a time when young boys barely went to school and took over from their fathers at an early age, now that they were moving into the twilight of their lives they seemed to be making up for lost time. They were two men who had grown old but who had never really grown up and – faced with the challenge of finding the Tullymore lottery winner before anyone else did – Jackie felt like a schoolboy on a treasure hunt. It was not a question of Who-dunnit, he told Michael (a man with a penchant for detective stories), but Who-wonnit.

'How long can a man sit on a fortune without spending a penny, Jackie?' Michael shouted over the driver's shoulder as he clung on for dear life.

'As long as he wants, Michael,' Jackie called back, laughing dementedly. 'But the longer it is sat on, the bigger our share.' Adjusting his goggles with a grin and tightening his grip, he accelerated away even faster, as Michael lurched backwards, nearly falling off. Shouting at the top of his voice, his expression delirious with exhilaration, he added: 'We find the winner and make sure we're their best friends when they cash the cheque.'

Chapter
Two

*We are all in the gutter, but some of us
are looking at the stars.*

– Oscar Wilde

Brendy Tooley was filling a large plastic bowl of water in the courtyard of the tatty workshop that bore his name. A modern-day blacksmith-cum-carpenter-cum-mechanic, Brendy had taken over from his father Kevin as a young boy and expanded the old smithy into catering to the needs of horse-powered vehicles as well as horse-drawn ones. Now, anyone with a car, bicycle, goat cart, pony trap, truck or motorbike came to him when things went wrong and expected him to fix it. His tools were simple and his knowledge limited, but his innate understanding of the mechanics of how something worked generally got him through and he could mend anything from a broken wheel spoke to a fuel-injection system – given a little time and a fair wind.

Fifty-five years old, a divorced father of two, it was the general consensus in Tullymore that Brendy had lived without a wife for far too long. Ever since Bridgid had walked out on him twelve years ago for a slick city bible-seller, his world had pretty much fallen apart. His garage was a scrap metal graveyard of old car parts and horse carts dating back scores of years, bowls of dirty oil and greasy rags littering the ground all around him and tyres and parts hanging haphazardly from the thick stone walls lining the narrow lane to his yard. An old home-made wooden trap, minus the pony, was parked on its end outside the garage, its wheel missing.

Brendy himself was a picture of dejection, dishevelment and disarray. He had largely lost the ability to smile and was generally as miserable as sin – that was, until it came to his daughter and grandson.

This morning, however, in his blue overalls spattered with the usual squirts of sump oil, diesel and brake fluid, and worn over his trousers, shirt and tie, his face showed no signs of cracking spontaneously into a grin. Tall and thin with a sprinkling of hair on the top of his balding pate, Brendy gave the appearance of someone with nothing to live for.

Maurice Tooley, Brendy's contemplative seven-year-old grandson, was playing with a piece of chalk that he had taken from his grandfather's tool box, and was using it to draw patterns on the blackened stone floor. Maurice spent most of his leisure time in his grandfather's garage, being baby-sat while his mother Maggie worked on her greetings cards messages – anything from confirmation cards to wedding congratulations – in the little room they shared above the workshop. Although Brendy liked to think that he was the chief breadwinner of the family, it was actually the small but steady income his daughter received from her commercial writing which kept the family in food and drink.

Brendy's youngest, Maggie's little sister Roisin, had left Tullymore ten years ago, running off to marry a Spanish sailor, and when Maggie had fallen pregnant out of wedlock eighteen months later, swearing never to name the father, Brendy had quelled his fury and resisted calls from some in the village to throw her onto the street, promising instead to care for her and the baby. After all, they were the only family he had left. Ever since then, Maggie had been in charge of all the domestic arrangements, feeding and clearing up after the two men in her life and trying to suppress her growing feelings of disappointment with her lot.

Spirited, passionate and just thirty-two, she had a mop of long curly black hair, big brown eyes and an attractive smile. Setting aside whatever dreams she may once have entertained, she had transformed her father's place from a veritable health hazard into a comfortable, if frugal, home, although she had long ago given up on trying to get him to clean up his workshop. In private, she daydreamed of the world outside Tullymore, reading her sister's postcards from foreign lands and wondering if she would ever venture beyond County More's wide boundaries or find true love and happiness.

As a teenage girl, she had been the sweetheart of the village and could have taken her pick of any young man. Donal Finn had been her first true love and they had frolicked together many a summer's night in the long grass behind his father's barn. In truth, she still loved him, but they had drifted apart in their twenties, after Finn followed his older brother Liam to Ballyneath to find work, and she was left alone and afraid. Her rosy red lips had not been kissed in over a year by the time Finn came back alone and broke. Finn could only find work as a swineherd and Maggie was repulsed by the smell. After a brief but unsatisfactory attempt to rekindle their passion, she finally sought solace in the arms of another man, a brief union from which baby Maurice had been the only consequence. Now she had learned her lesson and, although she still secretly loved Finn, she kept her distance from all the men of the village, although there were plenty who would have welcomed her warmly in their beds.

Turning off the tap, Brendy lifted the bowl of water and carried it over to where his grandson was playing on the floor, telling him to leave his drawing. Setting the bowl down next to the boy and reaching for the inflated inner tube of a tyre, he dipped it into the bowl of water to show his grandson how to check for a puncture. The boy was always interrupting, asking why this was so and what happened then, his strawberry blond hair falling over his eyes as he peered up at his grandfather with his latest question.

'There's a hole because it's punctured,' Brendy would say brusquely, in a tone that allowed for no further questions on the subject. But there was wonder in the boy's eyes and he would keep asking more. Brendy would sigh and speculate how long this incessant questioning of Maurice's was likely to continue. If he didn't know better, he might think the child was doing it on purpose, to test his patience. Secretly, he feared that the child really was as inquisitive and thoughtful as he seemed – a prospect that bothered him even more. Curiosity would get Maurice nowhere in Tullymore, Brendy felt. He should keep his nose out of other people's business and get on quietly with his own life. It would only cause trouble in the end; Brendy had learned that the hard way.

This particular morning, however, Maurice seemed to be paying heed to his grandfather and Brendy was glad to have his full attention at last. It was hard enough getting him to concentrate on anything remotely technical; Maurice seemed obsessed with thoughts of philosophical and religious matters that went way over the old man's head. He spent far too much time with that new young priest, Father Patrick – as he had with Father Mulligan before him – and Brendy had already warned Maggie to take the boy in hand. It was good to have the child finally taking an interest in something so mundane; after all, the garage would one day be his. But Brendy's pleasure was short-lived. A blast from a car horn made them both jump and look up as a shiny, red open-top sports car roared up the lane and slid to a halt outside the workshop. At the wheel of the brand new Mazda MX5 was Donal 'Pig' Finn, the thirty-three-year-old farm hand, now a swineherd – hence his new nickname – whose cap was still very firmly set at Maggie.

Looking as if he drove such a vehicle every day of his life, Finn brought it to a halt right by Maggie's front door. Brendy scowled; he knew Finn was there to show off and, hopefully, to catch a glimpse of his beloved girl. The ploy worked. Brendy's daughter, as startled as anyone else by the unfamiliar noise the car had made, threw open her bedroom window breathlessly, her long dark ringlets dishevelled but looking nothing less than an angel to the swineherd.

'Jesus, man!' she cried excitedly, 'where's it from?' She had never seen the like on the little cobbled streets of Tullymore before. Had he robbed a bank? The last time she'd seen anyone at the wheel of anything quite so fancy was when the mobile cinema came to town the previous summer and showed *Thelma and Louise*. Maurice had been completely bewitched by the film and had made her take him to see it five times. She herself had been unexpectedly moved by the free spirit of the two leading women characters, as they sped through America being chased by the police, and had survived for weeks afterwards feeding on the memory of their daring.

Finn, seeing the sparkle in Maggie's eyes, was delighted with the success of his little scheme. Looking up at her from the leather driving seat, he asked: 'Does it suit me, Maggie?' With his black hair long and scruffy, his face and sideburns unshaven and his eyebrows thick and dark, he looked completely out of place in the expensive sports car, dressed as he was in a denim jacket, jeans and dirty old T-shirt. But his expression, as always, was one of a devoted, if slightly over-exuberant, puppy, and Maggie couldn't resist.

'It does at that,' she admitted, seeing him, for a brief moment, in a completely different light. How lovely it would be if he were rich, she mused. Then he wouldn't have to work with pigs and she would be his.

His confidence boosted, Finn pulled himself up so that he was sitting atop the driver's seat and threw his arms open in a flamboyant gesture. 'Ah, will you marry me then?' he asked, his eyes ever hopeful. It was his tenth proposal in as many months and he already knew the answer off by heart.

Giggling uncontrollably and looking down at her father's stony face, his eyebrows raising to the heavens at the suggestion, Maggie cried: 'Oh, da!'

Seeing her laughing and knowing that he would once again get no firm reply from the woman of his dreams, Finn turned to her father. 'Brendy, can I marry your daughter now I'm drivin' a convertible?' he asked. He knew the garage owner didn't really approve of him and enjoyed pretending that a flashy car would make all the difference.

Treating the question with the contempt it deserved, and deeply sceptical of where the vehicle came from, Brendy remarked gruffly: 'It must be stolen, that?' as he walked slowly around the sports car, checking it over, running his hands down its polished steel bodywork, hoping to find fault.

Giving up on the older man, Finn turned his attention once more to Maggie. 'Come for a ride, like the old days?' he asked. His heart was in his mouth, awaiting her reply.

Maggie could think of nothing finer on such a marvellous day. She had spent the morning on bereavement cards, and was quite glum at the thought of several more hours of writing rhyming words of solemn condolence for the cheap black-edged cards that would be fronted by smudged photographs of drooping white lilies or leather bibles draped with rosary beads. An apologetic expression on her face, however, Maggie grimaced. 'Finn, darling,' she started, her tone soft, 'you know I would – if it wasn't for the smell of them pigs.'

He knew the answer already, it was the one she had been giving him ever since he had started working with old Tom Riley's swine after coming back, out of work, from Ballyneath. Long ago, when they were both much younger and there had been a spark between them, there had been some real flares of passion. In the few months before the village was stunned by her pregnancy, she and he had been courting, and he was convinced that young Maurice must be his, even though there was little family resemblance. Both Finn and Maggie had dark hair and eyes, while the boy looked to be of paler stock – probably a modern-day descendant of the Viking lords who once ruled the Celtic chieftains in their province.

Turning to the boy now, Finn tried a different tack. If only he could get Maggie to see how well he and Maurice got along, regardless of who the father really was, she might overcome her unreasonable objection to the smell of pigs and allow him to get close to her once more. 'What about me young man there,' he asked. 'Maurice, would you come for a ride in the racing car?'

The boy's eyes lit up. Looking to his grandfather, he asked: 'Grampy, can I go?'

'No,' snapped Brendy, shaking his head. He didn't even know where the car came from, and he wasn't going to let his only grandson be killed just because Pig Finn was trying to impress the boy's mother.

'Please?' the boy asked, but stopped when he got a glare from his grandfather that told him not to ask again. Maurice shrugged his shoulders at Finn helplessly and turned back to his chalk drawing. He didn't mind too much; he'd have secretly enjoyed the ride, but didn't like the smell of pigs either and no amount of wind blowing through a convertible sports car could disguise the fact that the farmer stank to high heavens.

Clearly disappointed, Finn slid back down into the driver's seat dejectedly and returned to his original reason for calling. 'Brendy, is me puncture mended?' he repeated, his face miserable. The previous day, he had blown a front tyre driving his old Bedford truck along a tractor-rutted track up on Killian Point and nearly gone over the edge of the cliff with his prize boar in the back. Bringing the vehicle to a juddering halt a few inches from the cliff edge as seagulls winged and called overhead, he had rested his head on the steering wheel and thanked Sweet Baby Jesus for his life. The sheer stone escarpments at Killian Point were over a hundred feet high in places and anyone unfortunate enough to fall over the edge would be smashed to smithereens on the jagged rocks below. The crashing waves and wheeling gulls would be the only witnesses to such a desolate and deadly end.

Eventually recovering his composure, Finn had limped his vehicle back into the village at a few miles per hour, and needed three stiff whiskies at Fitzgerald's before he had stopped shaking. Replacing the blown wheel only to discover the new tyre had a slow puncture, he had dropped it in to Brendy to fix it for him as a matter of emergency. He needed to get the boar to the market at Ballyneath the following day. But the dour-faced mechanic held up the inner tube from the water ominously. 'Come back tomorrow,' was all he said by way of apology.

Finn winked up at Maggie, pretending to be angry. 'I could have done it quicker meself.' Starting up the sports car after a last glance at Maggie's smiling face, he revved the engine and took off in the wrong gear, only to kangaroo-jump back down the lane, badly crunching the gears.

Holding the inner tube so firmly under the water that it looked as if he was strangling it with his bare hands, Brendy watched him go and muttered under his breath.

Later that evening, as the sun dipped down behind the grey-green hill known locally as the Old Man of Cragimore, where Bronze Age pilgrims had worshipped at ancient rings of stone, soft lights glowed in the windows of the houses of Tullymore and trails of yellow peat smoke wafted into the darkening sky behind the chimneys. At the O'Shea farm-house, set in a small courtyard overlooking the sea, a dim light shone in the kitchen window, and a brighter one at an upstairs window. Raised voices could be heard.

Inside, Jackie O'Shea was soaking in the blue painted bath tub, soaping his body down. His hair was fully lathered, whipped up into soft peaks, and as he splashed around in the tub, hot soapy water was cascading over the side and drenching the pale grey shag pile carpet. Shouting out to his wife, who was downstairs at the kitchen table, her hands covered in flour, putting the finishing touches to a pie crust, he encouraged: 'Well, come on then?'

Annie, pricking the pastry lid between stirring something furiously at the stove, wiped her forehead with the back of her hand and shouted back: 'I'm not sure.' She didn't want to be pushed into speaking too soon; she needed to do more research and she knew that her husband would only jump to the wrong conclusions if she said anything now.

'So you think it's a woman?' Jackie called, egging her on. She had hinted as much when she was scrubbing his back a few minutes earlier.

Annie refused to rise to the bait. 'I'm just saying it might be,' she called, shaking her head in wonder at his tenacity. Placing the lid on the old black broth pot her grandmother had given her, she checked the bread baking in the oven and licked the spoon. Mussel soup with wheaten bread was the supper she was making that night. It was a local speciality made with the fresh mussels she had picked off the beach that morning on her daily walk along the thin strands of pale shingle, picking up her quarry watched by the waders dabbling at the edge of the breakers. There was something else going in the oven, something very special, and she didn't want to be distracted from her domestic tasks and have it spoiled by the rantings of her husband.

Sitting up in the bath tub, lathering his broad, hairy shoulders, Jackie O'Shea chuckled softly, and allowed himself a wry smile. 'If it's a woman, I'll chat her up and we'll be off before you know it,' he yelled. Annie stood stock still in her kitchen for a moment and wondered how far her husband really would go to get his hands on this lottery money. Ever since the game had started, he had been like a man obsessed. She had even asked Father Mulligan's advice about it at confession earlier in the year, but the priest had simply smiled and confided through the window of the ornately carved wooden confessional that he, too, was a weekly sinner. Now, here was her husband, living, breathing and eating the experience to the detriment of all else. It had been bad enough before he found out about the Tullymore win, but now that he had got it into his head to get his hands on some of the jackpot, he was possessed. The gentle opening and closing of the front door woke her from her reverie. She looked up nervously, wondering how much their unexpected visitor might have heard of her shouted conversation with Jackie, but she was relieved when a face she knew almost as well as her own peered shyly round the kitchen door at her. It was Michael O'Sullivan, the widower who had never really grown up, her husband's best friend and someone they had both known all their lives.

Annie smiled at the sight of him. She had always had a soft spot for Michael, from the earliest days. There was something very attractive about his unassuming air, the way he blushed coyly and tilted his head to one side. When Jessy had got sick with the cancer, Annie's heart had gone out to him and she had done all she could to help. Remembering her own loss, she had promised Jessy on her death bed that she would always look out for Michael, and make sure that Jackie didn't lead him astray. Michael, in turn, had leaned heavily on his best friend's wife for support in his grief, and was as devoted to her as any friend could be.

He entered the kitchen now, as sheepishly as usual from the hallway. Largely unfamiliar with the ways of women after years of living alone and always slightly uneasy in their company, even Annie's, he reminded her of a nervous schoolboy. But tonight there was something different about him; his eyes were bright and he seemed eager to speak. Finally unable to contain himself, he blurted: 'I'm bursting with news – I think I know who's won.'

Annie turned and stared at him in astonishment, her hands on her hips, an apron tied around her waist. 'That's mighty, for I've an idea I know meself,' she said with a grin.

Hearing voices murmuring somewhere deep within his house, Jackie sat upright in the bath, releasing yet another deluge of water, and called out to his wife impatiently: 'Annie, what's the noise?' He would hate to be missing something.

'It's Michael,' she replied with a yell, putting her pie deep in the bottom oven of the stove. Teasingly, she added: 'And he knows the winner.'

Pouring a jug full of water over his head to rinse off his hair, half-flooding the bathroom in consequence, Jackie was dripping wet but desperately eager to hear the news. Distracted from his bath, he stood up to dry himself off, towelling his body furiously. 'Well, come on, I want to hear it up here, so,' he shouted, as his wife and Michael – knowing full well what was expected of them – began to climb the stairs.

Leading the way up the narrow wooden staircase, a tea towel thrown over her shoulder, Annie called to her husband: 'Jesus, Jackie, do you think you're the Pope? Shouting out the bathroom window for the whole village to hear?'

Opening the door and walking in, Annie was met with the vision of her half-naked husband wrapped in a large towel and using the corners to dry his ears. She shook her head and waited for Michael to join her in the doorway. Hastily drying off his face, Jackie stood dripping, staring at the pair of them, and waited. When no revelations were forthcoming, he prompted angrily: 'Well, come on, out with it!'

Both apparently reluctant, Annie broke her silence first. 'It's Mrs Kennedy,' she announced triumphantly, relieved to be free of the burden of her news.

Michael's face was equally full of confidence. 'Oh, now,' he said buoyantly, 'I've got someone else.' This was like a proper detective story, he thought – piecing together the clues and all the evidence until the right suspect is found. He hadn't enjoyed himself so much in years.

As Jackie and his wife waited, Michael bit his tongue and bided his time to keep up the suspense. Annie couldn't wait and urged him on. 'Well, speak up man,' she said, her eyes narrowing.

Gulping hard, Michael announced: 'Pig Finn.'

Annie looked sceptical, but her husband was clearly completely unfazed by the discrepancy and delighted with their efforts. 'Huh! Will you look at that?' he cried, grinning from ear to ear, pleased with them both. 'Well, there's forty-nine possible winners and we're down to two already.'

An unexpected knock at the front door wiped the smile off his face and broke their euphoria. Jackie scowled and shouted: 'Go away out of that, we're in the bath,' angry at the interruption. The last thing he wanted at this momentous moment was to be buttonholed by some miserable farmer, moaning on about the weather or the prices at market.

A distant voice called up from the yard: 'Jackie, it's Finn. Are you up for a pint?' There was a pause, and then he added: 'I want to ask your advice on something.'

Startled and excited, Jackie leaned into his wife and best friend and whispered: 'He's after advice on his money.'

Both Annie and Michael agreed and nodded. Annie whispered back: 'Say you will.'

Shouting out of the window in a completely altered tone of voice, Jackie called: 'Aye, Finn, I'm up for a pint.' Inside the O'Shea bathroom, the three co-conspirators were frozen to the spot, waiting for him to respond or go on his way. Jackie looked helplessly at his wife. Michael did likewise.

The swineherd, dressed uncharacteristically smartly in a dark suit and tie, was taken aback by the instant acceptance. Shielding his eyes from the bright light of Jackie O'Shea's bathroom window, he thought about asking Jackie to get Annie's permission first, to avoid any arguments. He still remembered the night that Annie O'Shea had dragged her husband kicking and screaming from O'Malley's bar in the early days of their marriage when he had failed to come home for his supper for the second night running. Everybody liked Annie, but they knew she had her father's temper when riled, and Finn did not care to witness a repeat performance.

Prompted by Annie now, Jackie called: 'Finn, I'm just out of me bath. I'll see you in Fitzgerald's in ten minutes.'

Deciding to let sleeping dogs lie, Finn called out: 'Right,' and walked away without another word, scratching his head and hoping that Jackie and Annie were all right. As he sauntered off into town, Jackie rushed around the room searching for his trousers, the look of the demented in his eye.

* * *

Dennis Fitzgerald was the sixth generation of his family to run Fitzgerald's Bar in Tullymore's main street. It had first opened in 1837 as a shebeen, one of the hundreds of illegal drinking dens which had flourished under colonial rule and which disguised themselves primarily as shops, with drinking rooms hidden through a secret door behind the counter, known only to the locals. Its customers over the years had lived through the famine, eviction, abject poverty and two world wars. It was the only bar to have survived in Tullymore and that was largely due to the fact that it was still two businesses in one.

Half of the room was now occupied by an old wooden bar, complete with shiny brass beer pumps, bottles of spirits and well-worn bar stools; the other was set aside as a general repair shop and boot menders. Televisions, radios, hairdryers and kitchen appliances cluttered the sagging shelves, all covered in a thick layer of dust. Unclaimed boots, boxes of shoes and patched rubber wellingtons hung from rusty nails and the remaining shelves. The bar had entirely escaped modernisation, due in part to lack of funds, and was very much a practical place to go for the 'crack' – a bit of fun. In the main room, scrubbed wooden tables rested on a wooden floor and the room was heated by a large open fire, its neatly cut squares of turf burning merrily in the grate in the winter.

Dennis had initially fought against his natural destiny of becoming the landlord, by serving a three-year apprenticeship as a cashier in the local bank and then, when that closed down and the regional branch office transferred to Ballyneath, he decided to put his natural aptitude with his hands to good use and open up a small electrical repair store. With dwindling custom, however, and not enough income to pay the shop's rent, he had begrudgingly taken over from his father a year before the old man died, and had been behind the bar ever since, although he still dabbled in the mending business to help pay the bills. To differentiate between his two occupations and to let the people of Tullymore know which 'hat' he was wearing at any one time, he wore everyday clothes when he was pulling pints and slipped on a brown gabardine overall when he was doing repairs. Tonight, he was in a pair of corduroy trousers and a white and brown check shirt.

All was quiet as Jackie and Michael entered and looked around. The little bar with its low beamed ceiling and rendered walls looked cosy and snug in the soft lamplight. A darts board hung above the fireplace and, in the cramped space behind the bar, shelves groaned under the weight of whiskey bottles, cracked china measuring jugs and personally inscribed pint glasses.

Pat Mulligan, a slippery young farmer, was supping on a Guinness at the bar, an old timer was in the corner reading a newspaper, while Dennis was trying to mend an ancient Roberts radio, its many tiny components strewn across the bar. Pat was speaking in a half-whisper to Dennis about Finn. 'Yeah, I'd noticed a terrible stink on him lately.'

Looking up as the front door creaked open and shut, the landlord nodded a greeting: 'Evening Jackie, Michael.' Never one for many words, this giant of a man had the perfect physique for a publican – square shouldered, thick curly black hair, a great block of a head sitting on a thick neck, brawny arms capable of lifting any drunk by the seat of his pants and kicking him out onto the street. But in the quiet fishing village that had always been his home, there was rarely any need for his muscle, and instead his huge hands tapped tiny nails into the soles of shoes, or delicately fiddled with pieces of wire as he mended the villagers' few domestic appliances.

Pat Mulligan also nodded a hello to the two men as they settled onto stools at the bar. 'Boys,' he acknowledged stiffly,

41

before returning to his solitary pint. Mulligan wasn't much liked in the village, he was far too full of himself for the older folk. He spent as much time as possible in the bars of Ballyneath and took himself across to Dublin once every three months or so for a weekend of debauchery in a favourite brothel he knew. Or so he said. Pat's father, Sean, had been much the same, a ladies' man who ended up a drunk and finally died of the whiskey. It was only out of courtesy to Pat's poor long-suffering mother, Bridie, that anyone was even courteous to the boy.

Extremely anxious by the apparent lack of Pig Finn anywhere in the smoke-stained room, Jackie asked Dennis if he was in. The big man nodded to the table by the fire. 'His glass is there, and himself is in the toilet.'

Enormously relieved, Jackie reached into his pocket for some change. 'Er, two pints for us and one for me old friend, Pig Finn,' he ordered, as Dennis's jaw almost fell open.

Almost as an afterthought, Michael added: 'Oh, and let me buy him a packet of his favourite Mexican crisps there as well, Dennis.' He liked being magnanimous; it felt different.

All in the bar were surprised by the unfamiliar generosity of the two old men, but the landlord quietly got on with pouring the thick black stout, knowing better than to open his mouth unnecessarily. The young farmer at the bar, however, had a habit of being unable to keep his shut. 'Your old friend?' he exclaimed, repeating Jackie's description of Finn. 'You must be needing an operation on your nose, Jackie. Have you smelt the pig lately?'

Bristling at the suggestion that he and dear Finn were not the very closest of bosom buddies and always had been, Jackie replied defensively: 'I have, and I'd say it was not half as bad as the smell of your aftershave.'

Smarting from his rebuff, Pat Mulligan, in white open-neck shirt and black jacket, his hair slicked back with Brylcreem, sniffed himself surreptitiously and bragged: 'Well, this aftershave is a knockout with the girls.'

Michael curled the corner of his mouth and asked sarcastically: 'And tell me, Pat, which particular girls are you knocking out at the moment?' Pat Mulligan glowered at the two old codgers and went back to his pint.

The knock at the front door of Mrs Kennedy's small stone cottage made her jump for the second time that day. Rising unsteadily to her feet, a half empty bottle of champagne in her hand, she opened her little front door to be faced with the smiling face of Annie O'Shea.

Glancing at the champagne and looking quickly away, Annie beamed a smile of utmost warmth and friendship at the older woman and spoke in her most reassuring tones. 'Well hello, Mrs Kennedy, don't be afraid,' she said. 'It's only meself ... I've been baking, and Jackie had no room for this.' In her hand she held something large and round under a gingham cloth which she pulled back to reveal a crusty pie, its deliciously meaty contents still steaming through the hole in the lid and scenting the air. 'So I thought we'd share it between us,' she added, coyly, knowing how much of a weakness Mrs Kennedy had for good shortcrust pastry.

Stumbling slightly, the postmistress – dressed in a psychedelic patterned dress – opened the door wider and waved her bottle of champagne wildly at the room, spilling a few drops on her carpet.

'Share your pie with me, Annie O'Shea, and I'll share a mighty secret with yourself.'

Annie O'Shea stepped quickly inside and closed the door behind her with a smile.

At Fitzgerald's bar, Jackie and Michael sat with a packet of tortilla chips next to Pig Finn's untouched half pint and waited for their Guinness to settle at the bar. It was ten to eight on the clock and they had been waiting three minutes. Dennis always said that a decent pint took at least five minutes to settle, its creamy contents swirling and blending together to create the bitter nectar. He often regaled the men in the bar with dreadful tales of pints poured in a matter of seconds in London pubs he had visited as a youth, and how he was kicked out for spitting the watered-down contents of his glass out on the carpet in disgust.

At that moment, Finn finally emerged from the lavatory, still buttoning up his flies, and walked over to his table. Michael nudged Jackie to warn him Finn was coming and the two of them smiled up at him expectantly. 'There's the man!' Michael called across the room.

'How are you, boys?' Finn replied, walking towards them, surprised at the warmth of greeting he was getting from his drinking companions.

'How are you?' Michael asked.

Finn grinned. 'I'm grand,' he replied.

Jackie sniggered conspiratorially. 'The old sparkle in your eye, eh?' he said and pointed to the vacant seat next to Michael.

Finn grinned again. 'Ah, you're a devil, Jackie,' he ribbed as he smiled at them and sat down. On cue, Dennis carefully carried three pints over from the bar, placing one next to Michael and two in front of Jackie as Finn picked up his original half pint.

'There we are, boys,' Dennis announced before walking rather reluctantly away. O'Shea was definitely up to something, or his name wasn't Fitzgerald, and he wondered what on earth it could be.

Jackie winked at his retreating back. 'Thank you, Dennis,' he said, making sure the barman was well out of earshot. Patting Finn on the back and ignoring the stench from his clothes, Jackie said warmly: 'Mud in your eye, eh?'

The pig farmer looked down at the two pints in front of Jackie O'Shea in astonishment. 'Jesus, Jackie, you must have a terrible thirst on you tonight,' he said. 'I've never seen a man drink two pints at the same time!'

With a nod and a wink, Jackie slid one over towards him and told him: 'Here, this is yours, Finn. I've bought you a pint, so.' He said it quite casually, as if it was something he did every day; but the pig farmer was almost speechless with surprise.

'You're joking me!' he said, concerned now.

'No,' Jackie replied, his expression one of indignation.

'You never bought me a pint!' Finn gasped, amazed at such a strange turn of events.

'Go away with you,' Jackie responded. 'I brought you home many a night.' Entertaining no further discussion on the subject, he sipped deeply from his beer, giving himself a white cream moustache.

Finn was even more taken aback when Michael pushed over the packet of tortilla chips and added, with feeling: 'And I bought you a packet of your favourite Mexican crisps.' His head was nodding like the toy dog in the back window of old Ma Hennessy's ancient Morris Minor.

Reaching into the pockets of his old woollen cardigan, Jackie pulled out some scented soaps in the shape of fruit his sister-in-law Roisin had once sent Annie from Paris, and which had been sitting untouched in a bowl on the windowsill of the bathroom ever since. He'd grabbed them as he was leaving earlier that night and considered them his trump card. Placing them carefully in front of Finn like a sacrificial offering, he said: 'Aye and no offence now, Finn, I bought you some expensive fruity soaps. Take them home and try them out.' He sniffed deeply on his own fingers after handling them and pulled a face that suggested they were just the thing to keep Maggie Tooley happy.

Pig Finn stared down at the soaps and the pint and the Tortilla chips with a frown and then looked up at the two men with a puzzled expression on his face. 'Ah, boys, what are you up to?' he asked, deeply suspicious.

Jackie shrugged his shoulders and tried to look as innocent as possible. 'Nothing. Can I not buy you a pint?' he asked, attempting to look hurt. Michael nodded so hard in agreement that Finn thought his head might fall off.

The young farm-hand was highly cautious. In all his life, Jackie O'Shea had never bought him a pint. In fact, all his life, he had never seen him buy anyone other than his old friend Michael a pint – and then only grudgingly. Leaning forward, he whispered: 'Did you come into some money, Jackie?'

Michael threw his head back and laughed at the ridiculousness of the suggestion and Jackie shook his head, although he was delighted that the question had been asked. Patting the table firmly, he leaned towards him and replied with a twinkle of his eye: 'No. But you'd be the first to share in it if I had, Finn.'

Three hours later, back at the O'Shea farmhouse, Jackie lay naked in bed, more than a little tipsy, and watched as his wife Annie crept into the room, kicked off her shoes and started to undress. He had been home some time and she had been nowhere to be found. He had eaten his soup and cold meat supper alone and wondered where on earth she had got to.

Now, here she was, trying to keep quiet because she thought he was asleep, but staggering around the room and bouncing off the walls and furniture like a pinball. 'Where have you been, woman?' he groaned as she tried to take off her skirt without falling over. 'I've been in bed an hour!' His outburst made her sigh. Burping slightly with chronic indigestion, she told him to shut up. Rolling over to get a better look at her through his half-closed eyes, Jackie announced indignantly: 'You're drunk!'

Slipping into her blue chiffon night-dress and switching off the bathroom light, Annie countered with equal indignation: 'I am not!' Wanting to change the subject as her head span, she asked her husband: 'What's the news?'

Jackie's face fell at the memory of his disastrous evening in the bar and he slumped back on the pillows, his own head thumping. 'I spent ten pounds on Finn and all he wanted was some advice on his sick pigs.'

'Is the sports car his?' Annie asked, sliding into bed next to her husband.

'Not at all. He's looking after it for his brother,' he moaned, adding dolefully: 'Then I spent another forty on the locals, in case the winner was hidden among them.'

Annie raised her eyes to the heavens and tutted out loud as she puffed up her pillows. 'You're acting like you've won the lotto yourself.'

'Aye, yeah, Rockefeller, that's me,' Jackie joked.

Recalling the events of her own evening, Annie leaned on her elbow and told him: 'I followed me nose to Mrs Kennedy's, and I took a meat pie to soften her up.' Ignoring his mounting excitement as he urged her to go on, she added: 'I found her on her own, drinking champagne.'

Opening his eyes wider, Jackie had a triumphant expression on his face. 'It's her then!' he cried. Champagne was an extremely rare commodity in Tullymore and nobody drank it unless they had something pretty mighty to celebrate. He'd pay the postmistress a call first thing in the morning with a bunch of heather and offer her the benefit of his sound financial advice.

Seeing his mind racing ahead of himself, Annie stalled him: 'Hold on,' she said glumly, patting his arm to hold him back. 'No sooner was my meat pie in her belly than she tells me that

47

her daughter's belly's filled up with a new baby. That's why she was singing the golden goose. Sure, she's over the moon!' Her expression was one of deep dismay.

Falling back on his pillows in despair, Jackie clasped his head in his hands. 'Lord, would you look at that! We're already fifty pounds and one meat pie lighter.' Reaching over to switch off the light, he closed his eyes and tried to get to sleep.

Chapter
Three

If we command our wealth,
we shall be rich and free:
If our wealth commands us,
we are poor indeed.

– Edmund Burke

Dennis Fitzgerald was not having a good morning. Not only did he have an almighty hangover from the previous evening's celebrations, courtesy of Jackie O'Shea – although neither he nor any of his unsuspecting fellow drinkers had a clue what they had been celebrating – but Lizzy Quinn had called at his bar to collect something that she had put in for repair.

A miserable old woman with a fearsome temper and an acid tongue, Ms Quinn was the spinster of the parish and a skinflint. Regarded locally as an antagonistic old witch, she had spent her life carping and griping at all around her and no amount of pleading or bargaining or flattering could induce a better frame of mind. Orphaned as a toddler by the influenza epidemic of 1927, put to work in the local priest's house to pay for her keep, she grew up bitter and twisted at the unexpected loss of her parents and siblings, with not a single good word to say to or about anybody. It had been a terrible thing that had happened to her, no one could deny, but in a remote and gale-lashed region of Ireland in the 1920s, where death and disease had been commonplace – with fishermen lost at sea, women dying in childbirth, and infants stillborn – there was hardly anyone untouched by tragedy, and yet each made the most of it. Not, however, Lizzy Quinn.

By the time she was eighteen and legally old enough to make her own decisions, she had fled from the kind priest's care to Drumdolan Cove on the fringes of the village, moving back into the derelict and draughty red brick house once owned by her father, where she had lived alone ever since. A more inhospitable house did not exist in County More, situated as it was behind a high wrought iron gate, down a forbidding tree-lined grass drive. Local children believed the house was haunted and a few of the adults did too. The garden was so overgrown that it shrouded much of the house, and spiders spun the only curtains in most of the windows. Huge yew trees, their branches like long gnarled green fingers, scratched and scraped at the walls. Many of the windows were shuttered, cobwebs hung round the arched stone porch, and the wind made strange noises whistling through the roof slates at night.

It suited the old woman well. Few dared venture down the spooky drive to see her, and those that did only caught the sharp edge of her tongue.

In 1987, when she was well into middle age and more embittered still, a wealthy great uncle from Belfast died and left her all his money, but she had never once shared her good fortune with her fellow villagers and remained locked away in her spartan home alone. Her only extravagance was reluctantly to pay towards the cost of a disabled electric buggy, which she used to get down into the village. The three-wheeled machine, complete with turquoise velour seat, had been provided largely at the expense of the diocese on her insistence, and with the hesitant endorsement of Dr Moran – browbeaten into backing up her claims of chronic arthritis.

With only her dozen cats for company, she ventured into the village as little as possible during the sixty-odd years she had lived at Drumdolan Cove and had little contact with her neighbours. The children of Tullymore – and occasionally a few irresponsible adults – often made sport of her spectacular gruffness, playing practical jokes on her, placing obstacles in the path of her whining buggy when she came trundling down the street. Having heaved a boulder or log in her path, they would hide and watch as the old woman, seeing that it was impossible to get past, would rant and rave and manoeuvre her buggy jerkily around the obstacle. Having run the usual gauntlet of jibes and laughter from the village children that morning, she was in an even more foul mood than usual as she made a beeline for Fitzgerald's to collect her burnt-out toaster.

The pain in his head still pounding in his ears despite the three aspirin he had already taken that morning, Dennis tried his best to keep a clear head as he stood in the low doorway of his bar in his brown overalls listening to Ms Quinn berating him for the nominal two pound fee he had asked for repairing her toaster yet again. She had bought the blue-painted item from him eleven years earlier when he was still running his electrical shop and she had come into her inheritance. It had been one of the few personal treats she had allowed herself with all that money. Since then, the machine had been in for repair more times than he had had hot dinners – initially under guarantee and then, for some time, under the imaginary guarantee she insisted it should still be entitled to.

Five years on, after she had let the toast burn for the umpteenth time by having the setting up too high yet again,

Dennis had insisted that any future repairs had to be paid for, and his declaration had started a never-ending war of wit and words that he was far from up to this morning. 'You're not getting your toaster, Lizzy, and let that be an end to it!' he shouted, riled that she should be causing him so much grief on such a morning.

'I'm an old disabled person with no money, Fitzgerald, and you're taking advantage,' Lizzy squawked from under the grey rain bonnet she lived and slept in, her expression thunderous as she refused, once more, to pay.

Dennis Fitzgerald sighed and looked disdainfully at the sour-faced old bat in her tired red anorak and black woollen scarf, sitting at the wheel of her buggy. He had long ago given up all attempts to be reasonable. 'Your toaster is mended, but you can't take it until you've paid for it,' he said, defiantly clutching it to his side in the crook of his right arm.

Scowling furiously, the old woman shouted: 'You're ripping me off, Fitzgerald!' hammering her fist on the button on the handlebars that made the buggy move backwards with a judder. It was an insult he was well used to and one which, he knew, signalled the end of this particular hostile engagement. He hoped she would allow him a day or two to recover before the next barrage. As she turned her machine jerkily in the cobbled lane outside the bar, allowing its irksome whine to further aggravate his headache, she looked daggers at Dennis Fitzgerald. She had never liked the man, or anyone from his family. When she came into her uncle's money, Dennis was still working in the bank, and she always suspected him of being the one who leaked the news of her inheritance to the rest of the village. How else would they have known? Certainly not from her extravagance.

Now that he was the landlord of the only bar in Tullymore, he still had a lot to answer for, in her opinion. It was when they spilled out of his bar late at nights that the men of the village would sometimes make a special drunken journey to her house simply to rattle on her windows or tease her beloved cats. And if Dennis hadn't persuaded her into buying the wretched toaster in the first place, she would never have had all these problems. It was clearly his responsibility from the start.

Rubbing his already overheated temples with the palms of his hands, Dennis Fitzgerald refused to let her have the last word. 'And I'm fed up with you taking without paying, woman,' he called after her. She owed him at least ten pounds for previous repairs and he no longer worked in a bank, as he had pointed out to her many times before. This little business was his livelihood.

Her back to him now, her buggy trundling down the narrow cobbled lane as fast as it could go, she almost ran over Jackie O'Shea and Michael O'Sullivan as they rounded the corner and inadvertently walked directly into her path. 'Get out of my way!' she yelled, hooting the irritating little horn on the front handlebars of her buggy. Jackie did a little dance in front of her and laughed, before doing as he was told. Yelling over her shoulder at a laughing Michael, she called: 'You're a little gob shite!' – her final words on the matter.

Still clutching the toaster to him like a comforter, Dennis watched as the buggy headed off back up the lane with steam still coming from Lizzy Quinn's ears. It looked like she was headed for the post office. Poor Mrs Kennedy, Dennis thought. He felt like ringing her to warn her what was coming her way. But his mind was diverted from that duty by the arrival of Jackie and Michael. Pulling himself up to his full height and pretending that he was completely unaffected by the six Guinnesses and three whiskey chasers he had foolishly sunk the previous night, Dennis moulded his face into a smile and asked cheerily: 'Morning boys, how's the heads?'

Jackie, paler than usual and a little dark round the eyes, smiled but gave up any similar pretence. 'Oh Lord, we were heavy drunk last night,' he moaned. The expression on Michael's face told a similar story.

'The whole bar was heavy drunk, thanks to you,' Dennis reminded him. It was his best takings in a long while – and Jackie O'Shea had even settled his account, something he had once thought was as unlikely an event as Lizzy Quinn coughing up for the toaster. Leaning forward to speak privately to the retired farmer, Dennis said: 'Listen, there's a rumour that you've come into some money, huh? What? Eh?' His eyes were wide with anticipation.

Jackie O'Shea rocked back on his heels, hands in his pockets and chortled aloud. Michael, silent until now, giggled at his side. Shaking his head sorrowfully, Jackie bemoaned: 'Oh, Janey Mac, I wish I had.' It still hurt to think of the cash he'd wasted and the meat pie gone and he was still no nearer to finding the winner. Composing himself at the sight of Dennis's disappointed face, he added, in a well-rehearsed speech: 'No, no, you know. I was just treating me friends with the little I've got.'

When that still failed to bring a smile to the landlord's ashen features, Jackie spoke the words he had rarely, if ever, spoken to the man before. Clearing his throat and keen to make the right impression in case Dennis was the secret jackpot winner, he said: 'I came over this morning to make sure I'd settled up for those last few rounds.' Slapping Dennis playfully on the chest, he added: 'I'd hate to be owing you anything, you know?'

Dennis blushed visibly at the offer. He was still overwhelmed by the forty pounds the farmer had already put in the till for him. Patting Jackie on the back, he grinned and said: 'Ah, go on, on you go. Good luck.'

It was twenty minutes past ten in the morning before Annie O'Shea, nursing her own hangover, eventually emerged from the bedroom in her cardigan and night-dress to see what all the noise was about downstairs. She didn't care how much champagne cost, she reasoned with herself, give her a glass of milk stout any day. Shuffling into the kitchen in her slippers, she half-nodded at Michael and Jackie, who bid her good morning.

Holding her head as still as she could as she took the kettle to the old enamelled butler sink to fill it with water, Annie grimaced. 'That Mrs Kennedy is a fine one for the champagne,' she said, her voice weary. 'I thought it would be you boys who would have the heads this morning, not me.' She put the kettle on the stove and leaned against it for support.

Michael flashed her a shy grin, unaccustomed to seeing her only partially clothed. Jackie, sitting at the green painted kitchen table between them, writing something onto pieces of carefully cut up card, beamed up at her. 'We *do* have heads,' he admitted, 'and they *are* sore, but at the same time, filled with the very best of Irish brains.' As he spoke, Michael reached into a sack, and pulled out six fresh, unplucked white chickens, laying them on the kitchen table one by one in an untidy heap of wings, beaks and feet.

While Michael picked up the last bird by its horny yellow feet and held it aloft for critical examination, Annie, hand on her hip, standing behind her husband, asked with a nauseous sneer: 'And will those dead chickens find the winner?' She couldn't imagine what the boys were up to, but she sensed that she wasn't going to like it.

Her husband lifted his face to hers and she recognised the sparkle in his eyes. Unless she was very much mistaken, that look meant mischief and trouble, in that order. 'They will, they will,' was all he said, chuckling in a manner that implied a great deal more. She leaned over his shoulder to see what he was writing.

It was left for Michael to explain as Jackie scribbled away.

'Jackie talked Mrs Kennedy into giving us a list of the regular Lotto players,' he said gleefully, clearly delighted at his friend's master stroke.

Jackie nodded, his countenance triumphant. 'There's eighteen,' he cried, unable to contain his excitement. 'And each of those'll be invited to a chicken supper. We'll sit them down, feed them up, and during the night ... we find the winner.' Evidently delighted with his ruse, which had instantly reduced their target group by two thirds, he had crowed to Michael he was that sharp, he was in danger of cutting himself.

There was no time to waste, Jackie told Michael. The invitations must be delivered immediately. The chicken supper would take place the following night, Wednesday, at eight o'clock. 'But, Jackie,' Annie had reasoned. 'You'll miss the Wednesday night lottery draw if you have it at eight o'clock.' She could hardly believe that he would countenance such an intrusion on his twice-weekly ritual. His response made her feel even more under the weather than she had when she had first got up and been sick. 'Never mind all that!' he had snapped. 'This is far more important.'

Sending his underling out to do his dirty work, Jackie stayed at home to gloat on his own brilliance, telling Annie how he had duped Mrs Kennedy into giving him the names. 'It was sheer genius!' he bragged, pacing up and down in the kitchen and doing a little dance. 'I told her that I needed the names because I had been asked by my cousin Colm to undertake a little local market research on lottery players for his company in County Wexford. She always had a soft spot for Colm, if you remember, and she handed them straight over without even giving it a second thought – especially when I took her a dozen fresh eggs.' Annie cupped her hands around her hot mug of tea and sipped on it gingerly. She had to admit, he was a cunning old fox.

Michael set about delivering his hand-written invitations to a fine supper at the O'Shea household the following night. Taking his job very seriously and clutching the invitations close to his chest for fear they should fall into enemy hands, Jackie hurried around the village to complete his task. One by one, the little white cards were carefully posted through the assorted letterboxes belonging to Pig Finn, Dennis Fitzgerald, Pat Mulligan, Brendy and Maggie Tooley, and the other suspects on the list.

With only a couple of invitations left to deliver, Michael arrived at the grey pebble-dashed cottage of Kitty Moore. He dropped the invitation through the door and tried to creep away unnoticed. But Kitty's well-coiffeured head was out of her bedroom window before he could take more than two steps towards freedom.

'Yoo hoo!' she called out, a vision in a pink blouse and skirt, covered by a pink apron, all complemented by pink lipstick. 'It's not me Christmas card already, is it, Michael?' Silver-haired, with a pretty face, she beamed him her most seductive smile, her pearl earrings dangling.

Michael stopped and turned, smiling up at the oversexed sixty-five-year-old widow who had been teasing him for years. 'Christmas has come early this year, Kitty,' he smiled shyly.

'Oh, how exciting,' Kitty squealed, delighted to see him at her door. Beckoning him closer with perfectly manicured fingernails, she said: 'Come in, Michael, come in – I've been baking.' The quickest way to a man's heart was always through his stomach, she had come to learn, and she had been unsuccessfully trying to woo Michael O'Sullivan with her delicious barm brack ever since his Jessy passed away. A doughy, fruity bread normally only made at Easter and Halloween, it always concealed a small brass ring, hidden in the middle each time she made it, in the hope that Michael would get the message when he found it and marry her by the following year, as Gaelic tradition dictated.

Ever since her beloved Niall died of a heart attack in her arms in bed (some say she wore him out) eight years before, she had survived financially by taking in sewing and making home furnishings which her daughter sold in her shop in Dingle. But it was a struggle and, quite apart from the money, she longed for a man in her life again. Michael was the most eligible widower in the village. Kind, gentle, with a tiny but comfortable crofter's cottage and a small pension from the fisheries company he had worked for until he retired, she firmly believed that he was her best chance of happiness.

Michael stayed rooted to the spot. 'Oh, it's tempting, Kitty, but I've more cards to deliver,' he said, patting the ones still held firmly in his hand. Much as he found Kitty quite attractive, with her elegant clothes and pretty eyes, and as much as he missed the company of a woman, she frightened the living daylights out of him. It had been far too long now for him to embark on any passionate affair; and besides, he wasn't even sure he could remember what to do.

Leaning further forward out of the window, Kitty made one final attempt to lure him inside. Gesturing to the card he had just posted through her letterbox, she purred: 'Is it a little love note, Michael?' But by the time she looked up again, Michael was long gone, scurrying off down her path in a little jig with a hand half-heartedly waving, ignoring her calls at his heels.

Jackie O'Shea had graciously condescended to deliver a few of the invitations to his chicken supper, and the first on his list was an old fishing cottage situated on an isolated cove, just over the hill from Tullymore. Whistling as he strolled along the steep cliff path, Jackie's heart was filled with joy as he soaked up the bright sunshine. It was a golden morning. Wood pigeons cooed and a mule could be heard braying far away. Bounding down the meadow came a huge hare, red-brown in hue and covering vast distances leaping on its great long legs.

Rounding the headland as Ned Devine's little whitewashed cottage came into view, Jackie started down the lane which wound to the house. Nearing the cottage, he saw the old fisherman's hand-sewn fishing nets drying on special stakes out the back and his grey cat, Gnasher, mouse-hunting under an outbuilding. He laughed at the old man's threadbare pink undergarments flapping on a washing line in the sea breeze.

Ned was a good sort, although a man who kept himself to himself. With his distinctive blond hair and sea-green eyes, he had the look of a Nordic about him. A confirmed bachelor, he had lived in the tiny cottage owned by his father before him, each generation eking a living from the sea, and supplementing their income from the land around the cove by cutting the turf from ancient family sites. They worked all summer long out in their boats catching what fish the seals and dolphins had left them, and then – when the seas were too rough – they would spend the days using special spades called sleans to dig in and lift out the peat in thick square clumps. There was a special art to cutting each piece the same size and it came from years of backbreaking practice.

Ned's bothy had originally been two cottages and had walls three feet thick which kept it cool in summer and warm in winter. Buffeted as it was by the wind and the rain on its desolate spot surrounded by brooding mountains, it needed every inch of the wattle and daub that held it together, and the green grass that sprouted from its neglected thatched roof. There was many a night that Jackie, Michael and Ned had sat around the blazing turf fire with a tot or two of whiskey or a glassful of the illegal potheen. Ned was a keeper of Tullymore's age-old stories – horrific tales of fishermen's ghosts rising from their graves on foggy nights, and salty superstitions from the times when his ancestors went out in curraghs and the hookers or turf boats flew in and out of the main harbour at Tullymore on wind-filled sails.

Ned was also the owner of the finest ballad voice in Tullymore, and when he opened his mouth to sing, the spirit of the Gaels rose up into the air and gladdened every heart. Annie always said that he sang as if he had spent his entire life standing on the deck of his battered old boat, communing with the waves and serenading the mermaids.

With just his cat for company, Ned was nonetheless a man who did not like to be disturbed uninvited. He was probably sitting at his kitchen table now, dressed in his spare pair of long johns, eating lumpy porridge and contemplating the day over a mug of milky tea. Keen not to arouse his ire and perhaps risk his refusal of the chicken supper, Jackie quietly pushed the invitation under the door and crept away.

Pig Finn was having a good day. Having fed and mucked out the pigs, he had cleaned himself up and called round to see Maggie, only to be told she was up at Craigarron Woods on her own. It was a place they had often gone when they were courting and he hoped to catch her in their favourite spot now. Rounding the top of a small copse, he looked down and smiled. There she was, the girl of his dreams, reclining in the crook of an ash tree, writing some lines of poetry into an exercise book.

Strolling down the hill towards her, his hands stuffed deep inside the pockets of his denim jacket, he remembered the many picnics they had enjoyed in this wooded glade. With Doheny Bay glinting through the trees in the distance, and the water babbling over the peaty brown rocks in the adjacent brook, they would sit and eat a lunch fine enough for an Irish President. There would be ham sandwiches and cooked sausages, hunks of crusty white bread, local cheeses and a delicious mackerel pâté made by his sister. They would wash it down with some cider and crunch through fresh red apples for dessert. Sated, they would fall back on the soft woodland floor and make love for hours, before falling asleep, their naked bodies intertwined in the bracken. When they finally, reluctantly got up to go, Maggie's long black hair would be covered in leaves and twigs, her lips red raw from kissing and her cheeks flushed.

Today reminded him of those golden days. The brilliant summer sunshine illuminated the coastal scenery like a manuscript, picking out all the greens and golds and blues vividly. Maggie looked up from her notepad, breathed in deeply and comforted herself with the fact that even if she had never yet seen the lands beyond Tullymore, she was lucky enough to have this to be going along with for the time being.

Startled from her thoughts by the sound of someone approaching, she turned to see Finn smiling down at her from the top of a hill. 'What are you up to?' he called, making his way down towards her. He looked scrubbed clean underneath his T-shirt and mottled green camouflage trousers.

'Been writing,' she called back up at him.

Coming still closer, leaping a small brook and sitting a few feet above her on a tussock, his face lit with a smile, Finn asked: 'Ah, Maggie, will you read me some of your poetry?'

Maggie threw back her head and laughed. He saw the curve of her neck above her low-cut floral T-shirt, and was momentarily dazzled by the whiteness of her breast in the sunlight. 'Jesus, Finn, that's not poetry,' she said. 'It's just – words for a greetings card. There's a big difference.'

Finn sighed the sigh of a man with a Byronic spirit. 'Ah, it's poetry to me,' he said, smiling.

Maggie, ever the cynic, spelled it out for him. 'My cards are bought by men on their way home from work, who give them to their wives who give them a bollocking for leaving the price on the back – and they never even read what I've written inside.'

'*I* read them,' Finn promised, his puppy dog eyes moist. 'Go on, Maggs, read us one.'

'No' she said, defensively burying her notebook in her jacket. She had always been quite coy about her work; the words seemed all right to her when she wrote them on the page, but if ever she had to read them out, or let someone she knew read them, they seemed corny. Brendy, her father, was the worst; she had long ago stopped reading them out to him for fear of his ridicule. He simply didn't understand – he could barely write, he had never bought a greetings card in his life and had no idea why anybody would want to. Only young Maurice really understood Maggie; she believed he truly had a poet's soul.

'Ah, will you go on now,' Finn asked, his tone softer as he reached the tree where she sat and leaned against it.

'I can't,' she said shyly.

'Make my heart sing,' Finn pleaded.

Looking suddenly bashful, Maggie smiled. 'No,' she protested, but her lips belied her words.

'Ah, go on, Maggs, just the one – just for me, please,' Finn asked again, his expression serious now.

Maggie looked up at him for a moment. 'Promise you won't laugh,' she pleaded, thinking of her father's reaction.

'I certainly will not,' he said most emphatically, hurt at the suggestion that he might even consider doing so.

Closing her eyes momentarily for courage and opening her book, she chewed on her pencil nervously before clearing her throat and starting to read. '"Sometimes ...",' she began, but then giggled and shook her head.

'No ... "*Sometimes*" is good,' Finn encouraged. '"*Sometimes*" ... it's a lovely start. Go on.'

Maggie stopped smiling and started to read slowly. As she spoke the words, her eyes left the page and she looked up into Finn's big brown eyes, reciting the words she had written to him from her heart. '"Sometimes – some things are special. Sometimes – someone is close. Sometimes – you feel that you'll never quite say, the somethings that matter the most."' Pausing, she gave him a look of such pure affection that he felt quite moved.

Finn beamed her a smile and clenched his fists in appreciation. 'That's poetry, Maggie. You've a real talent there.' He edged an inch closer, sliding down towards her.

Suddenly angry with herself for revealing her feelings, Maggie stood up, and snapped her notebook shut. 'It's bollocks, Finn,' she retorted, her eyes flashing. 'It's a bit of extra cash is all it is.' She knew exactly what she was, and Elizabeth Barrett Browning she was not. Although she may have had delusions of being a fine writer some day when she was younger, the cold harsh realities of life had taught her that such foolish schoolgirl dreams didn't pay for the food on her plate.

Creeping another inch closer, Finn stopped when he saw Maggie had spotted him nearing her and slipped round to the other side of the tree, teasing him. 'I've been using some fruity soaps, Maggie,' he reasoned, remembering with discomfort the itchy rash his skin had broken out in immediately after soaping himself down with Annie's peach-scented Savon de Paris.

It was worth every minute when Maggie softened and smiled. 'I've noticed,' she said, flirtatiously. Seeing the desperation in his eyes, she added cautiously: 'Well, come on then – let's get closer,' before ducking around to the other side of the tree.

Finn almost fell over himself as he jumped to his feet. 'Oh, yes please, Maggie,' he urged. Awkwardly, tentatively, he shuffled another few inches towards her, but she turned and ran, hopping across a babbling brook and up an incline, looking breathlessly across and down at him, still on his side of the divide.

'It's been a long time, hasn't it, Finn?' The fresh air was bringing the colour to her cheeks and a warm feeling in the pit of her stomach. How she longed for a man to hold her in his arms once more. How she wished it could be Finn. 'If it weren't for the pigs,' she added, 'we'd be settled by now.'

Finn stood in the long grass on his bank of the brook looking up at her. He closed his eyes and imagined burying his face in her black tresses. 'We might,' he said. In his fantasy he was already fumbling at the back of her dress, trying to unbutton her bra, then moving his hands round to cup her firm white breasts, his breathing starting to come harder and faster.

'The pigs is all, you know,' Maggie started to say as she, in turn, imagined his hands caressing her body and stroking her hair. She wanted nothing more than to be naked with him, rolling in the long grass, satisfying those hot pangs of desire that haunted her dreams and woke her in the night.

Finn desperately wanted to kiss the soft white flesh of her neck. 'Maggie, can we forget the pigs for the moment?' he urged, his arms open to her, ready to leap across the brook at her at any minute. It was doing nothing for his sexual fantasy.

Maggie grimaced. 'I know, Finn, I'm sorry. But if it weren't for the pigs, well then ...' Her voice trailed off as her would-be seducer looked her straight in the eyes.

'Oh, can we get – closer, Maggie?' he said, with meaning, his pupils dilated.

'We can,' Maggie conceded, '... but I can't wait for ever, is what I'm saying.' She edged a few feet towards him, carefully picking her way through the ferns and down the bank, as his eyes followed her every move.

'I know, darling, come on down,' he urged, wanting nothing more than to get her onto his side of the brook and pull her onto the soft bracken bed at their feet.

'Ah, Finn – I have missed you,' Maggie moaned as she turned to face him once more, just a few feet away across the water now. She still had the fondest memories of their sexual encounters all those years ago, before he started working with pigs. He had always been the most considerate of lovers, unlike some she knew.

'Come on, Maggie,' Finn urged.

'Here, you could work with my da,' Maggie argued, not even minding the thought of him coming to her bed covered in sump oil and diesel. Anything but the smell of pigs.

'Oh, he hates me,' Finn stated, truthfully. 'Come on, Maggie,' he begged, holding out his pink scrubbed hands, as she scurried closer, giggling like a schoolgirl. There was a new urgency in his voice as he willed her even closer.

'Well, in Fitzgerald's then?' Maggie pleaded, thinking how fine it would be to have her lover smelling of beer and pipe tobacco, anything but hog swill.

'He doesn't need anyone,' Finn muttered. 'Come on, girl.' His eyes implored her to jump across and into his arms.

'There must be something you're good at,' Maggie begged, just a foot or two from him now.

'Come here and I'll show you, girl,' Finn winked, a few inches away now, as she giggled. 'Come on, Maggie.' Whatever else he had been good at in his life, he knew he was more than satisfactory in the bedroom stakes. Maggie had been among several women who had told him so and he longed to prove it to her once more.

Laughingly taking a step back and running forward, Maggie launched herself across the brook and into Finn's arms, rocking him backwards and kicking her feet high into the air behind her. Throwing her arms around his neck, she closed her eyes and wanted nothing more than to allow her passions free rein. Finn, too, squeezed his eyes shut, for fear the moment would be lost if he opened them. But, even while they were closed, it was suddenly and violently pulled away from him.

Maggie's top lip curled. 'I caught a whiff of something then,' she said, warily. Her nose wrinkled with disgust. She started to remove herself from his embrace.

Finn let out a laugh which bordered on the hysterical, his hand fondly brushing back a lock of hair from her face. 'Oh, no. It's peaches ... peach soaps, Maggie.'

Maggie shook her head vehemently and sniffed the air. 'No, it's something else.' Each shake of her head pulled her a few centimetres further away from him.

'Could be strawberries?' he suggested in desperation. Burying his head in her neck, he whispered: 'Maggie, Maggie.'

But Maggie had other things on her mind. Even though she let out a small cry of: 'Oh, Finn,' as he nuzzled sensuously in her hair, her nose was twitching and sniffing the air like a rabbit all the while.

'Oh, Maggie,' Finn moaned, his passion aroused, as he kissed her throat.

'Finn,' Maggie murmured, her head thrown back and her eyes closed once more. But, in an instant, her head had jerked forwards again and she was distracted from their imminent moment of passion by the unmistakable scent of pigs. Dismay written all over her face as she recognised and finally identified the scent which repulsed her, her final verdict came with the south-easterly wind that whipped up suddenly around them and left him downwind. 'Oh no, I'm sorry love, it's still there,' she said, freeing herself from his grip.

He'd seen that look before and he knew it heralded the

cruel shattering of all his hopes. 'No, Maggs, no Maggie, please, no,' he implored, holding his hands up defensively, willing her to reconsider. He had spent over an hour in the bath, scrubbing and scraping, topping up the hot water by manoeuvring the taps with his toes. He had used two whole bars of the fancy French soap, then topped it up with deodorant, aftershave and strawberry-scented talcum powder. He couldn't possibly still smell. Could he?

'No, no. I'm sorry,' Maggie said, finally, firmly, as she swallowed and tried hard to overcome the repulsion she felt. Hurrying away up the hill, looking back on his disappointed face with an apologetic shrug, she was gone.

Finn sat down hard on the ground, his dreams in tatters once more. She might as well have stabbed him in the heart and left him in the woods to bleed to death.

Back in Tullymore, young Father Patrick O'Riley, the temporary priest-in-charge, wearing his black robe and white dog collar, sat on the stool in front of the little church organ and allowed his fingers to run idly over the keys. Sitting at his side in a green anorak was young Maurice Tooley, recently a regular visitor to the grey stone St Anthony's Church, and the only person in the village who had been genuinely friendly to him since he arrived.

Father Patrick had found the boy outside, hanging around, and as the stiff breeze whipped up from the bay and tugged at the cloth of his cassock, he had suggested to young Maurice that they move inside the church. Walking up the pathway between Catholic graves, ancient and modern, they pulled open the heavily studded oak door and slipped inside.

Accustoming their eyes to the half-light, they strolled companionably down the aisle between the gothic wooden pews and settled side by side on the organ stool. Built in 1840 of hard grey stone brought down from the headland when the former church's roof had caved in, the building was simple but finely crafted, with pale stained glass windows in hues of red and green, arched between elegant hand-carved wooden columns. The polished flagstone floor was cracked in several places and the ornately carved font was leaning precariously after some unexpected subsidence in the crypt, but the altar looked beautiful in the slanted shafts of sunlight, with its tall gilt candlesticks, and both their eyes came to rest on the large wooden statue of Jesus on the cross that adorned the middle of it.

'What can you play?' Maurice asked through the large gap in his front teeth, his freckled face pointed up to the young man next to him. They could have been brothers, they looked strangely alike, one only twenty years older than the other but with a face as fresh and mottled as the boy's.

'Oh, nothing really, I just like messing around,' the priest answered.

'Can you play songs about Jesus?' Maurice asked, his blue-green eyes pensive.

'No, I wish I could,' Father Patrick laughed.

Both of them studied the organ keys silently as the priest pressed them in turn, making gentle music in the big steel pipes somewhere high above them.

'So, did He come to you, then?' Maurice suddenly asked, his expression still thoughtful, as he examined the pained face of Christ at the altar beyond them.

'Who's that?' Father Patrick asked, although he suspected he knew.

'Jesus,' Maurice replied, nodding at the statue, the carved droplets of blood dripping realistically from the hands and feet.

'Oh, Jesus ... Well, He did in many ways, yes.' The young priest thought back to his own childhood, shy and lonely as an only child. He had sought solace early on in his local church, the one place he felt truly at home. When he had reached his teen years and the complex emotions of adolescence, he had prayed for strength at the little shrine to the Holy Virgin in his bedroom, invoking the saints nightly. By the time he was seventeen and alone, young Patrick knew that he had the calling.

'But, did you see Him?' Maurice asked, his forehead furrowed. The sputtering rows of votive candles flickering behind him gave the impression that he was wearing a halo.

'Well, not exactly, no.' Father Patrick tried to suppress a smile.

Maurice looked surprised and studied the profile of the man in black. 'But you're working for Him?' he asked incredulously.

'I am,' the priest concurred. 'Doing the best I can.'

There was a long silence between them.

'Do you get paid for it?' Maurice asked. His childhood had been dominated by talk of money – or the lack of it – and he knew whatever line of work he eventually went into, he would need to earn enough for his keep.

Thinking of the pitiful stipend Rome granted him in return for his devotional duties performed morning, noon and night, seven days a week, including a double shift on Sundays, the young priest winced. 'Well, it's more a payment of the, er, spiritual kind, Maurice,' he was forced to admit.

Unconvinced, the boy looked away. 'Oh, right,' he said.

Leaning towards him and speaking gently, Father Patrick asked: 'Do you think you could be drawn to the church, Maurice?' It was a thought that had crossed his mind more than once in these last few weeks, with the boy so much in evidence at the church.

The lad sneered and turned up his nose. 'I don't think so,' he replied, truthfully. He had clearly given it serious consideration.

Sad-eyed, the priest shrugged his shoulders. 'Well, you never know.' He hoped that Maurice might one day reconsider and he wanted to leave the door open for him to do so. There was another long pause as they both lost themselves in quiet contemplation.

Finally, after due thought, Maurice reasoned: 'I don't think I could work for someone I'd never met and not get paid for it.'

Stifling a laugh, the priest nodded his head in understanding. He couldn't help but admit it; the child had a point.

Chapter
Four

Of all the money that I ever had,
I spent it in good company,
And all the harm that ever I done,
Alas it was to none but me.
And all I've done for want of wit,
To memory now I can't recall,
So fill to me the parting glass,
Goodnight and joy be with you all.

– 'The Parting Glass', *a traditional Irish song*

The sun dipped behind the hills and made way for the dusk of a mournful Wednesday evening. Dark clouds rolled in from across the sea, creating patchwork hues of blues and greys. The winking lighthouse at Louismore Head could just be seen on the headland across the open waves and a gentle moon rose from the east and settled uneasily in the path of the impending summer storm.

Soft lights shone in the window of Jackie and Annie O'Shea's four-square farmhouse and a persistent murmuring could be heard from within. The chicken supper had just been served and as glasses were filled and chilled feet warmed by the fire, a growing air of excitement and anticipation pervaded the crowded living room, hall, kitchen and parlour. The kitchen table was groaning under the generous gifts of wine, beer and whiskey brought by the supper guests. The living room was thick with smoke from the peat fire and the various guests who had been invited along, people who had known each other all their lives, stood around or sat on the stairs chatting animatedly with each other as if they had never met.

Michael, armed with a bottle of whiskey, was doing the rounds, filling up glasses and handing people plates of food. Passing a second helping to Kitty Moore, who was dressed impeccably in yet another completely pink outfit, he felt his arm grabbed. 'Did you enjoy your supper, Michael?' Kitty asked him, for the third time.

Thinking of the delights that had just been laid before them, Michael replied: 'Oh, I did, indeed, Kitty,' plying her with even more whiskey. The food had come out of the kitchen in a never-ending conveyor belt of home-cooked delicacies. As well as the tender roast chickens, there were Colcannon potatoes, glazed carrots with herbs, Brussels sprouts, roast and mashed potatoes. Waiting in the wings were four giant apple tarts, and huge chunks of freshly baked soda bread to be eaten with runny wedges of locally produced Cashel Blue cheese and smoked Durrus. Fresh fruit had finished the sumptuous feast.

'It was generous of Jackie to splash out like that,' Kitty said, slurping her whiskey as her perfectly plucked left eyebrow arched inquisitively. Her face was so close to Michael's that he could see her moist lips and smell the whiskey on her warm breath.

'Oh, he's a generous man, Kitty,' he said, nodding energetically, slipping past her to top up even more glasses. As agreed, he, Jackie and Annie had split up in an attempt to gather information from the eighteen suspects, to see who had been splashing out or who was about to spend some money. Annie had been entrusted to approach the women on the list – Mrs Kennedy, Maggie Tooley, Kitty Moore and a few others – while Jackie and Michael would concentrate on interrogating the men. Mulling around, stopping for a quiet word here and there, they hoped to catch the winner off his or her guard.

Jackie found a place next to Brendy, dressed in a threadbare cardigan and trousers, but wearing a tie, opened a new bottle of Jameson's whiskey and started pouring him a large measure. He couldn't remember the last time he had seen Brendy this merry. The man was positively radiant with alcohol and enjoyment, his bushy ginger eyebrows wiggling up and down as he laughed.

'Did you see Pig Finn in his brother's racing car this week, Brendy?' Jackie asked, as the normally morose garage owner stood, grinning inanely, leaning against the wall for support.

'I did,' he replied, chortling. 'I thought it was stolen.' Swigging from the glass and rinsing his mouth satisfyingly with the amber liquid, he asked: 'Now Jackie, they tell me that you might be splashing out on a sports car yourself.' His twinkling eyes peered up into Jackie's for a reaction.

Jackie chuckled and shook his head ruefully. 'Oh, if I had the money, Brendy, I wouldn't waste it on a car when me bike's outside.' Pausing slightly, he asked: 'How about yourself?'

Taking another huge swig, Brendy was momentarily distracted. 'How about meself what?' he asked, confused for a moment.

'Will you be splashing out on a sports car?' Jackie asked cautiously, his tone conspiratorial.

Brendy stared at Jackie in disbelief before he threw his head back and laughed heartily. It sounded like the bray of a donkey and it had been such a long time since anyone had heard it that several people in the room turned to look. 'Are you mad, man?' Brendy asked, his face purple with glee, as Jackie's own paled visibly.

'Just asking,' he said sorrowfully, shaking his head at Annie who was stood watching him from the doorway.

Michael homed in on Tom Flannery, the village postman, wearing his regulation uniform and tie and warming his bottom by the fire. Pouring him a whiskey, he said: 'Tell me, Tom, would you be looking for a bigger house now that you've had your baby?' Tom's wife Mairead had just given birth to their fourth son in as many years. He certainly had his hands full in his two up, two down cottage in Main Street.

Tom shook his head and looked as tired as he felt. It was already way past his bedtime. He had to be up at four in the morning and the new baby would undoubtedly keep him awake for the few hours that he had left. He would have loved nothing more than to move somewhere bigger, where the baby could have its own room, instead of sleeping in a cot by their bed, but he told Michael he was thinking more of building an extension on the back.

Michael winked knowingly, his expression impish. 'I see you've got a little bit put away then?'

Tom shook his head sadly and said: 'No, but I've started saving.'

Jackie approached them, took the whiskey bottle back from Michael, and they exchanged a sorrowful shake of the head. Catching sight of Annie standing in the kitchen in her best white blouse, black skirt and waistcoat, Jackie raised his eyebrows hopefully, but she too shook her head negatively. They were getting nothing but false leads. He was devastated. Whoever the winner was, they were playing their cards very close to their chests and that meant they would be even more unlikely to want to share the money with their friends. Old skinflints.

Back in the kitchen, Annie and Kitty were still clearing up while the other guests talked. Annie washed as Kitty dried and the two women remained companionably silent for much of the time, listening to the guffawing and chit-chat in the room beyond as the drink continued to take effect. Stopping for a moment, Annie poured Kitty a large measure of Jameson's and handed it to her in one of her best Waterford crystal tumblers. Kitty put down her cloth and drank greedily.

'So, Kitty, how did you like your breast?' Annie asked, her tongue in her cheek. She had heard poor Michael being ribbed all evening by the lascivious seamstress and wondered at her nerve.

'Me breast, Annie, was tasty,' Kitty smirked.

'So tell us,' Annie went on, as nonchalantly as she could, 'are you going to take a holiday this year?'

Slurping the whiskey, Kitty snorted. 'Now where would I get the money for a holiday?' she asked derisively as Annie dropped her cloth to the table and put her hands on her hips. Watching the two women from the door and listening in on the conversation, Dennis Fitzgerald smiled. Politely reaching across them for the whiskey, he poured himself a large measure. 'Oops, sorry, girls, there we go,' he said, pouring them both a drink after Annie told him to help himself.

Standing in the doorway of the lounge, watching Pat Mulligan sitting on a low stool and using all his charms on pretty Maggie Tooley, Jackie thought what a great injustice it would be if Mulligan was the secret winner. Maggie, intoxicated with drink, was kneeling on the floor at Mulligan's feet, her laughter tinkling across the room, while he stroked her arm and called her his girl. Pig Finn staggered along the hallway, rebounding off the walls, before arriving at Jackie's side and clapping him warmly on the shoulder. 'Am

I smelling sweeter, Jackie?' he asked, smiling. 'I tried one of your banana soaps.'

Jackie nodded towards Maggie in the corner with Pat Mulligan and said, rather cruelly: 'Not sweet enough by the looks of it.' Finn surveyed the scene miserably, feeling deeply wounded as he watched Pat laying his charm on thick.

Feeling sorry for hurting the pig man's feelings and seeing his pained expression, Jackie whispered encouragingly: 'There's a raspberry soap upstairs, try that tomorrow, huh?'

'Raspberry?' Finn echoed, sadly.

'Yes, raspberry. Try that,' Jackie reiterated as Finn wandered off despondently and Dennis Fitzgerald took his place.

Slightly the worse for wear, his voice raised above the general hubbub, the big publican had been listening in to conversation after conversation and he wanted to know what was going on. Slurring, he finally asked: 'Jackie, am I right in thinking that you've booked one of these Caribbean cruises?'

All the conversations in the room stopped dead as the other guests listened in and waited for their host's reply. It had been the topic of conversation on everybody's lips all evening. Why had Jackie invited them here? Had he come into some money? What were he and Annie and Michael doing asking all these questions about how much or how little they had? Was he going to be giving some money out to those in most need?

Jackie, maudlin through drink and disappointment, stammered slightly as he spoke, almost addressing the room. 'If I had the money, Dennis, I wouldn't spend it floating around the Caribbean when I can float in the cove for free, eh?'

Pat Mulligan, his patience running out, jumped up and shouted from the other side of the room, speaking for all of them. 'For Christ's sake, Jackie,' he cried, 'would you mind telling us what you *would* be spending your money on?'

Almost as an afterthought, he added sheepishly: '*If* you had any, that is?' The room fell silent with anticipation once more.

Jackie thought for a moment as all eyes rested on him and then said, in all seriousness, 'Well, I'd take what I needed, Pat, and treat me friends with the rest.' Excited conversations resumed instantly as each guest toasted their host and discussed how lucky they were to have a friend like Jackie O'Shea.

Only when every drop in the house had been drunk and almost every morsel of food eaten did most of the guests finally leave, disappearing into the raging storm outside, which had worsened considerably since the supper began. The wind howled around the chimney pots and rattled the latch doors of the old farmhouse. Rain lashed at the windows, and the dark, dank night matched the mood of those left inside. In the living room, Pig Finn and his toothless father Rennie sat side by side on the sofa, finishing a bottle between them and drunkenly singing 'The Mountains of Mourne' and other ballads remembered from Rennie's far distant youth.

In the kitchen, Jackie was slumped wearily in a chair next to Michael, who was pouring the very last drop of whiskey into his glass, before resting the empty bottle next to five others. Annie was clearing up in another room, and both men sat half-leaning against each other, their heads in their hands, drunk.

Jackie's face was like thunder, his large silver-haired hand rubbing his tired eyes. 'Oh, jeepers, the chickens and the whiskey were wasted,' he complained bitterly. Lowering his hand and looking across at the alcohol-induced smile fixed on Michael's face, he growled: 'What are you staring at?'

Hiccuping slightly, Michael shook his head to try to clear it. 'Oh, I wasn't staring at anything,' he said slyly, his elbow on the table, his chin resting in his hand.

But Jackie knew the old rogue better than that. 'Come on, out with it!' he snapped.

Michael smirked, his eyes bloodshot and glazed. 'I know who it is ... I've worked it out,' he said, a cheeky smile tugging at the corners of his mouth.

Jackie sat up suddenly, his attention caught. 'No!' he gasped. He could hardly dare believe it.

'Oh, yes!' Michael grinned, eager to share the secret.

Intrigued and leaning forward across the table, Jackie smiled at Michael and urged: 'Go on.' Perhaps all the expense would have been worth it, after all.

Michael stared at him a little longer before lifting a drunken index finger. Giggling, he announced knowingly: 'It's you,' and pointed straight at Jackie O'Shea's face.

Jackie snorted and leaned back angrily. 'Me?' he cried. He knew he should never have put Michael in charge of topping up the glasses, it was virtually inevitable that he would top up his own more than anyone else's.

Michael was not to be deterred. 'I think it's you and I think you're having us all on,' he said, with logic worthy of Sherlock Holmes and the other great detectives he knew so intimately from his bedtime reading.

Leaning his face even closer to his, Jackie scowled. 'Michael, go home!' he said.

Expecting just that reaction from someone who was pretending not to be the winner, Michael smirked once more and got unsteadily to his feet. He started to pull on his best tweed jacket, but was having difficulty finding the arm hole. Jackie eyed him suspiciously. Finally fully inside his coat, Michael slurred: 'I'll leave you in peace to count your winnings.'

Watching him, Jackie's face lit up suddenly. 'Here, wait, wait a minute,' he said, his index finger wagging back at Michael. 'What if it's you? You've never said it wasn't.'

Michael stopped and thought for a moment, considering the issue. Coming to his senses, he smiled and then started laughing. He tapped the side of his nose, knowingly. The more he laughed, the more he couldn't stop. And as he laughed, leaning over the table lopsidedly, Jackie looked at his inane expression and realised that the man he had known all his life was physically incapable of telling a single lie, let alone maintaining a façade for several days. Getting up to see him to the front door and chasing him out into the storm, Jackie shouted: 'Get home, you're drunk. Get to your bed. Get yourself a hot chocolate.' Pushing him out of the door and watching him rush off, his umbrella bent against the wind and the driving rain, he yelled affectionately: 'Get home, yer hoodlum!' Just as he closed the door, and for good measure, he shouted: 'Stupid eeejit!' but the howling gale snatched his voice and carried it skywards.

Slamming the front door shut and staggering back inside, Jackie was met by his wife, standing in the hallway, her expression excited. She was holding up a plate with both hands. In the middle sat a single cooked chicken leg. Jackie wondered what was wrong. 'I've a chicken leg left over,' Annie said, her eyes bright.

Jackie burped silently and rubbed his overextended belly with his left hand. 'I'm full, Annie,' he complained, frowning at the thought of another mouthful. 'Put it in the fridge for dinner tomorrow, huh?'

Annie sighed, realising that her husband was missing the point. 'Jackie,' she said, glaring at him. 'I counted those joints precisely.' She paused. 'If there's a leg left over, it means someone was missing.'

His face illuminated by the sudden revelation, Jackie said: 'The winner's smelt a rat?' Looking around frantically, patting his clothes, he asked her: 'Where's me list?' before suddenly remembering that it was in his waistcoat pocket.

Pulling out a crumpled piece of paper and trying to focus through the haze of Irish whiskey that had fogged his vision, he examined it carefully.

Looking up at his wife, his mouth falling open, he cried: 'Ned Devine! Ned Devine was missing!' Angry with her suddenly, he chided: 'God, Annie, did you not notice?' Before she could voice her indignation, he had grabbed his waterproof greatcoat and a torch. Annie shook her head in disbelief, but Jackie was on a mission. 'Make up a dinner, sweetheart, I'm going over,' he told her firmly. Knowing that nothing she could do or say would change his mind, Annie took the plate back into the kitchen to top it up with leftover vegetables and gravy.

The storm was coming in even harder from the sea as Jackie struggled along the coastal path, trying desperately to keep the metal saucepan lid on top of the chicken dinner and hold the torch at the same time. Giving up on the torch and slipping it back into his pocket, he bowed his head and ploughed on, the rain beating hard on his face, the wind whipping back the hood on his black waterproof greatcoat and lashing his face as he staggered drunkenly towards Ned's isolated house at the bottom of the cliffs.

It was nearly two o'clock in the morning, pitch black, and fearful stormy by the time Jackie reached the property with its wooden-built fishing boat upturned outside, and called Ned's name above the howling wind. Banging on the door but not waiting for a reply in such foul weather, he lifted the latch on the little wooden front door and entered the darkened house, his face wet from the rain, his hair dishevelled.

Shaking himself off, and clearing his throat, he called softly: 'Ned, Ned, I've brought a chicken dinner.' Switching on the light, all looked normal in the sparse yet tidy living room with its fishing hooks, oilskins, kit and tools all neatly

Jackie sat bolt upright in his seat and stared at the television in disbelief.

Annie was as transfixed as her husband by the flickering screen.

'Ah, will you marry me, then?'
Finn asked Maggie, ever hopeful.

'I'm bursting with news. I think I know who's won,' Michael blurted out.

Pig Finn looked at the two men with a puzzled expression on his face.

Jackie was keen to make the right impression in case Dennis was the secret jackpot winner.

Michael pulled out six fresh unplucked chickens, laying them on the kitchen table in an untidy heap of wings, beaks and feet.

Michael tried to creep away unnoticed, but Kitty's head was out of her bedroom window before he could take two steps to freedom.

Above: Maggie's top lip curled. 'Oh, hang on, Finn, I caught a whiff of something then,' she said warily.

Below left: 'Jackie's a generous man, Kitty,' Michael said, nodding enthusiastically.

Below right: Michael slurred: 'I'll leave you in peace to count your winnings.'

I've a chicken leg left over,' Annie said, her eyes bright.

Sitting up in bed opposite him was the pale, frozen figure of Ned Devine, long dead.

Jackie gently slid Ned's eyes shut. Examining his handiwork, both men looked at each other and smiled.

Discarding their clothes, they trotted side by side into the sea stark
naked, as they had done for nearly sixty years.

stacked on wooden shelves. Yet, there was no sign of the old fisherman. Dripping wet and still holding the dinner in one hand, Jackie's eyes came to rest on the rough stone floor where his untouched invitation to the chicken supper still lay.

A little fearful now, in case his friend should be sleeping, Jackie called once more. 'Ned, I've brought you a chicken supper. Ned? Ned? Are you in there?' He moved cautiously towards the half-open bedroom door under which he could see the flickering light from a television. Pushing the creaking door further open and calling Ned's name softly, he was momentarily dazzled by the mesmerising grey mottled fuzz on the screen and the hiss of a television channel shut down for the night. The room was bitterly cold, the fire in the small grate expired, and the chill northerly winds outside still pounded at the windows and billowed the net curtains.

Feeling along the wall with his hand for the light switch, he finally found it and turned it on, noticing that dangling from around the switch's simple plastic housing was a string of brightly coloured rosary beads and a small crucifix. But it was the next sight that met his eyes which made his blood turn cold.

Sitting up in bed opposite him and just a few feet away was the pale, frozen figure of Ned Devine, long dead. Propped up against the pillows, dressed in pyjamas and with a tray of congealed Irish stew and tea resting neatly on his lap, his head tilted back, his blue-green eyes staring straight ahead of him, a smile set deep within his craggy face. Letting out a cry of shock and horror, Jackie dropped the chicken dinner to the floor with an almighty clatter, spilling the meat, vegetables and gravy all over the hard linoleum floor with spectacular coverage.

Regaining his composure slightly, he moved forward with great trepidation and touched Ned's ice-cold arm. Studying his strange expression and sitting down on the edge of the

81

bed, his legs trembling, Jackie noticed, for the first time, a small piece of paper in Ned's right hand. Reaching forward and carefully releasing the piece of paper from the corpse's stiffened, outstretched fingers, he examined it closely. It was a lottery ticket.

Following the line of Ned's frozen gaze to the now hissing television set and realising what must have happened, Jackie shook his head. 'Dear God!' he said, and sank further onto the bed, the ticket still in his hand, his expression one of genuine pity. 'You'll be cursing in heaven tonight, Ned Devine,' he said, with real sympathy for his old friend.

Sodden to the skin, frozen to the marrow and drying his bare feet by the warm kitchen stove back at his farmhouse, the only light glowing in on them from the hallway as he and Annie sat in near darkness, Jackie O'Shea was shivering with more than a chill after his late night excursion. The sight of Ned sitting stone cold dead in bed was one which would haunt him for many years to come, he reckoned. He thanked God Michael wasn't with him at the time; his old school chum was more than a little squeamish and he would probably have ended up with two dead men on his hands instead of just one.

Sitting opposite him in the half-light as he dried himself out, Annie rocked back in her chair, staring in wonder at the lottery ticket and studying a newspaper. 'They match,' she said, her voice no more than a whisper. 'It's a winner. It'll be at least a half a million.' The two of them stared at the ticket in awe. Thinking of poor Ned and what a great carouser he had always been, Annie allowed herself a wry smile as she added: 'He'd have spent it too. There'd have been a mighty party.'

Her husband nodded, already mourning Ned Devine's angelic singing voice, which would be so greatly missed at the usual village *ceilidhs* and celebrations. 'Is there a greater twist

82

of fate, Annie?' he mused. 'To win half a million and the next minute, die from the shock of it?'

Annie murmured her sad agreement.

'God rest him, the poor fella,' Jackie added, softly.

Annie bowed her head. 'Ned, the sweetest man in the world. They say money changes a man, Jackie, and there's no greater change than moving him from life into death.'

'It's the cruellest twist,' her husband concurred.

Silent for a while, the two of them conjured up happy images of Ned, working away on his boat, hauling in the nets, his hair ruffling in the breeze, or in Fitzgerald's bar, standing by the fire as his voice lifted and carried across the room, capturing hearts and minds as it caressed their souls.

'Half a million pounds,' Annie repeated, thinking of all the fun the old codger would have had with such a haul. Generous to a fault, he would have undoubtedly seen to it that all his friends were well taken care of. He had no family, after all. 'Should we be phoning? Police? Or the doctor?' she asked, waving the ticket at her husband.

Jackie sighed. 'It's a call to both, but there's nothing to do tonight. His bedroom is as cold as any fridge they'd put him in. Make the calls in the morning.'

It was a frightful night as the storm raged on, lifting roof tiles and shattering them, claiming debris from the beach and skidding it along Main Street. Pulling on her warmest woollen night-dress, Annie O'Shea climbed into bed next to her husband with a pensive look on her face. 'I think we should make room in this day for some prayers,' she said softly.

Jackie emerged from the covers and they both adopted a praying position, hands clasped together, eyes closed. In unison, they recited a familiar prayer at a whisper: 'God bless mothers and fathers, and grandparents too, aunties and uncles, friends old and new. Amen.'

Opening her eyes and holding her hands up higher as she looked to the heavens, Annie added: 'And dear Lord, we pray tonight for a little man from Tullymore. Ned Devine, as sweet a soul as ever was blessed. A gentleman, who loved his life, and carried a heart the size of his head, within his chest.'

Together, they chanted 'Amen' and turned the lights out, only to lie awake listening to the water from the guttering cascading into the overflow and the winds screaming and howling through the rafters.

Jackie's slumber, when it eventually came, was restless and disturbed. Tossing and turning, pulling up the bedclothes, then pushing them off, it took him an hour finally to drift off to sleep and when he did his dreams were full of Ned Devine with his staring eyes and blue lips. Finally, after what seemed like an age, he fell into that still, silent world of sleep that insomniacs crave. But his relief was short-lived, for through the haze of his subconscious came the sensation of flying low across a golden sea, the light and the water dazzling beneath him. Straining to see more of his dream, Jackie found himself sitting in a boat, miles out to sea with no land visible. Then, suddenly, a voice and the sound of cutlery on crockery made him look up. Sitting opposite him was Ned Devine. They were seated either end of the old man's fishing boat, floating on still waters out in the middle of an orange sea. In the far distance, sitting on rocks, mermaids sang and seals basked and cried an accompaniment.

Both men were dressed, Ned in an open-neck shirt over a string vest and trousers, Jackie in his usual cardigan. Ned was balancing a plate on his lap and greedily devouring the chicken supper Jackie had brought him, laughing all the while about how delicious it was and seemingly heedless to the fact that the oars were up and there seemed no means of keeping direction. 'There would have been a mighty party, Jackie,' he told his friend, with a twinkle in his eye.

'There would indeed,' Jackie agreed, warily.

Pointing to his plate and eating voraciously, Ned asked: 'Would you ... would you like some chicken?'

'No thanks, Ned,' Jackie said.

'Are you sure?' the dead man asked, still tucking in, but Jackie shook his head.

'Are you angry?' Jackie enquired. He knew he would be if he had just dropped dead at the one moment when the dream of his lifetime had finally come true.

But Ned seemed strangely placid. 'Not at all,' he smiled warmly. Biting into a juicy drumstick, he said: 'Are you sure you wouldn't like some chicken? It's delicious.' He had always enjoyed Annie's home cooking when he was invited to their house for supper. Had he ever been inclined to get married, she would have been the ideal wife, he had always thought, but Jackie O'Shea got there first. Now that he was dead, he seemed delighted to be able to enjoy one last sample of her cooking skills, a final meal with his old friend.

'No, thanks Ned, I'm full,' Jackie sighed, as he looked around at the golden shimmering haze on the water which shrouded the boat from the land. 'Where are we going, Ned?' he asked, peering out to sea.

'Into the light,' Ned answered, pointing to a distant horizon.

'It seems far off,' Jackie commented, concerned now.

'Aye, but don't worry, man, the tide'll bring us there safely,' Ned responded, in the relaxed way of a seasoned fisherman completely at ease.

The next time Jackie looked out of the boat, it was stranded high and dry on some jagged rocks at a beach edge. Ned and he were still sitting facing each other and Ned was still eating. Woken suddenly by a huge clap of thunder overhead, Jackie's eyes opened and he lay quite still on the pillow, afraid to move and staring straight ahead of him, blinking back the sweat pouring off his brow.

Dressed from head to toe in waterproofed clothing, with oilskin coats, rubber boots, hats, gloves and an umbrella, Jackie and Michael leaned into the wind and clung to each other as they trudged along the coast path less than an hour later, shouting at each other in order to be heard above the terrible storm. 'It's a premonition, Michael, a vision,' Jackie insisted, yelling from under the hood of his coat as his face was lashed once again with wind and water. It had certainly been the most vivid and spiritual dream of his life, lost at sea with Ned, the old fisherman repeatedly inviting him to share his meal, intent on it in fact. It was an omen, nothing less.

Michael was deeply worried about his friend. 'It's a chicken dinner, Jackie,' he said, turning his head so that he could hear his response amid the thunderclaps.

But Jackie had a determined gleam in his eye. In the space of a few hours, Ned's spirit had become his driving force. 'It's obvious, Michael. He wants us to claim the money. Share the chicken dinner, share the winnings,' he cried.

'What a great man he was,' Michael conceded, struggling to keep his umbrella the right way up. He was truly amazed that Ned should have come to Jackie in such a way. He so wanted to believe it was true, but – ever cautious – he still wasn't convinced.

Jackie, however, was hooked on the idea. 'Yes,' he agreed, more impressed now by Ned than he ever had been in life. 'And his spirit's in me head.'

'What'll you do with the ticket?' asked Michael, utterly oblivious to the ways of fraud.

Jackie had it all figured out. He had been unable to sleep after his dream for working it out in his mind. Unable to wait a moment longer, he had dressed quietly and rushed round to Michael's cottage to tell him his sensational news and ask for his help. Reluctantly, and only after some serious persuading, Michael had agreed. 'Well, he wrote his name on the back,

Michael,' Jackie explained. 'But we pretend to be Ned and we claim the half million.' It sounded so simple, so utterly plausible the way he said it, that Michael was almost convinced.

Then the thought occurred to him that Jackie would almost certainly expect to enlist his collaboration. Stopping halfway along the well-worn goat track, now treacherously slippery with the rainwater, Michael said cautiously: 'Oh, I'm not sure Jackie, I couldn't be Ned, I'm no good at pretending.' That, indeed, was true.

Thinking that he had better take charge of this rather more delicate situation himself, Jackie nodded. 'I'll be Ned meself,' he said. Seeing Michael's still doubtful expression, Jackie grabbed his old friend's arm and stopped him dead to spell it out for him. 'Michael, Ned's no family,' he explained. 'The money'll go unclaimed. He plays the Lotto for the last twelve years of his life and dies from the shock of winning it. Can you imagine the anger of his spirit, man?' Allowing his fearful words to sink into poor old Michael's squeamish, superstitious mind, Jackie stood for a moment, staring wild-eyed at him, before moving off again down the path. His companion stumbled on behind.

'Does Annie know we're going back up tonight?' Michael asked, comforted by the thought that somehow all of this would be all right if Annie had agreed to it.

'No, no,' Jackie conceded, rather reluctantly. 'She's left cuddling me pillow.'

Very jittery, and not fully understanding what it was that Jackie intended to do, Michael asked: 'Do we report the death in the morning?' He wanted only to do what was best and stay on the right side of the law.

Stopping his friend mid-step, this time with anger and frustration in his eyes, Jackie shouted: 'Michael, are you thick? If we report the death and are found to be claiming, we'll surely be questioned for murder.'

Michael shivered visibly. 'Murder is a mighty word to use at this time of night, Jackie,' he said, wishing more than anything in the world that he was tucked up in his bed.

Jackie looked hurt. 'Yeah, well, I'm sorry if it gives you the willies, Michael,' he said, but his expression belied his words. Moving on and into the night, he decided not to say another word until they had reached Ned's cottage.

Checking fearfully around the little building as they arrived, looking for any unwelcome visitors, the two men approached with the utmost caution, their figures casting giant shadows up the cliff walls. Jackie, much more confident than before, warned his friend to mind the step and entered first, while Michael peered nervously around the door and followed him in. Turning on the light and picking up the untouched invitation to the chicken supper from the doormat as he stepped inside, stuffing it into his pocket, Jackie started looking around the room for the necessary documentation he would need to impersonate Ned and make the lottery claim.

He had it all figured out. He'd phone the lottery company in the morning, demand privacy about the win, get the cheque in a day or two, cash it and then report Ned's death to the proper authorities. He doubted if Dr Moran could tell how long Ned had been dead as long as the weather stayed this cold and the corpse remained pretty well frozen. Meanwhile, they would have their hands on the money and no one would be any the wiser.

'Where is he, Jackie?' Michael whispered from the doorway, water dripping off him and onto the floor in a great puddle. His voice was tremulous and his knees knocking together so hard he was sure they could be heard above the wind rattling at the windows.

Flicking through some correspondence in a side cabinet as if he owned the place, Jackie pointed momentarily to the open bedroom door. 'Through there,' he said, casually. 'Take a look.'

With an uneasy feeling in the pit of his stomach and the palms of his hands clammy, Michael gulped and screwed up his face in disgust as he gingerly approached the bedroom and stepped inside. 'Jesus, there's a stink in here!' he spluttered, coughing and wheezing to clear the sweet, acrid stench from his nose and the back of his throat.

'Ah, nature's taking a hold, Michael,' Jackie said matter-of-factly. 'He's been gone a few days now.' He hoped that the body wouldn't decompose too badly, despite the cold, or Dr Moran might start to suspect something.

Quelling his rising nausea and trying not to dwell on the details of Ned's decomposing body, Michael stepped bravely forward and turned on the light, as Jackie watched in great amusement from behind. Scanning the room quickly, Michael jumped physically when his gaze settled on Ned's smiling face. Calming himself, he studied the corpse's strange expression. Finally able to speak, he called over his shoulder: 'Jackie ... he's smiling.' Sliding along the wall and round to the end of Ned's bed, he sat down nervously on the end of it.

'Ah, that'll be the winning smile,' Jackie called from the other room. 'With a little luck, we'll have one ourselves in a week,' he added, with a chuckle.

Unable to take his eyes off Ned's face, Michael was still lost in his own thoughts. 'And I always thought it would be the sea that would take him,' he said absent-mindedly, placing his hands palms down on the bed beside him. 'He survived all those storms only to be swept away by a few lottery balls.'

Feeling something sticky under his hands and looking down at a growing dark stain on Ned's candlewick bedspread, he touched it once more and lifted his hands to his nose, sniffing. Physically repulsed, and quivering visibly, he called out to his friend: 'Jackie, come quick, oh, sweet Jesus, the man's beginning to melt!'

Rushing back into the room in great haste, Jackie slipped on the wet floor. His feet slipped from under him and he writhed around on the ground, laughing hysterically as he tried to find a footing. His face one of abject horror at the sight, Michael screamed aloud. 'Oh dear God, you've slipped on his intestines,' he cried. Watching Jackie slither and slip over something green and brown on the lino, he added: 'Ah, will you get up – ah, for God's sake, Jackie.' Seeing Jackie laughing, he pleaded: 'Jackie, for the love of God, will you stop it!'

Finally finding his footing in the mess and rising on one knee, Jackie stifled a laugh and urged him to hush. 'Oh, be calm, Michael. It's only a chicken dinner,' he told him, holding out a handful of dollops of congealed gravy and vegetables.

Michael clutched his hand to his heart and looked faint. 'A chicken dinner? God, I thought it was his intestines.'

Getting up from the floor and sniffing his jacket, Jackie laughed: 'I've never smelt intestines on my jacket before, but it surely can't be as bad as Annie's Brussels sprouts.' He laughed at the pale features of his friend and told him to help him set about the important job in hand.

Set to one side of Ned's living room was a simple open plan kitchen. Working by the light of the single light bulb overhead, Michael reluctantly wiped Jackie down, his face screwed into a grimace. 'Come on, you missed a bit,' Jackie complained.

'Oh, God,' Michael groaned, dabbing his greatcoat and feeling decidedly queasy. He still wasn't convinced that this was chicken and not innards that he was dabbing off, and did not relish having to clean up the rest of the mess. 'The floor'll need to be cleaned proper before we go,' he said, physically turning his nose up at the thought.

Jackie nodded. 'What time it is?'

Michael looked at his watch. 'Er, ten to five.'

Jackie cursed. 'The morning's on its way.'

Still feeling sick to the stomach, Michael asked sheepishly: 'Jackie, can you clean up the chicken dinner on your own?'

Impatient with his squeamishness, Jackie pulled off his coat and told his friend: 'There are two things to do before we go, Michael, and the chicken dinner is by far the least gruesome.' Michael gulped, his eyes darting from side to side as he tried to fathom out what Jackie could mean.

More than an hour later and now working by the pinkish purple morning light as the seagulls wheeled and called outside the cottage window, Michael was on his hands and knees in Ned's bedroom, wiping the last of the Brussels sprouts and gravy from the floor with a wet cloth, while Jackie sat on the bed staring at the corpse's expression. Lifting his arms and hands slowly towards the dead man, Jackie's face was a picture of concentration. He looked to all intents and purposes as if he were about to strangle him. Michael, rising to his knees in horror, moved closer to watch. 'Is it necessary, Jackie?' he asked, concerned.

Startled at Michael's intervention, Jackie checked himself and lowered his arms. Tilting his head to one side to better view Ned's face, he reasoned: 'Well, it's sort of unnatural as it is, Michael.' There was something about Ned's winning smile that troubled him. If the police or Dr Moran saw it, he thought it might give the game away. Raising his arms again and moving his hands closer and closer to the corpse, he finally took Ned's cold cheeks firmly in his hands and tried to twist them outwards. Despite his efforts, the dead man's expression remained exactly the same.

Michael offered some advice. 'Take hold of his mouth. You won't get rid of a smile by twisting his cheeks.'

Not keen to touch the dead flesh once more, Jackie sneered: 'Ah, you think you're awful smart. Leave me in peace ...

Finish wiping those intestines from the floor.' With Michael backed off a few feet, he tried again, once more raising his hands and closing in on the dead man. Gently opening Ned's mouth, and mimicking the dead man's expression with his own face, he shunted his lower jaw to the left, and tried to transform his expression. Pleased with his work, he looked round to Michael for approval, but got none.

'What expression were you thinking of?' asked Michael, his tone wholly disapproving.

Still manipulating the stiffened flesh and with his hands poking around inside Ned's open mouth, Jackie snapped: 'Be quiet, I'm trying to ...' but at that very second he stopped himself mid-sentence and leapt back as a half-set of yellowing dentures flipped out and onto the grubby bedspread, their false teeth stained and tarnished and still flecked with food. With a fit of the giggles, Jackie recoiled and pointed at them, laughing.

'God Almighty!' Michael scolded. 'Oh, dear God,' he moaned when his friend couldn't stop himself laughing. Picking them up reluctantly between his finger and forefinger, he handed them back to his giggling friend. 'Here you are. Ah, come on, for God's sakes, Jackie.'

Taking a few deep breaths and attempting to put the dentures back into the gaping hole they had come from, Jackie told Michael, 'Stop, you're – you're panicking me, man,' he told him. He bit on his lip to stop himself from laughing as he proceeded to attempt to fit the dentures back into Ned's toothless mouth with his fingers. 'You're panicking me.'

Starting to see the funny side of it and chuckling quietly to himself now, Michael said, dryly: 'Now, now, watch he doesn't bite again, Jackie.'

'Oh, shush, would you!' chided his friend. Fiddling around inside the dead man's mouth, he finally succeeded in replacing them. All his inhibitions lost now, he continued roughly to manhandle Ned's facial muscles until the mouth was closed and he had changed the smile to an unhappy expression.

Michael leaned his head to one side for a better look. Critical, he said: 'No. It's – it's not natural, Jackie. It's too grim.'

Jackie had to admit his point. 'You're right there,' he said, trying to readjust the cheek muscles once more. But still it didn't work. There was an oddness about his face, they both agreed.

Staring hard at the dead man to try and figure out what was wrong, the answer suddenly came to Michael. 'It's in his eyes, Jackie,' he said, nodding at the staring orbs. They were milky and dry, like those of a dead fish.

Reaching forward for the last time, his two forefingers outstretched, Jackie gently slid Ned's eyelids shut. Examining his handiwork, the men looked at each other, smiled and nodded. 'Ah!' they agreed, in contented unison.

Chapter
Five

But I, being poor, have only my dreams;
I have spread my dreams under your feet;
Tread softly because you tread on my dreams ...

– W. B. Yeats, 'He Wishes for the Cloths of Heaven'

At Tooley's garage, Brendy was at the top of a metal ladder dressed, as ever, in his blue overalls, repairing guttering blown down by the previous night's storm. It was still very breezy, the wind riding in from the sea on crested white horses, and Brendy had to concentrate hard to keep the brackets holding the guttering in place. So preoccupied was he with the job in hand that he did not hear Pat Mulligan approach or see him standing at the foot of the ladder for a while, silently admiring his handiwork. There was no doubt about it, Brendy had a winning way with his hands. He could turn them to anything and work out in his mind how something held together or what to mend to make it work again.

'You're doing a fine job there, Brendy,' Pat complimented him, alerting the old man to his presence. In a beige check suit and a white open-neck shirt, Pat looked somewhat out of place amid all the rusting exhaust pipes and scattered car parts. He had always been a bit of a spiv – he always bought his clothes in Ballyneath or Dublin instead of mail order catalogues like the rest of the village. The only thing that gave away the fact that he, too, had had a skinful last night at Jackie O'Shea's chicken supper was the fact that, unusually for him, he hadn't bothered to shave.

Looking down at him from his position half way up the ladder, Brendy nodded a greeting. 'Oh, hello there.' There was not a trace of a hangover in the old man's eyes despite the impressive quantity of drink he had consumed at Jackie's. Clean shaven and up with the lark, he looked as fresh as a daisy. But the laughter that had lit up his face with the oiling of alcohol the previous evening was all gone.

'That was a storm, wasn't it?' Pat remarked, still recovering from the howling gale that had battered Tullymore all night. Damage had been done; roofs needed mending on cow sheds and barns, and one of Pat's heifers had been badly cut by a flying piece of corrugated iron that had lifted from the roof of a byre and hit her on the flank.

'Oh, it was,' Brendy answered, wondering what was coming next as he climbed further down his ladder and wiped his hands on an oily cloth.

Idly biding his time to tell Brendy what he really wanted to say and finally summoning up the courage, Pat stuffed his hands in his pockets and enquired, almost casually: 'Is Maggie around?'

'She's having a bit of a lie in after last night,' Brendy told him. The storm had kept most of the people of the village awake and when the guttering had come crashing down around their ears, Maggie – still quite intoxicated from the drink she had consumed – had leapt from her bed with Maurice like a frightened rabbit and called on the saints to save them all.

'Oh, right,' Pat said, unable to hide his disappointment, thinking of the pleasant evening he'd spent with Maggie at Jackie's chicken supper. The more she had drunk, the more she had flirted with him, or so he thought, and he very much wanted to keep up the momentum. Maggie was the best-looking young woman in Tullymore, and the only one Pat Mulligan hadn't bedded yet. She was a challenge waiting to be overcome – and unless he was very much mistaken from the signals she put out to him the previous night – she was ripe and ready for the taking.

Awkwardly, shyly almost, he inched closer to the man he hoped might one day be his father-in-law. 'Well, look, Brendy,' he said, shuffling from foot to foot, the breeze lifting his fringe and flapping it. 'I'll get straight in here.' He paused and wondered where to begin. Launching into a speech, he finally added: 'I spent some time with your daughter last night. Now I don't know how you feel about Finn, but – I think your daughter deserves a lot more than the local pig farmer.'

Brendy, who agreed Finn was a bit of an idiot, but who despised Pat Mulligan as a pompous coxcomb, arched an eyebrow and countered: 'Oh, Finn's not so bad.'

Pat was slightly taken aback. 'No, he's not – No, you're right there,' he faltered. 'He's a good man.' It pained him to even say the words, but he was wily enough not to alienate Brendy at this early stage. Continuing with his own testimonial, and looking way up to the hill high above Tullymore to the isolated and rather soulless farm he now lived in all alone, he boasted: 'But look at what I've got to offer, Brendy. I've inherited the farm now, I'm up there, rattling around on my own. I could look after Maggie and little Maurice.' Eliciting no response, he spelled it out for the garage owner: 'I'm looking to settle down, Brendy, and there's plenty of girls would jump at the chance.' He hoped he hadn't over-egged the pudding, but he didn't think so. It was fair comment, after all.

Brendy shot him a sideways glance and the corner of his mouth twisted into a half-smile. 'You're very much like your father, aren't you, Pat?' he said. He could still remember the old rogue Sean vividly. He had that same slicked-back hair, the shifty eyes and untrustworthy mouth.

Pat suspected that, when it came to his father, an insult was coming his way, but he didn't want to lose ground so he just smiled. 'Well now, Brendy, I'll take that as a compliment,' he replied, hoping Brendy would take that as a warning not to carry on.

Brendy wasn't one to be so easily deterred. Turning to face Pat, he told him of his father: 'He was always after me wife right up till we were married,' he said, coldly, his grey eyes narrowing. 'And, as I remember, he didn't stop there.' Bridgid had been a wild one from the start; she had Maggie's long dark hair and Romany looks, and she knew how to use them. Before she'd finally run off for good with that bible seller in his vulgar car, she'd had an affair with Sean Mulligan and God knows how many others, and Brendy could barely look at the fruit of the dead man's loins now without evoking feelings of anger and revulsion.

Nervous now, Pat stepped back a little, but kept smiling. Ever the charmer, he quipped light-heartedly: 'Ah, well, now, Brendy, that just goes to show that you both had good taste, doesn't it?' Seeing his joke fall flat, he went on the defensive and tried another tack. 'Look, Brendy, I know I've always had a bit of a reputation with the ladies and that – but this is different, Brendy. This is serious.' He tried to appear as earnest as he could under the circumstances. Truth was he had no intention of stopping seeing all the girls he knew in Ballyneath or the hookers in Dublin, he just wanted to get one over on Finn by wedding Maggie, before moving her and the child in to cook and clean up after him, look after the house and keep his bed warm.

Lying upstairs in her own bed now, her son curled up fast asleep in the crook of her arm, Maggie's eyes were wide open and staring as she eavesdropped on the conversation in the yard below her open bedroom window. The breeze was billowing the net curtain into the room and rustling the leaves on a single red geranium plant that stood on the sill next to a favourite shell. Her face close to Maurice's soft hair, she held her breath as Pat carried on with his appeal to her father.

'Maggie wouldn't want for anything,' Pat continued. There was no doubting that the man had money; everyone in Tullymore knew it. But seeing the look of mistrust in the old man's eyes, he added, a little too hastily: 'There'd be no other women, and she'll be well looked after.' Thinking of the old man's own needs and his devotion to his daughter, he concluded: 'She could stay in the village, she'd be here if you needed her. What do you think?'

Closing her eyes against the tears she felt welling, Maggie rolled over, hiding her head under the pillows to shut out the conversation.

In the post office a little further along main street, Mrs Kennedy, dressed in her purple floral overall, her blonde hair parted to one side, happily hummed 'The Golden Goose' while she studied a knitting pattern for a baby's woollen jacket. Annie O'Shea was right. She was over the moon at the prospect of another little grandchild. The scans had shown that it was a boy, and he was to be called Miles. She already had four grandsons, the eldest were in their teens now, and the late and unexpected arrival had been a great surprise to all.

In different circumstances, Maeve Kennedy might well have had a large family of her own. When she had returned to Tullymore penniless and with baby Flora in her arms, after her brief dalliance with fame and stardom, she had told everyone that her husband, a Mr Tom Kennedy, impresario, had been killed in a tram accident in Dublin. Few believed she had ever been married, and only Flora knew the truth. Now married to a Scottish schoolteacher, with four boys of her own – George, Edward, Hamish and Archie – all living over in Galway, Flora had been a good and dutiful daughter and had never given away the secret of her own conception. She had helped her mother financially, and visited as often as she could. Maeve had been invited to stay in Galway when the new baby arrived, and she could hardly wait.

The strident hooting of the horn on Lizzy Quinn's buggy outside made Mrs Kennedy jump. The old woman had just arrived at the doorway of the post office and was hooting impatiently – her usual method of signifying that she needed serving. She wanted bread, she told the postmistress sourly, and she didn't want to be kept waiting. Hurrying inside to fetch a selection of loaves, Mrs Kennedy had just reached the door again when Lizzy hooted her horn once more. 'Come on, girl, come on,' she called, as the postmistress emerged with two large loaves.

'Here you are, Lizzy,' she said, 'have your choice.'

Reaching out her long spindly fingers, Lizzy Quinn took one loaf and squeezed it hard to check its freshness. Her fingers left deep imprints in the flaky crust. The postmistress was not at all amused but said nothing at first. She knew of old that it was generally more trouble than it was worth to cross Lizzy Quinn. Few were a match for her acerbic tongue. But when the old woman started squeezing the other loaf in the same way, Mrs Kennedy could no longer keep quiet. 'Lizzy, stop squeezing the bread, please,' she entreated.

''Tis all stale anyway,' Lizzy growled, quite unfairly.

Indignant at the suggestion, Mrs Kennedy cried: 'It certainly is not! It came in fresh this morning.' All the village's bread was made by Tom Flannery's mother, Mary, and was of the highest quality, everybody said so. Only Ms Quinn ever complained.

'I'll take two loaves and pay half price due to the staleness,' Lizzy snarled, her mind clearly made up. Her expression was so malevolent that poor Mrs Kennedy felt ill equipped to argue and begrudgingly wrapped them for her.

On the very outskirts of Tullymore, along a deserted stretch of coast road bordered by a steep, sheer drop to the sea, Jackie and Michael sat astride Jackie's motorbike and sped up and out to the hills beyond the village. Pulling up alongside an old-fashioned green-painted telephone box right at the cliff's edge, they wore glum expressions on their faces and had the stooped shoulders of two schoolboys caught smoking behind the bicycle sheds.

'Ah, jeepers, Annie is livid,' Jackie said morosely, removing his helmet and climbing off the bike. He was still smarting from the clip round the ear and the torrent of verbal abuse she had given him when he told her what he was planning to do. Her hands on her ample hips, her eyes spitting venom, Annie had berated him fearfully. The last time he had seen her this angry was in 1969 when she had found him face down and snoring in Kitty Moore's cleavage on the village green after the midsummer *ceilidh*, when everyone had got fearful drunk on Dennis Fitzgerald's home-made cider. It would have been enough to stop a lesser man dead in his tracks, as he sat cowed before her, but not Jackie O'Shea.

'Did she give you an earful?' Michael asked, remembering only too well that Annie O'Shea had her father Eamonn's temper and no mistake.

'She did,' Jackie admitted, removing his goggles and draping them over the handlebars as Michael did likewise. 'She locked me in my room. She said we should never have gone back up last night, she said we're too – we're too old for prison.' He chuckled at the thought.

Michael was deeply uncomfortable at the realisation of how much Annie was against it. He had always so valued her opinion. 'Maybe we should stop it all now, Jackie?' he suggested sheepishly. He had never been very happy with the idea anyway. Looking at his friend and imagining the two of them locked up in the Ballyneath gaol, or worse, in a Dublin prison, he prompted: 'Come on, man, what do you say?' putting his hand on his friend's back to keep him from his quest.

But Jackie's heart was set. He had already spent his share of the money in his mind and by the time Annie had been on her third Caribbean cruise and bought her fourth diamond ring he was sure she would come round to his way of thinking. 'No, I – I'm all prepared,' he told Michael, determinedly. It had taken him nearly an hour to negotiate his way carefully down the porch roof on his bottom from the bedroom window and he had nearly broken his neck in the process. He wasn't giving in so easily. 'Come on,' he urged, marching towards the phone box, that stubborn gleam in his eye which Michael had seen so often over the years.

They had driven to the only public telephone box for miles for several reasons. Quite apart from the fact that the storm of the previous night had knocked most of the telephones out back in the village, they wanted to avoid any suspicion. There was no private telephone line at Ned's cottage, way out as it was on the cove, and Jackie, locked in the bedroom, could not have made the call from his own house. There was a pay phone at Fitzgerald's Bar, but there was no privacy there and they needed to be completely alone. No, it was this telephone or nothing, even if it was in the windiest and most Godforsaken spot on earth, with only the seagulls for company.

Pulling open the heavy glass-panelled door and shuffling

101

inside together, their bodies squashed together, the two old men fumbled for small change and loaded it onto the coin slot, listening to it drop into position. Taking a deep breath, Jackie lifted the receiver and, after placing a small red plastic bag on top of the telephone directories, he reached inside and pulled out Ned Devine's winning lottery ticket. Passing it to Michael to hold up in front of him and squinting to see the telephone number printed on the back of it, Jackie carefully began to dial, wishing he had brought his reading glasses with him.

'What's in the bag?' Michael asked, seeing that it was stuffed full of papers.

'I pinched these from his house last night,' Jackie said, opening it to show Michael Ned's few personal documents. 'Birth certificates and stuff.' Ned had never been anywhere outside County More so he didn't have a passport, and he never drove a car so he didn't have a driving licence. Jackie had to make do with his birth certificate, pension book and insurance documents.

Jackie's whole demeanour changed as soon as the phone was answered at the other end. A woman switchboard operator at the National Lottery headquarters in Dublin said: 'Hello, National Lotto, Maureen speaking, how may I help you?'

Pulling himself to his full height and adopting his very best telephone voice, Jackie replied: 'Yes, Maureen, hello. Now I'm wanting to talk to someone about a claim that I'll be making.' He winked knowingly at Michael, whose heart was in his mouth as he watched his best friend take the first tentative steps along a path which he sensed would lead to disaster.

Annie O'Shea was on the warpath. Once she had calmed down a little and made herself a soothing cup of tea, she had thought again about Jackie's plan and decided to talk it

102

through with him once more. Going upstairs to try and talk some sense into her deranged husband, she discovered the bedroom window open and her prisoner escaped across the roof. Fearing the worst, she marched down into the village, still in her apron, to look for him. Popping her head round the doorway of Fitzgerald's bar, she found Dennis and Dicey Riley fiddling around in the back of an old television set. 'Have you seen the boys?' she asked, curtly, her eyes ablaze.

'Not today, Annie,' Dennis answered truthfully.

'I'll kill them,' she said and hurried out, closing the door behind her.

Dicey Riley watched her go and thanked his lucky stars he was single. It was said around the village that there was no bone in Annie O'Shea's tongue but she had often struck a man down with it. Dennis and he sat in stunned silence, watching her marching away up the street, almost holding their breaths in anticipation of the fate awaiting Jackie and Michael when she eventually got her hands on them.

Their mighty deed done, Jackie and Michael left the telephone box solemnly and put their helmets on with great ceremony, as if signalling the end of some important ritual. Jackie turned to his old friend and clutched his arm. 'Michael,' he said, a little fearful now that he had actually set the ball rolling and knew it couldn't be stopped. 'We'll go down to the beach and get the story straight.' There was a pause while he gulped. 'They're sending a man from Dublin.'

Michael also swallowed hard at the thought. 'Are they convinced?' he asked as they both sat astride Jackie's motorbike, fixing the leather straps on their helmets under their chins.

'They are,' Jackie replied, starting up the bike with a single kick of his left leg. It was just as he had expected. Unless he was very much mistaken, the lottery company would act quickly to confirm that the claim was genuine and send someone from Dublin in the next few days. It might even be sooner, he wasn't sure. Calling back over his shoulder, he told Michael: 'But there's some preparing to do. I need to spend the night at Ned's in case the Lotto man comes first thing tomorrow.'

Michael crossed himself silently and thanked God it was Jackie, and not he, that was going to have to go back to that stinking cottage and spend the night alone with its grisly, decomposing occupant. Michael knew he'd never be able to eat another Brussels sprout again. Clasping his hands tightly around Jackie's waist, his long fingers interlocked, he hung on as the bike skidded on the gravel and sped off back down the hill towards the beach.

Outside the church, Father Patrick spotted young Maurice Tooley lying full length on a wooden trestle table normally used to sell vegetables, his hands behind his head, looking skyward and smiling.

'What are you looking at, Maurice?' the priest called, following the lad's gaze up to the blue sky and white clouds, peppered with circling seagulls.

The boy looked thoughtfully down his nose at the young man from Galway with the soft white hands and the lilting accent. Staring skywards again, he remarked: 'It's amazing how it just goes on and on, Father, isn't it?' A dog barked incessantly somewhere in the distance. Looking upwards, marvelling at the wispy veils of clouds floating majestically in the sky, he mused: 'On and on – into the universe and infinity.'

Father Patrick stood next to Maurice and, tilting his head upwards, drank in the scene, giving a silent blessing for this chance to share in the wonderment of a child. Now that he looked at what had seemed a perfectly normal sky from someone else's viewpoint, he saw how truly beautiful it was. 'Oh yes,' he said, breathlessly. 'It's a marvel, isn't it?'

He wondered where this was leading. What little he had learned of the boy in the past few weeks told him that here was a child with thought processes way beyond his years. He had already spoken to Mrs Shaunnessy, the sole teacher of the tiny village school, about trying to get Maurice some extra tuition or arrange to have him sent away to a better school when he was old enough. 'I think he's a remarkably bright lad,' he had told the kindly lady who taught just three children and none of them very well. 'You never know, Mrs Shaunnessy, Maurice may even become the first of your pupils to get to Trinity College.' She had thanked him for his suggestions and promised to see what she could do. It was something she had already considered for the boy, as he was way ahead of his fellow pupils, and the conversation echoed one she had privately had with his mother already; Maggie Tooley was very keen for her son to enjoy the chances she never enjoyed. She wanted him to see the world and escape from Tullymore, she had said. Of that she was quite clear.

Standing beside Maurice now, Father Patrick stared upwards for a while longer until the boy finally broke the spell. His brow creasing with concern, Maurice swivelled his legs round suddenly, sat up, and asked: 'How are you, Father?'

The priest, slightly bemused by the sudden concern, smiled and nodded. 'Oh fine, Maurice, fine, you know,' he reassured him, the breeze fresh in his face.

The boy, ever thoughtful, commented: 'You don't sound so sure there.' He watched the priest's face closely for any telltale signs of stress – twitching eye muscles, jaw clenched, trembling hands. He had watched a programme on RTE the previous night all about stress, about how it could affect people's health and make them ill. Doctors, lawyers and priests were high on the list of those affected, and it had troubled the boy. Having grilled his mother and grandfather about the stress levels in their own lives, and found there to be none, he had got bored. Father Patrick, he decided, was his next best shot.

Laughing off Maurice's consternation, Father Patrick dismissed it. 'Ah no,' he said. But then, seeing that he could not fool the child, he spoke from the heart for the first time since he had arrived in Tullymore four weeks earlier. 'It's just, well, it's been a difficult month for me, you know, Maurice, coming into a community like this,' he admitted. Thinking of the difficulties he had experienced trying to get the villagers to open up to him, to let him be their friend, he added: 'If I was here permanently I think people might be a little bit more, you know, welcoming.'

The boy nodded sagely. He thought as much. The television programme had mentioned the feelings of isolation from which parish priests sometimes suffer. He could just imagine Lizzy Quinn giving Father Patrick hell in the confessional, and wondered at the resilience of the man to listen to Pig Finn reeling off his sins in such close proximity. Then there was Pat Mulligan and all his lurid tales of sex with women. He supposed that Pat spiced up the details of his sexual exploits in order to shock the virginal priest. 'How much longer have you got?' Maurice asked, wishing that the young priest's posting wasn't just temporary. He liked him, and besides, he might be able to help him. The programme had said encouragement was vitally important.

Father Patrick sighed. 'Well, er, Father Mulligan should be back from Lourdes fairly soon, so then I'll be off.' It was a prospect which filled him with genuine sadness. In his short time in Tullymore, he had completely fallen for the place – hook, line and sinker. It had its own charm, trapped as it was in a time capsule, where nothing much had changed in generations and few outside influences had affected the simple ways. It was the sort of village he had always hoped to end up in as a priest, somewhere he could be loved and accepted by the community, able to inspire and comfort, and administer to their faith. The church was well attended each Sunday, the confessional was always busy and by and large there was a healthy respect for Catholicism, bucking the national trend.

Maurice sighed too, wondering what the future held for the cleric. 'Well you'll be missed,' he said kindly, remembering the advice given on the programme. 'You've done well,' he added, encouragingly, but rather spoilt it by adding: 'No matter what people say.'

Although a little taken aback, Father Patrick smiled and nodded at the backhanded compliment. 'Thank you, Maurice,' he said with feeling. 'Yes, well, I – I like to think I've made an impression.'

Two hundred miles away at Dublin's international heliport, an Augusta 109 twin jet turbine executive helicopter sat on the tarmac, its rotors spinning as a man in a suit and trendy beige overcoat and carrying a briefcase ran from a limousine and boarded. With a loud whirring noise, the seven-seater helicopter took off, its retractable undercarriage sliding into its belly as it lifted upwards and veered away over the city, bound for the Wicklow hills and thereafter the mountains of southern Ireland. It was to be a journey of some two hundred miles, which would take about ninety minutes.

The pilot, Tom Kidd, an inimitable professional and veteran of many similar flights, told his VIP passenger that, as arranged, he would drop him down on a hilltop road just outside Ballyneath, where a rental car would be waiting to speed him to his final destination. The passenger had been quite specific in his instructions; he didn't want to alert the villagers to his presence by arriving in a helicopter; he needed to be dropped off nearby and then make his own way in, discreetly, by car. Having delivered his passenger safely, Tom was to land the helicopter somewhere near Ballyneath and wait until dusk for his return. If for any reason he didn't make the agreed rendezvous, he was to fly back to Dublin and return to collect him at ten o'clock the following morning. Needless to say, when dealing with this particular company, Tom knew that the mission was top secret.

At Glenskellig Bay, Jackie and Michael were undressing for a swim after dismounting from the bike, but neither one was full of his usual *joie de vivre*. Michael had been uneasy all morning and as they reached the cove he had told his friend that he was having serious second thoughts about going through with the plan after all. Jackie had become uncharacteristically angry. He didn't welcome Michael's nagging doubts. He had plenty of his own. Snapping at his old friend, he had said that it would be no cause of concern for him, it would be Jackie doing all the lying, and Jackie sent off to prison if they were caught. Heartened slightly by the thought, Michael had decided not to press the point and to give Jackie all the support he needed. He would even come and visit him in prison, he promised, a prospect which did nothing for his companion's mood.

Discarding their clothes in a heap and trotting towards the sea stark naked and side by side, as they had done for nigh on sixty years, they both decided not to say another word about their private fears and concentrate instead on the matter in hand. Michael, his gaunt figure a contrast to the thickset man at his side, cupped his right hand over his genitals and prepared to step gingerly into the water. Jackie, marching into the waves, his arms pumping at his side, ploughed on without a second thought. Reaching the shore, each man privately wondered if this would their last time in the cold, clear waters of Glenskellig Bay.

On the designated hilltop road on the outskirts of Ballyneath, the Augusta helicopter came in to land with a deafening noise. The dust and wind from the jet turbines and the massive rotor blades flattened the grass and scared off all the sheep, who fled to the corners of their fields. The man in the suit ran from the aircraft, his head down to avoid the whirring blades and cursed at the duplicitous lengths he sometimes had to go to, just to do his job. It would have been so much easier if Tom could have flown him all the way to the village, even if that would have set tongues wagging and minds racing. No, this was the only way. Waving a farewell to the pilot, he ran towards a waiting silver Ford Mondeo hire car, where a woman in uniform was waiting to hand him the keys. Offering to drop her back at the hire car company in Ballyneath town centre, the man started the engine and headed towards Tullymore.

At Glenskellig, Jackie and Michael were at the edge of the water and calling to each other over the noise of the crashing waves. The overnight storm had cooled the water considerably and there were goose bumps visible on their lily-white flesh.

'Go on, ask me another one,' Jackie called to his companion with confidence, as he took another step further in, his naked body thick and flabby after too many platefuls of Annie's apple tart and other culinary delights.

Michael faltered and mumbled: 'Er, er ...' racking his brains for yet another question the lottery representative might ask the man he believed to be Ned Devine.

Losing his patience and flapping his hands in indignation, Jackie shouted: 'Come on, man. Use your imagination.'

Speaking in a strange falsetto voice, akin to one he though the lottery representative might have, Michael called: 'How old are you, Ned?' as he waded further in, his bones showing through his thin flesh at every joint.

'I'm sixty-six, sir,' Jackie answered proudly.

'And do you have any family, Ned?' the strange voice asked.

Jackie shook his head vehemently. 'No, there's just meself now,' he said. Delighted with his own answer, he launched his body forward into the waves at that point, splashing the skeletal frame of Michael and drenching him. This was going to be a piece of cake, Jackie decided, doing the doggy paddle briskly around the bay and chuckling to himself all the while. He'd have the winning cheque in his hands in no time at all.

Pig Finn had a face as long as a wet weekend as he led a small white pony up to Brendy Tooley's workshop. Brendy, having fixed the wheel of the little wooden cart as well as that of Finn's van, was wiping his trap down for him and telling Maurice about the old days when goat and donkey carts were regularly used in the county for fetching and carrying and motor cars were a rarity. Maurice had stopped listening to his grandfather ages ago and was sitting on the ground idly playing with a box of matches and an oily rag.

'Is she fit, Brendy?' Finn asked of the green-painted trap, as he slowed the pony beside it and scratched her nose fondly under the halter. He was inordinately fond of animals, he always had been, ever since he was a child, and this little pony had served him well.

Unable to resist a sarcastic dig at his expense, Brendy looked up at Finn's latest mode of transport and asked: 'Oh, so you're not in the convertible today then?' He hated flashy cars. It was a flashy car that had first caught his Bridgid's eye and which had ultimately taken her away.

'No, I'm not,' Finn snapped, wiping his nose on the back of his hand. Before Brendy could make a second comment, the attention of both men was abruptly interrupted by Maurice, who had set fire to the oily rag, frightening himself. Jumping backwards, he let out a cry. 'God Almighty!' Finn exclaimed. More nimble on his feet than the older man, he rushed over to stamp the fire out with his big green wellington boots. 'Maurice! Be careful there, son, there's petrol here,' Finn warned the boy. He grabbed a plastic bowl full of water and threw it onto the flames to quell the fire. 'Careful, son!' Finn called, as the flames finally died down and acrid smoke billowed towards him. He was not really angry, he was more taken aback than anything else.

Brendy, however, was furious. 'Oh, Maurice, you're a bad boy. I've told you time and time again not to be playing with matches!' he shouted, his expression thunderous. The boy stood watching the flames, his eyes fearful.

'Sorry, Finn,' Maurice called softly, emerging from the garage, genuinely contrite.

'You're all right,' Finn conceded, ruffling Maurice's hair, but he was still frowning. Taking the old man to one side, he hissed: 'Jesus, Brendy, would you keep the boy away from the petrol?' His heart was still racing. He loved Maurice like his own son, and he couldn't bear the thought of him coming to any harm.

Brendy sighed and shook his head. There had been numerous occasions recently when he had crawled out from underneath some car or other, to find Maurice about to embark on some potentially fatal escapade. It was too much responsibility for him, he had told Maggie so. He was an old man with a business to run and he couldn't be expected to keep the boy from harm. 'He needs a father,' he told Finn. 'He's too quick for me.'

Finn couldn't have agreed more and moved closer to

Brendy for a private word. 'He needs his real father,' he said, a sense of urgency in his voice. Pausing for effect, he added softly: 'Maggie needs me too, Brendy.'

Brendy scoffed and shook his head. 'Jeez, man, you're not the da.' He had no idea who the real father was, Maggie had never told him, despite his initial threats to beat it out of her, but one look at the pig man with his mop of dark curly hair and bushy black eyebrows told him all he needed to know.

Defensive, Finn bristled. 'I am so,' he said, 'and Maggie knows it.' There had been many a time when he had pointed to the boy and told Brendy to look at the similarities. 'Look at his eyes,' he would say, opening his own as wide as he could to reveal their colour. His were brown, and Maurice's were greeny blue. 'They're the same,' Finn would insist. Brendy, shaking his head, would look between the boy and the young man and scratch his head. Whenever Finn thought he had his attention, he would add: 'And the nose, look at it, look at those two noses,' placing himself in profile to give Brendy a better view. The older man would turn away rather than indulge the pig man further.

While the two men stood conferring on the matter, Pat Mulligan, dressed in a different suit – black this time, the collar turned up at the neck – swaggered smarmily towards them. Pointing to the pony Finn had brought to take the trap home, he sneered: 'What a mess your donkey's making.' A steaming pile of fresh dung littered the lane leading up to the workshop.

Finn shrugged. 'It's a pony,' he pointed out, indignant on the animal's behalf.

Pat wasn't finished having a dig at his old adversary. The two men had been at each other's throats since primary school when they had first fought over a girl. They had been sniping and vying with each other ever since, although Pat – smelling of aftershave, deodorant and hair gel – had considerably more success with women than the pig farmer. 'Christ man, the stink on your donkey's arse is almost as bad as yourself,' Pat added, for good measure.

Finn wasn't in the mood for this. 'Ah, piss off with you,' he said, waving his hand dismissively and turning back to Brendy to finish his conversation.

But there was a wicked spark in the eye of the village dandy and he decided to play his trump card. 'And I will at that,' he said, his face smug. 'I've a date with Maurice's mother tonight. Haven't I, Brendy?' he called, for endorsement.

Brendy frowned disapprovingly at having been dragged into their little dispute and turned away. Finn's face flushed red and he stood his ground. 'And that's a lie,' he denounced. 'Maggie's mine. We're just discussing it here now.' He turned to Brendy for support but the garage owner was busying himself with something suddenly.

Pat smirked. Moving closer to Pig Finn, he spoke under his breath so that Brendy couldn't hear: 'She wanted someone who could get close enough – to give her what she wants.' Walking away, still chuckling to himself, he left the swineherd red of face and speechless, as his pony dropped a huge pat of dung on the ground by his feet.

The man from Dublin had taken off his raincoat and his suit jacket and hung them both on the little hook above the rear passenger door. Hurtling along winding country lanes in his new Mondeo, he had a map unfolded and spread haphazardly across the steering wheel as he drove. 'Tullymore, Tullymore,' he whispered to himself, frowning and looking for the tiny fishing village that seemed to have been overlooked by almost every cartographer known to man. 'Where is it?'

The man on the telephone had been perfectly clear. Fifty miles south west of Ballyneath, past the ring of ancient pagan stones at the top of the moor and then left down the twisting lane that looked as if it petered out or led only to a cliff edge. He'd passed the ring of stones an hour ago and still there was no sign of his destination in the distance. At this rate, he'd miss his return journey rendezvous with the helicopter pilot.

Cursing to himself under his breath, the wind from his open window rippling his stylishly cut mousy brown hair, he wished to God he didn't have to find these Godforsaken places all on his own every time. The company really should send someone with him to navigate; especially when he had such an important task ahead and needed to keep all his wits about him.

Michael and Jackie, out of the sea and drying themselves off in the lee of a rocky outcrop at the top of the beach, were still chatting animatedly about the lottery win. Jackie, almost fully dressed, his skin still tingling from the cold water, felt invigorated and stood away from the shelter of the rocks, by a waterfall leading to the cove.

Michael, undressed but for his shoes and socks, and with just a towel around his narrow waist, his skin hanging in loose folds off his rib cage, lit up a cigarette from a Zippo lighter, took a deep draw on it and leaned into the rocks. Studying the ebullient expression of his old friend, he asked: 'So, what are you going to spend your half on, Jackie?' before exhaling deeply.

Jackie laughed out loud as he pulled on his polo shirt. 'Ah, oh, we agreed half, did we, Michael?' he teased.

Michael looked suddenly contrite. 'No, I just sort of assumed it,' he said, but realising that as the whole thing had been Jackie's idea – he had found Ned Devine dead, he was the one making the claim, and pretending to be Ned – then perhaps he was entitled to a bigger share. It wasn't greed on his part, it was simply a thought that hadn't entered his head before – the two friends had always shared everything fifty fifty, even their

114

sandwiches at school, and he had expected the same now.

'Oh, you assumed it, did you?' Jackie repeated, teasing his friend still further. There was mileage in this. Although he had every intention of giving Michael half, he could easily string him along right until the last minute, he thought, mischievously. It would keep him on his toes. Distracted from his scheming thoughts by the throaty sound of a car approaching, he looked up in genuine surprise. 'Who's that?' he asked, as Michael, out of sight behind the rocks, puffed on a cigarette and looked up inquisitively.

The man from Dublin swore under his breath as he pulled his car to a screeching halt at the end of a dead end lane that led only to a little cove. He was well and truly lost now; he'd been down every other lane in the area, or so it seemed, and they all led nowhere. Scratching his head and looking around hopelessly, he suddenly caught sight of Jackie, standing by some nearby rocks, and fervently hoped that he could help him. Stepping out of the car, the man smiled and waved, and held his hands up to his eyes, squinting into the sun. 'Well, hello there!' he called in his most friendly tone, across the roof of the vehicle.

'Hello,' Jackie answered, taking a few steps forward cautiously. It was not often that they got strangers in these parts. Michael, out of sight, stood half-naked to one side, curiously eavesdropping.

'I think I'm a little bit lost,' the city man explained sheepishly. 'Do you know where Tullymore is?' He had long ago tossed his map onto the back seat in a fit of pique.

Always happy to help a stranger, especially one in such a new car and with a posh accent, Jackie smiled back as Michael stood listening. 'Er, you're not far off, mister,' he said, helpfully. Pointing, he added: 'Back up the lane, left at the end and it's a long road that has no turning.'

The man nodded his understanding, although his heart sank a little. He was sure he had been down that road twice already. 'Are you from the village yourself?' he asked, politely, hoping for a little more help.

Proud to answer, Jackie puffed up his chest like an O'Connell Street pigeon. 'I am, all me life,' he said.

'Would you happen to know a Ned Devine?' the man asked, as Jackie's face fell and Michael's cigarette froze in mid air a few inches from his lips, his eyes like saucers.

Glued to the spot, and unable to answer, the penny finally dropped. 'Ned Devine?' Jackie asked, his voice cracking under the strain. Michael, still covered only by a towel, dropped to his knees behind the rocks as if he had been shot. Clinging to the boulders and straining to listen as he sucked on his half-finished cigarette, he looked just as aghast.

'Ned Devine,' the lottery representative repeated, waiting for an answer. When none was immediately forthcoming, he asked again: 'Do you know him?'

Bursting back into life, and while Michael crouched just a few feet away, Jackie nodded violently. 'I do – I do,' he said. Swallowing hard, he asked: 'Is it Ned you're wanting?'

'It is, yeah,' the driver replied, beginning to wonder if this rural countryman was in full possession of all his mental faculties.

Raising his voice to make sure that Michael could hear him clearly, Jackie shouted: 'Well, I can take you to Ned Devine's house if you want.'

Michael's heart stopped in his chest. What was Jackie thinking? He had just blown his cover completely. He should have said, 'Yes, I'm Ned Devine', but he had panicked. Now what was he going to do?

A little startled by the sudden offer, but grateful all the same after his nightmare journey up to this point, the driver readily agreed. 'That'd be very good of you,' he said. 'Want to jump in the car?'

Hardly daring to look to his right to see what horrified

expression was on Michael O'Sullivan's face, Jackie picked up his cardigan as nonchalantly as he could and strolled towards the waiting stranger and his car. Climbing into the passenger seat and parking his bottom on the leather seat, Jackie looked imploringly back at the little beach, on which there was no sign of Michael. He only hoped to God he had heard him and hadn't been washing out his ears or doing something else at the crucial moment. His train of thought was distracted by an enormous sneeze from the driver, who fished out a man size tissue and blew his nose enthusiastically.

'Oh, hey, I'm sorry,' said the man. 'Excuse me, it's, er, hay fever. I get it every time I come down to the country.' Jackie shut the car door, looking back earnestly for the last time as they reversed back up the single track.

The second they had disappeared around the bend, Michael threw away his cigarette, scrambled up from behind the rocks and rushed over towards his heap of clothes. In a mad panic, he pulled his white motorcycle helmet and thick black goggles on, before remembering his clothes. Dropping his towel to reveal a bony body naked but for brown leather shoes and socks, he hopped precariously around on one foot as he tried unsuccessfully to marry up his foot with a trouser leg. Realising that he simply didn't have time and abandoning all thoughts of dressing, he cried aloud: 'Oh, sweet Jesus.'

Running to the motorbike, he sat astride it as speedily as his nudity would allow, started it up, let the clutch in too harshly and did a wheel spin off the shingle beach, splashing dramatically through the little stream that cascaded from the waterfall on the other side of the road. Manoeuvring it awkwardly onto the tarmac lane, revving it up and speeding back in the general direction of Ned Devine's cottage, Michael had not a stitch on apart from his shoes.

Chapter
Six

If I had money enough to spend
And leisure time to sit awhile
There is a fair maid in this town
That surely has my heart beguiled

– 'The Parting Glass', *a traditional Irish song*

The driver of the silver hire car turned it around and headed back towards the village. Jackie's heart was beating so fast in his chest, he wondered if he would die of a sudden cardiac arrest, just like Ned.

'Sorry, I'm Jim Kelly,' the driver introduced himself, reaching his right hand across his body and extending a soft city palm.

'Jackie O'Shea,' the farmer smiled nervously, his own palms sweaty as they shook hands. 'How are you?' he asked out of habit and politeness. His voice was hoarse and he felt extremely close to death. How on earth was he going to get himself out of this one, he wondered.

'Not too bad,' Jim replied with a fetching smile that created dimples in his boyish face. Looking ahead at the fork in the road coming up in front of them, and remembering the farmer's instructions of a few minutes earlier, Jim asked: 'So it's just at the end of this road and then the next left, yeah?'

Jackie, his hair still wet from the sea, stalled desperately. 'Er, no, no, no.' he said. 'If – if you're going to Ned's house, then you'd better turn right and head back to the hills.' He eyed the driver and hoped he wasn't quite as smart as he initially appeared.

'Are you sure?' Jim asked, his forehead creasing. He didn't have the best sense of direction, but it seemed to him that they would then be heading completely the wrong way.

'Yeah. Sure I'm sure. Yes, I've – I've been here all me life,' Jackie said defensively, glaring at the stranger and daring him to challenge his local knowledge. Jim sighed and duly forked right and north, turning the car back in the direction he had just come.

On the road just behind him, a naked Michael whizzed past on Jackie's motorbike, his face ashen with fear, his bare genitals bouncing uncomfortably up and down on the cracked leatherette seat beneath him.

Snaking up the hill, the car continued on its journey for several miles, heading well away from the village and up into the hills. Passing a right turn, Jackie suddenly shouted out: 'Ah, now I think there's a right turn coming up here,' pointing a finger to indicate the turn they had missed.

The car screeched to a halt just past the turning, and reversed. Jackie, his heart already under incredible strain, called out breathlessly: 'Will you drive a little slower, mister, please?' He looked genuinely alarmed.

Remembering the far slower pace of country life, Jim apologised. 'Sorry,' he said. 'I'll try and take it easier now,' and duly did so. Counting off the seconds, Jackie wondered how long he could keep the stranger up in the mountains before he became suspicious. He wondered if Michael had made it to Ned's yet.

But Michael was not nearly as good a rider as Jackie and he wobbled along on the bumpy roads precariously. Whizzing past the phone box where Jackie had first staked his claim, he drove past an astounded Kitty Moore, out for a walk with her pet poodle, who both looked back in disbelief as he screamed past. Suddenly realising who it was, she turned in her tracks and started to jog after him, calling his name. She could not believe her eyes.

Jim Kelly was getting a little impatient. He had promised the helicopter pilot that he would only be a couple of hours, and he had just wasted the past twenty minutes winding his way along increasingly narrow and dangerous country lanes. Passing another turn, Jackie shouted: 'Whoaah! Left.' Jim brought the car to a screeching halt once more and glared at his passenger and navigator, in whom he was fast losing confidence.

'Haven't we just been up here?' he asked, clearly agitated.

'Er, it would seem that way,' Jackie nodded, shrinking under his stare, 'but in fact that's a different spot.' Slamming the car into reverse, Jim sped back to the turning and took it.

Stopping a few hundred yards further on to allow Jackie to get his bearings, and leaning over his steering wheel impatiently, Jim asked: 'Are you having trouble with the directions?'

'I am,' the old man conceded at last. 'You're going too fast. Yes.'

Putting the car into gear, Jim apologised: 'I'm sorry, I thought I was taking it slower now.'

Not making any attempt to direct him either way, Jackie explained: 'Ah, it's faster than a walk, and I've always walked me way round these hills in the mist and fog.' Jim raised his eyes to the heavens and sighed.

A few hundred yards on, Jackie O'Shea shielded himself from another almighty sneeze, as the hire car crawled along slowly, winding its way down towards the village at last.

'Yes, there – there's a left turn, left turn here,' Jackie called, as they passed yet another familiar landmark. Jim missed it and was about to slow down, only to hear Jackie tell him: 'No, it's a right turn, I think, yes.'

'Left or right?' Jim asked, his patience wearing thinner by the minute.

'No, right,' Jackie replied, hardly daring to look into the driver's face. 'Right, right, right.' He nodded his head emphatically each time he said it to indicate his certainty.

'Right? Okay,' Jim responded, ruing the moment he had agreed to the old man showing him the way.

The green hills flying past them in a blur and the coast coming once more into view, Jackie tried to distract Jim from the grotto a few hundred yards ahead which he would surely recognise as having passed before. 'What kind of business are you in?' he asked, touching Jim's arm to make him look his way just as the grotto neared.

'Oh ... business,' Jim answered evasively, completely missing the landmark on his left. It was not company policy to speak to anyone about the line of work their employees were in, for fear of letting the cat out of the bag about a local winner. Many lottery winners preferred complete privacy, especially when they lived in small communities like Tullymore, and if Jim Kelly went around telling people he worked for the National Lottery and wanted Ned Devine, there was a strong chance that people might put two and two together.

'Business?' Jackie echoed, studying Jim's profile and obviously expecting more.

'Business,' Jim repeated, his lips pursing as he felt increasingly uncomfortable under his passenger's gaze, but determined not to give anything more away.

121

'Yes ... business,' Jackie finally conceded, knowing that he wasn't going to get any further.

On the rough muddy track which led down the steep hill to Ned Devine's cottage, Michael O'Sullivan was off-road and hurtling out of control, throwing the old bike around the bumpy track like a motocross competitor. Speeding through a ford, splashing mud up his bare back as he did so, he rounded the corner and – with tremendous relief – spotted the bothy hugging the contours of the cliff bottom.

A few minutes later, the silver Mondeo pulled up at the front of the little white thatched cottage. There was no sign of Michael as Jim pulled the car to a halt. Jackie leapt from his seat like a rabbit, not bothering to shut the passenger door behind him, and scurried round to knock on the little front door. A cat ambled forward, hungry for food and attention and brushed itself up against the marigolds growing either side of the porch.

There was no answer at the front door. Jackie knocked again, this time even harder, but still there was no reply. He couldn't understand it; he had taken Jim Kelly round and round the back roads of County More West for so long that Michael simply must have had time to get to Ned's and be ready and waiting for them.

'Ned, Ned,' Jackie called through the door. 'Are you in there? I've brought a man to see you. Ned? Ned?' There was a note of real panic in his voice.

Jim, sneezing loudly now that he was out of the car and even more exposed to the country air, blew his nose once more and looked disappointed after his long and tortuous journey. 'I don't think he's in,' he said. 'I'd best take a look down the village,' he added, turning back towards the car.

Jackie, his mind racing at the unpalatable prospect,

suddenly spotted the muddy trail of a motorcycle leading to the back of the house. Anxious not to let the stranger anywhere near the good people of Tullymore for fear they would ruin everything, he said: 'No, no, I – I'll take a look around the back, he sleeps a lot in the afternoon.'

Jim nodded but couldn't answer, as another almighty sneeze welled up in his nose and erupted with great force. Clutching a large white handkerchief to his face, he waved his approval as Jackie disappeared round the back of the house.

Following the trail and calling to Ned's cat to follow him, Jackie gasped when he came across Michael, still naked but for his helmet and shoes, spattered with mud and crouched on all fours behind the overhanging thatch of the bothy. He was desperately trying to gain entry via a tiny bedroom window. 'Michael, Michael!' Jackie hissed. 'Where are your clothes, man?'

'There wasn't time,' Michael explained, covering his genitals self-consciously with his bony hands. He was cold, wet and shivering with trepidation after his naked ordeal. The last thing he needed was Jackie stating the obvious and his expression told him so.

'We're knocking at the front,' Jackie persisted, indignantly.

'I can hear that, but it's all locked up,' Michael hissed back, deeply unhappy with the turn of events. He had said from the start that he couldn't pretend to be Ned and now here he was, being shouted at through no fault of his own, and about to have to do the very thing he had been promised he wouldn't have to.

Pushing him to one side impatiently, Jackie whispered: 'Mind yourself,' and forced the tiny, salt-stained window frame with his foot.

Sauntering round to the front of the long thatched cottage a few minutes later, where he found Jim Kelly sneezing and blowing his nose, Jackie smiled broadly.

'You're all right,' he said. 'He was taking a bath there.' He wandered up to the front door and stood there, waiting expectantly for Michael to open the door and play his part in their great charade.

Jim finished wiping his nose with his handkerchief, put it away in his pocket and came to stand by his side at the doorway. Offering Jackie his hand, he said: 'Well, thanks very much for your help,' indicating that the business he had with Ned Devine was private and that Jackie's services would no longer be required.

'Oh, no problem at all,' Jackie nodded smilingly, standing his ground and wondering how he could find a way to remain and help Michael out. 'No problem.' There was an awkward pause, during which Jackie refused to take the hint and leave. The silence was broken by a shuffling noise from the other side of the front door as Michael approached. Then they listened for what seemed an age to the sound of someone struggling with the lock, clicking it back and forth in an attempt to open it as if they were not accustomed to its stiff mechanism. Finally, the door creaked open, and there stood Michael, naked from the waist up, with a large bath towel wrapped around his angular hips.

His expression was one of sheer terror as his eyes nervously flicked back and forth from one man to the other. 'Yes?' he asked, fearfully, wanting the ground to open up and swallow him whole.

Hoping to instil him with some confidence, Jackie beamed warmly at him and said: 'Er, Ned, I'm sorry to get you out of your bath, but there's a man to see you.'

'Oh,' was all Michael could say. His throat felt suddenly very dry.

'Can I come in, Mr Devine?' Jim asked, also smiling. Glancing askance at Jackie, he added: 'It's rather personal.' Getting no response, he explained in a slightly louder voice in case the old fisherman was deaf or simple: 'I'm Jim Kelly. You called my office in Dublin this morning?'

Michael, completely dazed and looking to Jackie for guidance, nodded. 'Oh, I – I see,' he said, but still stood there silently in front of them, the tension electric between them.

Ever helpful, Jackie prompted his trembling friend. 'Why don't you invite us in, Ned – so the man can tell you his business?' He bobbed his head up and down meaningfully at him.

Michael finally took the hint. 'Y-yes, r-right, in you come,' he said, stepping aside to open the little wooden front door wider.

Jim, seeing Jackie step forward as if to enter, turned to him politely and said: 'I think it's best we're left alone now.' Shaking his hand firmly by way of goodbye, he added: 'Thanks again.'

Helpless, Jackie faltered but could do no more. 'Right you are,' he said, moving back to allow Jim through.

'Er, watch your head,' Michael told the stranger, as Jim ducked to get in through the low doorway and went into the little cottage.

Staring anxiously at Michael, who was looking equally anxiously back at him, Jackie hesitated but then said, with a smile: 'All the best, *Ned*,' and gave him a wave and the thumbs up sign. 'All the best,' he repeated, before turning and walking away, leaving Michael speechless on the doorstep.

Once inside the little fishing cottage, Jim took a good look around. It was like stepping back in time. The floor was stone, the yellowing plaster walls were several feet thick, the little windows set deep within them, their sills filled with the flotsam and jetsam of a fisherman's life. Apart from the rather peculiar smell, it was quite charming in a humble sort of way, with its ramshackle appearance and organised clutter. Yuppies in Dublin paid thousands to create the same atmosphere in their riverside condos. It reminded him of a bar that had just opened in Grafton Street that had an old-fashioned seafaring theme. God, what they wouldn't give for some of these old fishing artefacts – nets and hooks, lines and sinkers, lobster pots and crab traps. It was a veritable living museum, a time warp.

Michael, his face ashen with fear, shuffled in stiffly from the doorstep and turned to shut the front door. Fortunately, Jim was so busy looking elsewhere that he didn't notice the thick stripe of mud that had sprayed up Michael's spine from his madcap dash across the fields and tracks on Jackie's motorbike.

More than a little flustered, Michael turned to his guest and stammered: 'W-would it be better if I was dressed, Mr Kelly?' At least if his guest agreed, that would give him a few moments to compose himself a little, he thought.

'It would indeed, Ned,' said Jim, not at all alarmed by Michael's nervousness and quite accustomed to the unusual behaviour exhibited by people who had just come into a lot of money. 'You take your time there now,' he reassured him, hoping to put him more at his ease.

'Right,' Michael said, backing into the bedroom and leaving the door slightly ajar.

Wandering around the low-ceilinged living room, peering into old sepia photographs and studying the strange and mysterious objects adorning the walls, Jim called chattily: 'Do you have any family living nearby, Ned?'

'Oh no, I – I'm all on me own now,' Michael called back, pleased that he had at least got one pre-rehearsed answer out of the way. Still wrapped in his towel and rooting through Ned's wardrobe, while desperately trying to ignore the corpse still sitting upright in bed a few feet away, he pulled out a quite unsuitable shirt and a pair of dress trousers and examined them critically.

126

'Oh, do you have much family yourself, Mr Kelly?' Michael called, trying to sound congenial and relaxed, when all the time he could feel an impending angina attack due to all the stress.

Blowing his nose once more, and selecting a dusty old hardback book from a shelf, Jim called back: 'Oh, I do. Too much at times, if you know what I mean. We've got three kids now, so there's always aunties and uncles and cousins coming over, wanting to visit.'

Still rooting through Ned's mahogany veneered wardrobe and examining the few clothes hanging on metal hangers, Michael pulled out a fancy blue and white patterned shirt and a pair of Ned's maroon suit trousers. Holding them up against his lanky figure, he had completely forgotten that the dead man had not been tall and was a good three sizes smaller than him. He wondered if it would matter.

Jim, meanwhile was studying a framed photograph on Ned's wall which showed a group of fishermen sitting smiling around a bulging net of fish next to an old trawler. In the middle sat the real Ned Devine, alongside his father and uncle. To the right was Eamonn Daly, Annie's late father, and to the left the trawler owner Phil McConville. It had been Ned's most treasured possession. 'Were you a fisherman, by any chance, Ned?' Jim called.

Breathing in as he buttoned up the gaily-coloured shirt, Michael called: 'Oh yes, I was at sea man and boy. This was my father's cottage originally, he used to run a boat from here.' Checking himself in the full-length mirror, he looked like a scarecrow. The arms of Ned's shirt and the trouser legs were at least three inches too short. Sighing hopelessly, he was just about to leave the bedroom and rejoin his guest but was stopped by the noise of Jackie tapping on the open window and fighting to get in through the net curtains.

'What do you think?' Michael asked his friend, posing in front of him, his arms angled at the elbow, hands in the air.

Jackie looked horrified. All his future hopes and dreams rested on the sight before him and he could feel it all slipping inexorably away. 'You – you can't, you can't wear that!' he exclaimed in a whisper, before struggling in through the window to take his protégé firmly in hand.

Flicking through the old book, a first edition *Moby Dick*, and talking to no one in particular, Jim chattered on with his usual spiel: 'You have to be careful, winning the lottery can bring as much bad luck as it can good. It's a real shame you don't have any family, Ned.'

In the bedroom, Michael had changed again and was now dressed in a set of well-fitting, yet familiar clothes. Behind him, stood Jackie, completely undressed but for his baggy white Y-front underpants, brushing some fluff from Michael's shoulder. 'Oh, you're doing grand, grand,' he reassured his nervous friend. 'Don't be worrying now. You'll have the lottery man twisted around your little finger.' He smiled and patted his shoulders. But his face suddenly fell and he clapped his hand to his forehead in shock. 'Oh, Holy mother of God!' he cried, his hands clasped together in front of him as if in prayer, his encouraging expression shattered by a sudden terrible realisation.

'What?' asked Michael, appalled. Looking into his friend's face, he knew that, somehow, something had gone terribly wrong.

Jim was still talking in the other room. Wandering over to a wall on which a simple wooden crucifix was the only ornament, he called absent-mindedly to Ned: 'You're gonna have to be careful of your friends after the win.' He had seen it so many times. He could tell Ned all about it, but he wouldn't. That would only spoil his dream. It was not a pretty picture, generally speaking. Once the initial excitement of a

128

win was over, the party hats put away, the new cars bought, cheques written to nearest and dearest and the cruise to foreign ports taken, then would come the awkward visits, the friends popping round to ask if the winner could spare a few punts for this project or that scheme. That was usually followed by the begging letters – hundreds of them – from people the winner may have never even met, asking for cash for terminally ill children, money to save destitute families or donations to local religious charities and good causes.

The winner would be inundated, literally, with appeals for money, even if they had chosen not to have their win publicised. The news would filter out through neighbours and family members, and before long they would have to change their telephone number, move house and hide away from the people they had once called friends. When those asking realised that there was no money forthcoming, the worms would turn. Hate mail, late night telephone calls, vandalism, malicious rumours – all born of jealousy and greed. It was all very distressing for the recipients. Former winners would call Jim Kelly at work and tell him their tales of woe. How they wished they had never won, how everything had gone wrong since they had.

Even getting together with other winners for group moral support didn't work. Millionaire's clubs, set up by the lottery companies, were generally disbanded after a while, because of the strict pecking order which was established. Those who had won the most, say, more than two million, tended to stick together and looked down their noses at the smaller winners of a million or less. Jealousy and rivalry was rife, even amongst millionaires, and people who had previously been quite content with their winnings suddenly felt quite underprivileged by comparison.

The strain on relationships was often enormous; there was the couple who won just before they celebrated their silver wedding anniversary, only for the husband to run off with a younger woman a few days later; the happily married couple who split up because they couldn't agree on how much they should give away to the wife's family; the single man who stayed miserable and lonely because he said that after he won he felt that he could never again be certain if a woman only wanted him for his money; the divorcee who blew the lot and ended up on welfare. There were some happy endings – quiet, everyday folk who had shared their winnings with their loved ones and lived happily ever after – but they were in the minority and, standing in Ned's tiny cottage now, Jim wondered idly into which category he would fall.

In the bedroom, Jackie was forcing himself to be calm. If he panicked now he knew he would lose Michael's co-operation forever. Carefully explaining his dilemma to his friend, he said, as matter-of-factly as he could: 'The winning ticket is in me little bag, me little bag's been left in the phone box ...'

All the colour draining from his face, his eyes now as large as dinner plates, Michael stuttered: 'Oh – great. Bloody great.'

Jim looked out of the window and admired the view across the bay as he carried on talking to Ned in the other room. 'Do you understand what I'm saying, Ned?' he asked again. 'You'll have to watch your friends.'

The door to the bedroom opened fully and out walked Michael, as white as a sheet. Jim hardly gave his garb a second look and thankfully didn't recognise Jackie O'Shea's clothes. Everyone he had seen in the country dressed much the same anyway – in thick cord trousers, woollen zip-up cardigans and tweed shirts; it was a kind of rural uniform.

'Ah, there we are,' Jim smiled a greeting at the man he knew as Ned. 'Ready for business.' He turned away from the little window to reach for his briefcase just in time to miss the extraordinary sight of Jackie running across in front of the

130

house pushing his motorbike, dressed only in his underpants and helmet.

Standing in the bedroom doorway trembling and reluctant to step into the living room, Michael dreaded the next few minutes. If he was nervous before, the lost ticket only added to his anxiety. Feeling in desperate need of something to steady his nerves and spotting a half-empty bottle of Jameson's whiskey on the sideboard, he asked: 'Will you have a drink, Mr Kelly?'

Jim shook his head. 'I won't, thank you, but you help yourself.' He had somehow to find his way back to the helicopter rendezvous point yet and then drive home once he got to Dublin. Besides, he had been in some of these back-of-beyond places before and had learned the hard way that most of these farmers and fishermen made their own moonshine, which was strong enough to blow a city boy's head off.

Michael helped himself to a large measure, his hand trembling so violently that the bottle neck rattled on the little glass tumbler, and finally sat down in the only armchair in the place, a well-worn example whose shortcomings had been covered with a patchwork rug.

Jim sat himself down on a simple wooden chair opposite and placed his briefcase on his lap, his palms face down on it. 'Well, basically, Ned, the reason as to why I'm here today,' he began, 'is that sometimes when people learn just how much they have won on the Lotto, they get a bit of a shock.' His tone was suddenly earnest.

Quivering from head to toe, his stomach full of butterflies, Michael was completely oblivious to the fact that he had drunk a large whiskey in one gulp to calm them. 'Oh yes, oh that I can imagine,' he said with feeling, his face flushed. Looking over at a photograph of dear old Ned, he poured himself another large whiskey.

Jackie O'Shea, half-mad with worry, headed for the phone box like a bat out of hell, wading through bogs and fords and driving across fields made muddy by the previous night's storm. How could he have been so stupid, he chastised himself all the way there. What had he been thinking of, leaving the bag in the phone box? He'd already landed Michael in hot water up to his neck and now he had let him down still further. What if someone had inadvertently found the bag, had looked inside and seen Ned's personal documents? They might go straight to his cottage to return them and find Michael in the middle of his impersonation, while Ned himself lay cold and dead in bed in an adjacent room. Events were hurtling out of Jackie's control and he had no idea how to harness them back within his grasp.

Reaching the phone box in record time and jumping off his motorbike, half-naked, he pulled open the door and almost sank to his knees in gratitude at the sight of the red plastic bag lying where he had left it, on top of the telephone directories. Grabbing it, he jumped back onto the motorcycle and headed back to Ned's as fast as the wheels of his bike could carry him.

There was an awkward silence in Ned's living room, which Jim had rather expected Michael to fill. It was at this stage that most winners could contain themselves no longer and were desperately keen to find out how much they had won. But, instead of asking the big question, Michael sat silently with his glass in his hand, blinking at Jim and waiting. It was the Dubliner who eventually breached the impasse. 'Right, so, I expect now you'll want to know just how much you have won?' he said, prompting the enquiry.

Michael drained his glass and poured himself another, desperately stalling for time. His mind was elsewhere and racing ahead of himself. It would take Jackie at least fifteen minutes, he reckoned, to get up to the phone box and back again. That was, if the little bag was still there. God, he hoped it was. Looking up and seeing from Jim's face that he was expected to reply, he gathered himself in at last and stammered: 'Oh, and – and you'd be in a position to tell me that now, would you, Jim?'

Jim Kelly was a man who really loved his work and this was his favourite part. 'I can tell you exactly how much, Ned,' he said, radiating happiness, pleased at last that the question had come, even if the recipient seemed a little, well, distracted. Never mind, he told himself, first there were some minor details to attend to. 'Do you have your ticket on you?' Jim asked breezily.

Michael was on the edge of his seat. Attempting some bravado, he smiled weakly at his guest but instead of producing the ticket he suddenly stood to his feet. 'Will you excuse me just a minute, Jim – um – I have a bit of an upset tummy coming on,' he said and rushed off to the bathroom, closing the door firmly behind him.

Jim had seen it all before. He knew how distressing and nerve-wracking this business could be. He quite understood Ned's nervous reaction and he sat waiting patiently on his chair, hoping that he would be all right. He wasn't a young man after all, and Jim had noticed that he seemed a little breathless.

Speeding back from the phone box towards Ned Devine's house, still dressed only in underpants and with the red plastic bag held firmly between his teeth like a dog fetching a stick for its master, Jackie O'Shea leaned his head and shoulders into the contours of his motorbike to try and make his huge bulk more streamlined. If only he had told the lottery man that he was Ned Devine when he had asked for him, if only he had thought of something, anything that would have enabled him to play the role of Ned. But instead, Michael O'Sullivan – the world's worst liar – was sitting there now, alone with the sharp man in the sharp suit, and with no one to prompt him or help him through.

Without a doubt, Jackie thought, he would be digging his own grave and making mistake after mistake. The lottery man had probably already smelt a rat and any minute Jackie would see the Mondeo coming back up the hill towards him, a furious Jim Kelly at the wheel, with Michael sitting beside him, under citizen's arrest and being driven to face the Garda at Ballyneath police station. Turning the accelerator lever as far back as it would go, he wished to God he's swapped this old motorbike for something with a bit more power when he had the chance.

Michael was away from Ned's living room for nearly twenty minutes by the time the flushing of the lavatory indicated his imminent return. 'Are you all right, there?' Jim asked, relieved to see him when he emerged from the bathroom door. He had been worried, he was on the verge of breaking it down, just in case the old fisherman had had a heart attack or something similar with the shock of his visit. Stranger things had happened.

Full of apologies, Michael was visibly more relaxed now that the whiskey was starting to take effect and he returned Jim's smile. 'Oh, yes, sorry about that. Must be the excitement,' he said, sitting back down in the armchair a little unsteadily.

'Of course,' Jim nodded his complete understanding.

'Now, er, where were we?' Michael asked. 'Oh yes – the ticket.' Chuckling to himself, he lifted his right buttock and reached into his back pocket, pulling out the small pink ticket, the one Jackie O'Shea had prised from Ned Devine's dead fingers two days earlier; the very ticket Jackie had slipped back into Michael's fingers through the toilet window a minute before. With a look of sheer triumph on his face, Michael handed it over for inspection, saying jocularly: 'Ah, there he is, there's the winner ... What a famous little chap he is.' He rubbed his hands together gleefully as Jim Kelly carefully examined the ticket and its distinctive bar code to verify it.

In a draughty lean-to goat house tucked away at the back of Ned Devine's bothy, Jackie O'Shea, still in his underpants, shoes and socks, sat on a low bench straining to hear the conversation inside. He heard Michael laughing from deep within the cottage and breathed a huge sigh of relief. If only he could hear the words being spoken between the two men, he wished, but the sound of Jim laughing back reassured him that everything must be going swimmingly.

Waiting for Jim to finish examining the ticket, Michael shunted further forward in his seat and asked the question Jim had been waiting for. 'Big win, is it?' he enquired, keeping up the conversation and trying hard to focus on the blurring image of Jim Kelly a few feet in front of him.

Happy that the ticket was genuine, and placing it carefully in the inner pocket of his suit jacket, Jim geared himself up for the big announcement, the highlight of his working week. Leaning forward, his hands clasped in front of him, he adopted his most conspiratorial tone. Speaking deliberately slowly, so as to allow Michael to take in what he was about to tell him, he paused for dramatic effect. 'Ned,' he began, 'you have won –' Michael had it in his mind that it was half a million pounds, the minimum jackpot. Sure that was plenty – £250,000 each between him and Jackie. That was, if Jackie relented and agreed to a fifty-fifty split '– six million, eight hundred and ninety-four thousand, six hundred and twenty pounds.'

A pin dropping in the room would have made an awful clatter. Michael, his eyes on stalks, sat stock still in his chair in a state of near physical collapse, unable to take in the magnitude of what he had just been told. 'Oh, er –' he started to say, but stopped when all the saliva in his mouth seemed to drain away.

Not twenty feet from him and through two thick stone walls, Jackie O'Shea, unable to hear a word from inside anymore, was still crouching anxiously outside, waiting for a sign that nothing disastrous was happening.

His big moment over, the best part of his job done, Jim Kelly had run out of superlatives. Anything he said after that would pale by comparison, he knew that of old. 'How does that make you feel?' he asked Michael politely, his eyes twinkling with delight. He had never once been envious of the winners he met.

With Michael, it looked like he would never know how it felt because the old man continued to stare at him, speechlessly, his mouth opening and closing like some species of giant guppy, a wheezing noise emitting from within the gaping cavity.

Jim smiled nervously. 'Take your time, now, there's no rush ... It's a big shock to the system, I know ... Just give yourself a moment to get used to the idea.' But Michael was still rooted to Ned's tatty armchair, strange guttural noises coming from his throat, his eyebrows rising and falling as he tried in vain to speak. From a wall-mounted shelf, a faded sepia photograph of dear old Ned smiled across at him, a wicked gleam in his eye. 'So what do you think, Ned?' Jim asked again, more nervously this time and wondering if he should call for medical help. Still Michael didn't move, apart from his flapping mouth and animated eyebrows. The noise in his throat had altered to a high-pitched squeak.

Stalling for time, and explaining the unusually large size of the prize, Jim went on: 'Well, it was a rollover week. The jackpot wasn't won last week, so they carried it over to this week, and you were the only winner ... Were you aware of that, Ned?'

At last able to manage a feeble laugh, Michael gradually came to his senses and tried his best to focus on the matter in hand. 'Er – er, no,' he said, blinking repeatedly, knowing now exactly how Ned Devine felt when he realised that not only had he won the lottery, but that the prize – announced after the draw – had been nearly seven million pounds. Michael's own heart felt close to seizure.

Hearing silence inside, Jackie rubbed his hands together against the cool breeze and wondered what on earth was going on. He had no contingency plans, no master scheme to save the day. If there was a sudden fuss inside, indicating that Michael had blown his cover and that the secret was out, then Jackie was all for running for the hills on his bike, clothes or no clothes. If Michael made it out in time, he might just consider taking him with him. But it was every man for himself under such circumstances. The longer the silence continued inside, however, the more jittery Jackie became.

Seeing the colour gradually returning to Michael's cheeks, Jim Kelly began easing him towards the formalities. 'Okay, well, look,' he continued, 'naturally enough, with a claim this size, there are a lot of forms to be filled out, and we can do that today, if you like.' Seeing that his words were still not quite penetrating Michael's brain, he added guardedly: 'But I can always go and come back another day if you prefer.'

Coming to his senses at last and realising that he had to keep Jim from coming back at all costs, Michael suddenly pulled himself together and seemed to be sure of what he wanted. 'No – no – no – no – no –' he said, his words stuck like the needle on an old record, although he was nodding his head. 'Fill 'em in now, Jim,' he added, his mind still spinning with the news.

'Right. Well, let's have a look,' Jim said cheerfully as he lifted his big leather briefcase onto his lap once more, clicked open the double locks and started to pull out the various forms and official documents he needed.

137

Still outside, shivering with cold and wondering what could be taking so long, Jackie O'Shea was losing confidence by the minute. How could it have gone so wrong? Michael O'Sullivan was the worst liar he had ever met in his life – and he'd met a few. He wished there was something he could do, but he couldn't even walk in and surprise them because he was half-naked. He would just have to sit and wait, and patience had never been a virtue he could boast of.

Hearing the sound of a twig snapping behind him, he turned quickly, whereupon a horrified expression fell over his face. 'Oh, hello,' he said, attempting to sound chipper and appear quite normal despite his state of undress, as he looked up into the furious face of his wife.

'And what sort of game is this?' she asked angrily, her eyes flashing, her fingers pointing to his paucity of clothes.

'Shush! Shush will you?' Jackie whispered, grabbing her hand and half pulling her into the goat house with him.

'Don't you shush me!' Annie exclaimed, incandescent with rage.

Bringing her face close to his, his eyes wide and bright, Jackie hissed and pointed at the cottage: 'Michael's in there ... with the man from the lottery.'

'What?' Annie gasped, her fury reaching new heights.

Inside, having been asked to fill in a few basic details about himself, Michael had pleaded the need to go to the lavatory again. Pouring himself another large whiskey, he locked himself in, sat fully dressed on the toilet, his legs crossed. Opening Jackie's red plastic bag, he tipped Ned's documents onto the rough screed floor at his feet. Behind him, wedged in behind the cistern pipe, were several old copies of *The Irish Times* to use as toilet paper. The walls were rough plastered, muddy brown and stained with damp.

'Right, can I have your full name and date of birth, please,

Ned?' Jim shouted through the thin wooden door from the living room, after Michael had assured him that he was still able to answer all his questions, despite his upset stomach.

Slurping from the glass merrily, pleased at how everything was going, Michael reached down and picked up Ned's birth certificate. 'Ned Patrick Devine. Born 17th July 1933,' he yelled through the door. Spotting something else on the certificate, he added, for good measure: 'Six pounds, two ounces.'

Sitting on the wooden chair filling in the various forms and laughing at Ned's remarkable powers of recollection, Jim continued with his questioning. 'Okay, now I'll need to find your, er, social insurance number,' he called through the bathroom door.

Quickly shuffling Ned's papers on the floor and swigging another gulp of whiskey, Michael picked up the relevant document and called back gleefully: 'I know it off by heart, Jim. It's, er, 86 – 43 – 67 – 4B.' He raised his glass in a silent toast to the man from Dublin and took another swig.

In the ten years he had been in this job, Jim Kelly had never once met a winner who knew his social insurance number off by heart. He was mightily impressed. Chuckling to himself, and genuinely surprised, he called: 'That's wonderful, Ned.'

Annie O'Shea was not amused. Crouching down beside her husband, her voice hushed, she continued her gruelling interrogation of Jackie until she was armed with all the dreadful facts. Horrified, she repeated: 'You let Michael go in there on his own?'

Jackie nodded, ashamed.

Aghast, Annie said: 'Jackie, he's never told a lie in his life.'

Jackie's eyes pleaded for mercy. 'Well, he's making up for it now, so,' he said. Both of them looked up suddenly at the sound of Michael's high-pitched tittering from within.

Back in the living room, the toilet flushing behind him, Michael emerged from the bathroom and pretended to be doing up his flies. Jim had gathered together all his papers and put them into his briefcase as he prepared to leave. 'Right, Ned, well it shouldn't be too long now before I can issue the cheque,' he told a delighted Michael, as he rose to his feet.

Fully ensconced in his new role, Michael chided playfully: 'Don't take too long now, Jim, I'll be losing interest on that money.' The pair of them laughed amicably and made their way towards the little front door.

Shaking Michael's hand firmly, Jim said: 'Right, well, I'd best get back to Dublin. There's a lot of paperwork to be sorted out.' Both men reached the door and Michael – looking well pleased with himself – warned Jim once again to mind his head on the beam above the doorway. Bending down and strolling out into the bright sunshine reflected off the waters of the cove, Jim remembered something just before he left. 'Now, Ned, you did write your name on the back of the ticket, didn't you?' he checked, his expression suddenly serious.

'Oh, I did indeed,' Michael nodded enthusiastically, squinting into the sunlight.

'Very sensible of you, it means no one else can claim it,' Jim pointed out.

'That's right,' Michael replied confidently.

'Only thing is it means it'll take a little bit longer,' Jim said, seconds from leaving. 'I'll just have to come back to the village to make some inquires; like to make sure that you are Ned Devine.' His face creased into a smile at the suggestion.

Michael, in turn, let out a sudden and rather forced high-pitched laugh, mocking the very idea of such a thing. Rocking back on his heels and laughing a little hysterically, his forefinger scratching at his head nervously, he was unable to respond.

'Oh, well, congratulations, Ned,' Jim told him again, warmly shaking his hand before walking to his car. 'Take care now.' He threw his briefcase on the back seat, jumped into the driver's seat and started the engine. Looking back and giving a last wave to Michael, standing watching and waving at the cottage door, Jim Kelly drove off, keen to be on the road and heading back to the bright lights of the city.

Stumbling backwards into Ned's living room, his throat like sandpaper, Michael wondered how he could have been so stupid as to allow himself to think that he could get away with the ridiculous ruse. It had all been going so well; he had handled all the lies with the expertise of an arch criminal, but it was all for nothing. Jim Kelly was coming back and he would soon find out that Michael O'Sullivan was many things – a liar, a cheat and a con man – but that he was not Ned Devine. About to sink into a chair to hold his aching head in his hands, he was stopped from doing so by the noise of Jackie and Annie bursting in from the bedroom, having climbed in through the window.

His face alight with optimism, Jackie, still dressed in just his underpants, shoes and socks, couldn't wait to ask. 'Now, are we rich, man?' he asked, his fists clenched in anticipation.

'Or are you off to prison?' Annie asked, stony faced, her arms clamping her cardigan tightly across her chest.

Utterly defeated by the exhausting events of the day, Michael looked up at the pair of them with shattered eyes. 'We're not rich,' he said to his crestfallen friend. To Annie, he replied: 'And I'm off to prison soon enough.'

Jackie could hardly believe his ears. 'But I saw the man's face when he left!' he insisted angrily. 'He thinks you're Ned!'

Michael nodded glumly. 'He believes it now,' he agreed. 'But he's coming back in a few days to ask questions in the village.'

'But all that laughing?' Jackie asked, his body slumping at the realisation of what that would mean.

Michael pulled himself up to his full height and drew a deep breath. 'Jackie,' he said. 'The winnings is almost seven million.' He still found it impossible to take in fully.

'God in heaven,' Jackie muttered, his knees nearly giving way under him. Annie's legs faltered too and she almost fell against her husband as she clutched her chest. Jackie whispered: 'And this is how Ned must have felt, coming so close to a fortune.' Ever the optimist, he added cheerfully to his wife: 'At least we've not woken up dead in heaven.'

But his wife was far from impressed. 'No,' she glowered. 'You're alive – with a prison to go to.' Turning on her heel, her eyes wide with fear, she stormed out past the two of them and hurried from the cottage as fast as her legs could carry her.

Michael glumly watched her go, his body language a picture of dejection, despair and defeat. Looking back to his friend, his heart sank still further at the sight of Jackie's eyebrows wagging at him mischievously, a most dangerous gleam in his eyes.

Chapter
Seven

Last night as I lay dreaming of
pleasant days gone by
My mind being bent on rambling,
to Ireland I did fly ...
I went to see my neighbours
to see what they might say
The old ones were all dead and gone,
the young ones turning grey ...

– 'Spancil Hill', *an Irish exile song*

Banned from his own home, the front door locked and bolted, the shutters barred, Jackie had no choice but to crawl back to Michael's humble crofter's cottage for the night, his tail between his legs. Having sat up around the kitchen table most of the evening, mulling their dilemma over and over in their heads, the two men retired to bed, sitting side by side, drinking hot chocolate.

In reflective mood, Jackie – dressed only in his underpants because Annie had refused him his pyjamas and Michael's didn't fit – sipped from his mug and placed it on the bedside

143

table before leaning back against the solid mahogany bed head. 'If I'd have known how much was won, I'd never have started in the first place,' he confessed, sombrely. 'Oh, Lord, this is getting awful serious … It's desperate.'

At Jackie's side, in his patterned cotton pyjamas, Michael nodded, unable to add anything. Jackie knew his friend was taking the idea of prison hard, and he wished he hadn't got him into it, especially when he had behaved so brilliantly. 'God, you did well today, man,' he told him, thinking of Michael's Oscar-winning performance as Ned Devine.

Michael nodded. 'Me and the whiskey,' he said. 'But Annie's still livid.' That bothered him more than it did Jackie. He hated to be on the wrong side of her.

'Ah, she'll come round,' Jackie told him, not giving his wife's fit of temper more than a second thought. Still thinking of Michael's master stroke of answering Jim Kelly's questions from the sanctuary of the toilet, he beamed: 'What a performance that was. Your Jessy would have been proud of you.'

Michael smiled fondly at the memory of his beloved wife, so full of life and mischief. 'That she would, God bless her,' he said, sadly, placing his empty mug on his bedside table next to a dated but cherished photograph of him and Jessy as a young couple. 'I'd swear she was there today … But Jessy or not, I can't keep it up.' Looking across at his friend, Michael asked quietly: 'Are we off to prison?'

Jackie thought for a while before he spoke. 'Ned doesn't want us in prison,' he said, as sure as if Ned's ghost was sitting on the edge of the bed, telling him exactly what he wanted. 'But I can't believe he wants us to be multimillionaires either.'

Looking suspiciously around the shadows in the corner of the room, half-expecting to see a ghostly vision of Ned, Michael asked: 'Was any of this in the dream?'

Jackie shook his head. 'No, no,' he said, his expression one

speeding back along the road, in the direction of Ned Devine's cottage,
Michael had nothing on but a helmet and his shoes.

'What do you think?' Michael asked, looking like a scarecrow in Ned's clothes.

'You have won six million, eight hundred and ninety four thousand, six hundred and twenty pounds,' said Jim Kelly. 'How does that make you feel?'

Jackie stood and looked around at the people he had known all his life and considered the seriousness of what he was asking them to do.

Lizzy Quinn sat in her disabled buggy fully clothed, surrounded by cats and told them she wanted more than a nest egg.

Inset: 'The village says that you're Ned, so that's good
enough for me,' Jim Kelly told Michael.

Ned had never
looked more
serene than in
his satin-lined
coffin.

Jackie and Michael watched the man from Dublin leaving as
melancholy funereal music floated out from the bar.

As the people of the village watched, Jackie pinned the cheque to the bull's-eye of the dartboard and a tremendous cheer went up.

Lizzy Quinn was on a mission as she bent her head into the wind and drove her buggy up to Killian Point.

ne telephone box was tapulted into the air high ove the sheer cliff face before ashing on to the jagged rocks hundred feet below.

When the string on Dicey Riley's fiddle snapped under the pressure of maintaining such a long and high-pitched note, the villagers in the bar screamed their approval.

The men stood on the hill above Tullymore and raised their spirits to the sky. 'God bless you, Ned, and may we be forever in your debt.'

of puzzlement. 'No, this is for you and me to work out, Michael.' The two old friends finished their night-caps together, before Jackie reached across and switched off the little bedside lamp as they slid beneath the candlewick bedspread, bidding each other goodnight.

Maggie Tooley was doing something completely unheard of. Dressed in her black leather jacket, striped skirt, jumper, brown leather boots and white leggings, she had walked up to the ramshackle stone barns on the edge of the farm where Pig Finn worked high on the moorland above Tullymore, and was looking for him. Calling out his name and causing the squealing piglets at her feet to scatter like nine pins, she cried: 'Finn, Finn, are you there?'

Pig Finn could hardly believe his ears as he recognised Maggie's voice and his head popped out from a hayloft like a cuckoo in a clock. Trying to appear noncommittal as he tossed a bale of straw down to the ground below, he said: 'Of course I'm here, I'm always here.' He was still angry with her for clinging to Pat Mulligan's side all night at Jackie O'Shea's, and for fixing a date with the man, his arch rival.

Ever since they were young boys, Pat Mulligan had taken the things that Finn wanted the most – Laurel, Anna, Rose and Delia – all pretty girls from the village he had set his cap at. Mulligan had beaten him at the yard of ale drinking competitions at Fitzgerald's; the pony and trap races up to Killian Point; he had his own farm, flashier clothes and a seemingly unlimited supply of cash. Defeated early on, Finn had eventually followed his brother Liam to Ballyneath to work on a big co-operative farm, hoping to earn enough to come back and buy his own smallholding. But while Liam went off into the insurance world and made a packet, Finn was laid off as a farm labourer a few years later and returned to Tullymore broke and broken-hearted, only to find that Pat

Mulligan was still getting one over on him. Forced to work with old Paddy Riley's pigs for a living, enduring the constant sniping about the stink on him, Finn looked now to be losing the ultimate contest to Mulligan – and the prize was Maggie's heart.

'I thought I'd come up and see you,' Maggie said breezily, as if it was something she did every day. A black and white sheepdog pulled itself lazily to its feet and nuzzled her hand. Finn disappeared back into the hay loft and re-emerged at a door further along. Coming down the stone steps, his big boots heavy on the treads, he heard her repeat her last sentence, but brushed past her rudely.

'Right,' he said, unimpressed. His look was stony.

'Are you all right?' she asked rather nervously. She had never known him to be this unhappy to see her.

'Great,' he said, his tone clipped, moving away to get on with his work.

'Are you sure?' Maggie asked, following him across the yard. In her hands was a piece of straw and she was twisting it round and round anxiously.

'Full of the joys, boys,' Finn replied sarcastically, as he turned away again, filling a black plastic bucket from a sack of hog nuts and shoving away a greedy sow with a playful slap of her backside.

Trying to bridge the enormous gulf that seemed to have opened up between them, Maggie helped him by picking up the bucket and, following him to one of the breeding pens, she asked: 'What have you been doing?'

Finn threw the straw bale over the galvanised steel gate into the pen and leapt effortlessly after it, to spread it around on the muddy ground. 'I've been thinking,' he said, raising Maggie's hopes momentarily as she followed and watched him from the other side of the gate. Perhaps he was so serious this morning because he was nervous, she thought. Perhaps he was going to make some announcement to her; tell her he was giving up the pigs and offering to make her his wife. She couldn't think why else he could have such a long face.

'What have you been thinking?' she asked, allowing herself a small smile.

Finn spun round, his eyes blazing, and her face fell. 'Oh, I've had a few thoughts,' he said, quietly. Then, with obvious rage, he spat his words out in a torrent: 'I thought about punching Pat Mulligan in the face last night. I thought about telling Maurice that I was the real father and I thought a bar of strawberry soap would make all the difference.' His words were those of an embittered and angry man. Turning away from her once more, unable to look into her eyes, he forked out the straw around the floor of the sty.

Realising how truly angry he was and wanting to calm him, to make him understand her position, Maggie pressed herself up against the gate of the pen and soothed: 'Finn, I love you, you know that, don't you?' She looked as if she meant it. 'If it weren't for the pigs,' she added, 'I'd marry you tomorrow.' It wasn't that she was being unreasonable, she just couldn't stand the smell of pigs. It repulsed her, made her sick to the stomach and there was nothing she could do about it. As long as Finn smelled of pigs, she couldn't bear him to be near him. It was as simple and as cruelly straightforward as that.

Finn listened to her words with bitterness in his heart, reached over the gate to snatch the bucket from her and turned away. 'It's all been said before.' He didn't know how many times, but it had been too often. What could he do? There was no other work available in Tullymore. He was a proud man, he didn't want to be unemployed, claiming social benefit. He wanted to be working, earning just enough to buy himself the odd pint, to take Maggie out every now and again, and maybe even save for a farm of his own one day.

Gesturing to the animals sniffing and snuffling around his feet, he added angrily: 'Anyway, I quite like working with the pigs.' He meant it, he really did. Pigs were warm, loving and affectionate – which was more than could be said for Maggie. They were highly intelligent, answering to their own names and constantly devising new ways of attracting his attention so that they could get their backs scratched or their tummies tickled. Looking down at the sows now, their little pink eyes looking up at him devotedly, he added, softly: 'I get very attached to them, despite the smell.'

Maggie's heart almost melted at his kind words. There was real affection in the way he spoke of the animals he cared for. If only she could overcome her objection and ignore the stench. But she knew she couldn't. The smell was just too pungent, too overpowering for anything else to override it. Plucking at her fingers nervously, there was an uneasy silence between them. Finally, thinking of Pat Mulligan and the offer she overheard him make to Brendy, she told Finn sadly: 'He's promising to look after me – me and Maurice.'

Finn put down his pitchfork and spun round. 'You mean look after, or do you mean pay for?' he said, snorting derisively. He knew exactly what Pat Mulligan's idea of marriage was, and it was a million miles from his. It would involve cheating, and maybe beating, and then making up for it afterwards with gifts and flowers.

'What?' Maggie asked, stung by his unexpected vitriol. She knew the two men were rivals, but she never realised the depth of Finn's despising for the man until now.

Finn rounded on her. 'Maurice belongs with his *real* father,' he said, for the umpteenth time. Closing in on her suddenly, his jaw clenched, he asked: 'Or is Pat Mulligan the father? Is that what this is all about?'

Saddened by his accusation and sadder still that he was

148

once again failing to appreciate her dilemma, Maggie said gently: 'I'm sorry, Finn.'

Seeing this was maybe his last chance to find out if he was Maurice's father, he asked bitterly: 'Well, will you tell me?'

Maggie moved back, as if to leave. 'I have to go,' she said, unable to answer his question, the burning question he had been asking her for nigh on eight years now.

Desperate to know, Finn came to within inches of her, his eyes pleading for an answer. 'Is he mine, Maggie?' he asked, his voice breaking. Turning and walking away quickly without answering, Maggie's own eyes were filling with tears.

Word had quickly spread around Tullymore that Jackie O'Shea had called an extraordinary public meeting in the village barn that night and that all fifty-two members of the village had to attend as a matter of great urgency. The buzz in the air was palpable, as people gathered in doorways, huddled in the bar and finally made their way, in small groups, towards the barn. Standing around in the small first-floor threshing room, people stamped their feet on the straw-covered floor and wondered what on earth it could all mean.

Before long, the whole village was assembled. Smoke and excitement filled the room as they waited for Jackie O'Shea to arrive and take the makeshift rostrum, to tell them what they all wanted to know. Wild rumours started in one corner of the room quickly spread to another, and then swept back again with added spice, all of it highly speculative. One suggestion was that Jackie O'Shea must have sold his land to a developer for a caravan park, and that he was going to break the news to them tonight. The very same thing had happened in County Mayo, when a farmer sold his plot overlooking the sea for millions, and his tiny community had been taken over by German entrepreneurs and ruined.

Others insisted that Jackie had come into some money

through a distant relative, just like Lizzy Quinn had, and was going to share it among the people of Tullymore. All the indications were there, advocates of that piece of gossip argued – the strange way he had been behaving lately, buying drinks at Fitzgerald's and settling his bills, not to mention Annie's recent kindnesses to the women of the village, baking Mrs Kennedy a pie and cooking that fine chicken supper.

Dennis Fitzgerald was among many who voiced concerns they had had for some time that Jackie O'Shea must be sick, terminally ill in fact, and wanted to tell everyone all at once, to save grief. If he was ill, the publican argued, his recent shenanigans all made sense. Others were shocked and upset by the news, unable to believe that a man as apparently as hearty as an ox could be so stricken. But now that they thought about it, they agreed, Jackie had looked a little peaky lately. Oh Jesus, poor Annie, they cried. No wonder she wasn't here tonight, waiting with them. She obviously couldn't face it.

Michael O'Sullivan wandered amongst the people of his village listening to their talk and stifling a smile. How incredible people's imaginations were, he marvelled. He really never thought they had it in them to dream up such wild theories. It was like Chinese whispers and, in the telling, the stories were getting wilder and wilder. Suspecting that he must know something, being Jackie's oldest and dearest friend, several villagers took him to one side and asked what he thought, but Michael only shook his head firmly and told them it was for Jackie to say and that he would be joining them any moment. He just wished he would hurry up.

At the O'Shea farmhouse, Jackie had put on his Sunday best, a clean shirt and tie, a mustard yellow cardigan and his best grey suit. The jacket was hanging ready on the wardrobe door. As he sat in front of the mirror, combing back his silver hair, Annie appeared in the reflection behind him, standing in the doorway, her hands deep in her cardigan pockets, her face creased with worry. He stopped combing his hair and stared at her. It was the first time she had even looked at him in hours. He waited for the outburst he had been expecting all afternoon. But there was none.

Instead, she spoke softly, almost in a whisper, as though to a child. 'You're a country boy, Jackie,' she reminded him, her eyes mournful. 'Do you think you can outsmart the man from the city?'

Jackie swivelled round on the dressing table stool to look at the woman he loved. 'I know what Ned wants, Annie,' he replied gently. 'I'm sure of it now.'

She wanted to scream at him, to remind him how hard he had worked at their farm for fifty years so that he could settle back and take a good rent from it. They were sure of a nice little retirement, something they deserved, and now all he could be sure of was a prison cell. As he turned back to his combing, her gaze remained steady and she said: 'Jackie, Ned is dead. The game's moved beyond talk of dreams and spirits. A crime's been committed. It's a fraud.' Her eyes were misting with tears as she spoke. How beautiful she looked in the lamplight, Jackie thought. How he would miss her if he had to go to gaol.

'I don't want you worrying about me,' he said, turning again and speaking very slowly.

Annie jerked back her head. 'I'm not worried about you, Jackie,' she half-laughed. 'You'll manage ... I think I could probably manage. But if anything happens to Michael ... then God help you, Jackie, for he *will* suffer.'

Jackie was suddenly enormously proud of his wife and of Michael, his best friend. They were two quite remarkable people, if he hadn't noticed that before. How typically selfless of her Christian spirit to worry about the widower; she had taken him under her wing ever since his Jessy passed away, and both men loved her all the more for it. Taking in all that she said, he turned to her once more, about to speak again, to reason with her, but she stopped him. To his very great dismay, he could see a hardening in her eyes, and in her heart. 'How much am I worth to you, Jackie?' she asked.

Jackie looked away. 'Oh, Annie,' he groaned. He wished she would leave it and let him get on with what he had to do.

'No, how much?' she asked, a steely glare fixing him in the reflection. 'How much for Michael? For the farm? For God's sake, what are you going to do with ... seven million pounds?' She almost laughed as she spoke the amount, it seemed so obscene.

Jackie grimaced. 'I – I know ...' he began, but she interrupted him once more.

'No ... Stop ...' she whispered. 'You're on your own from now on,' she said quietly, before leaving the room.

The sun settled into a moody sky. The barn was completely quiet, unlike before. A single naked light bulb dangled overhead, casting long shadows into the corners of the room, and onto the faces of those waiting. All eyes were transfixed, all ears were straining, all hearts beating softly, as the villagers waited quietly in front of the makeshift rostrum on which Jackie O'Shea now stood, about to make the most difficult speech of his life.

Not a word had been said, or a sound made for over ten minutes, ever since he had arrived and made his way through them to the front. They had hushed each other as he walked past, his face grim, the silence creeping across the room like a blanket of fog. Taking the stand, he had stood mutely for a minute, looking into every face, young and old, recognising those he had known all his life – farmers in their flat caps, housewives, fishermen, farm labourers and old age pensioners. He could see their anticipation, sense their anxiety, almost taste their eagerness to hear him speak. For a brief moment, he had wanted to run, to run all the way to Glennskellig Bay and throw himself to the mercy of the sea. It was a mighty thing he was about to do; a mighty thing he was to ask of them, and he wasn't sure now, as he stood like a priest at a pulpit, looking down on these good, simple, law-abiding folk, that it was fair to go on.

It was when his eyes rested on the face of Michael O'Sullivan that his heart soared once more. The old rogue, that lanky leprechaun of a man, was standing right in front of the rostrum, his arms folded across his chest, staring up at Jackie O'Shea, with such a look of mischief and excitement, his mouth twisted into an impish smile, that Jackie couldn't help but smile back. Michael's face, above all the others in the room, spoke to Jackie of the thrill of danger, of the sheer audacity of the risk they were about to take. It reminded him of all the tremendous fun the two friends had had over the years, and of the fun they could have now, with all this money. It reminded him of Ned Devine, the man who had come to him in a dream, who had told him he wanted the money claimed, and urged him to hold the party of a lifetime in celebration.

Breathing in deeply, Jackie O'Shea began to speak to the people of Tullymore. His words flowed eloquently, his delivery was perfect. The notes he had scribbled by way of reminder were left forgotten in the darkness of his pocket. He spoke from the bottom of his enormous heart. He spoke of Ned Devine and the great man that he had been. He told them everything, and he told it as it was, without embellishment. The villagers listened agog, their hearts and minds racing with the news, the adrenaline pumping the blood through their veins as they took it all in, and soaked up the enormity of what they were being told.

Coming towards the end of his explanation, his eyes

sparkling with hope, Jackie said: 'I am not a great man for telling things the way they are. I mean I've been known to add a little colour to stories and riddles for the benefit of those that will listen. Yet, here, tonight, I can swear that all that I've told you is true.'

At the O'Shea farmhouse, the only person missing from the barn was planning an early night. In her night-dress and dressing gown, cleaning her teeth, Annie tapped her brush on the side of the sink when she had finished and dropped it into a glass which already contained her husband's toothbrush. Catching sight of herself in the mirror on the door of the little bathroom cabinet, she looked into the eyes of the woman she was, and wondered where the woman she had once been had gone. Her face was lined, her hair grey. Yet she looked good for her years, despite the hardship and suffering. It had not been an easy life, living with Jackie O'Shea. It had not always been a very happy one. But it had been a good marriage to a good man, and it had brought her much joy and contentment.

She remembered their wedding night those many moons ago, preparing to join Jackie in his bed for the first time, preening herself nervously in front of the very same mirror and wondering how their marriage would work out. Way back then, after she had finished brushing her teeth, she had placed her new brush into the glass next to his and suddenly all her nerves had faded away. Everything was going to be all right, she had realised. This was what marriage was about; standing side by side, facing triumph and tribulation together, come what may.

Hesitating now, she looked carefully for a moment at his worn blue toothbrush and his shaving gear, neatly placed on the shelf beneath it. There was his bristle brush, used to lather the soap onto his face, usually while he sang, badly, at the top of his voice, his razor – the smart one she had bought him for his sixtieth birthday – a little pot of shaving cream and his tortoiseshell comb, its teeth still threaded with a few strands of his silver hair. Studying these small but significant objects, these artefacts of a life, symbols of the man she had married and the man who had helped her through life's trials with a wicked smile and an encouraging word, Annie O'Shea looked again at her own reflection and wondered at herself.

In the barn, now filled with an electric atmosphere like none before, Jackie was nearing the very end of his speech. The villagers were completely captivated. What he had told them was the stuff of dreams; they hardly dared believe it was possible; that Ned Devine had won the lottery, that he had died, and that now Jackie was telling them that it was Ned's most fervent wish that they share the money and all the joy and happiness that it would bring.

These were simple people, many of whom had diligently played the lottery themselves, week in, week out, for years and had never won more than a few pounds. They were willing shareholders in a dream, investors in a miracle and yet, like so many millions of lottery players around the world, they had never really expected to receive any return for their money. Now, here was the farmer from Tullymore, the one man they probably respected more than any other in the village, telling them that their dividend was due, their boat had come in. Wide-eyed and speechless, they stared up at him with near reverence as they listened to his words.

People like Pig Finn, with never more than two halfpennies to rub together and with no realistic prospect of ever getting his hands on any more; a man for whom money would mean he could finally give up working with the pigs and marry the woman of his dreams. Maeve Kennedy, poor as a church mouse all her life, harbouring sad secrets about her past, but never once allowing them to quell her spirit. Money to her would mean a chance to travel again, to see her daughter and grandchildren more often, to go to Dublin and maybe visit the theatre she so loved. Tom Flannery and Dennis Fitzgerald, working hard to make ends meet; men who could now buy their own homes and improve their working conditions; Dicey Riley, the best fiddle player in the village, who could travel with his music and treat himself to a decent fiddle; Kitty Moore, pretty in pink and desperate for love, already planning a coach tour to the Holy Lands in her mind, a holiday on which she might meet the man of her dreams; Maggie Tooley, eking a living from greetings cards, hoping one day to see more of the world and to give her son the experiences she had only ever dreamed of.

'The money will be claimed and divided equally between the fifty-two of us,' Jackie was saying. Bowing his head slightly to indicate his genuine shame, he added: 'Now, I was wrong to think I could claim the money myself, that's not what Ned wants. He wants us to share the winnings, a nest egg for us all. So now, if the Lotto man comes to the village, you say that Ned Devine is alive and well and you point your fingers at Michael O'Sullivan.' Just to remind everyone who he meant, as if they could forget, Jackie pointed him out, as Michael looked around him, smiling nervously.

There was an uneasy pause, as the village reflected on what was being asked of them. Excited as they were by the prospect of the money, dazzled momentarily by the dream, the harsh reality was that Jackie O'Shea was asking them to break the law and to risk their livelihoods – maybe even their freedom – for a share in the pot of gold, a pot whose size they still had no idea of. For such humble, law-abiding folk, people who didn't even need a police officer in their village because no one ever committed a crime, it was a mighty decision and one which would lay heavy on their Catholic souls.

Kitty was the first to speak, raising a hand shyly and

addressing their ringleader from the middle of the throng. 'Jackie?' she asked.

'Yes, darling?' Jackie answered.

'How are we going to recognise the Lotto man when he comes?' Kitty enquired, as people nodded in agreement and murmured that it was a very good question.

'He sneezes,' Jackie said, simply.

'He sneezes?' Kitty asked, incredulously.

'Sneezes,' Jackie repeated. 'He gets hay fever when he's in the country.' Many of the villagers laughed, relieved at last to release some of the tension in their chests.

There was a sudden shuffling in the room and a raucous hooting of a horn as the villagers parted and old Lizzy Quinn manoeuvred her buggy to the front of the crowd, her face as cold and hard as stone. 'Enough of the sneezing,' she said impatiently from under her rain hat and scarf. 'How much has been won?' The murmur that rippled around the room indicated, for once, mutual agreement with the old woman.

Jackie wasn't quite finished yet and waved a hand at her to pipe down. 'Yes, yes, in a minute,' he told her firmly, as she scowled. He had one last important thing to say. It was something that had come to him in the night, as he had tried to get to sleep and failed miserably. It was something he hoped that when, Annie heard about it, might put her troubled mind at rest. Addressing the crowd once more, his hands clasped together to emphasise his point, he added: 'Now, everyone in favour of claiming the money should visit me before sunset tomorrow. If we're not *all* committed, there'll be no claim, and I'll make my way to Dublin to face the authorities – alone.'

He stared down at Michael, standing before him in the front row and looking up in genuine surprise. It was the least he could do, Jackie had decided. He had pushed his old friend into it from the start, forced him into doing something quite against his honest character, and aided and abetted him in the worst possible way. If the village went against claiming the money, he would go and see Jim Kelly in Dublin personally and tell him everything. He would claim that Michael was an innocent, that Jackie had blackmailed him into going along with his harebrained scheme, and that he – and he alone – should stand trial for fraud. Annie was right, he would manage in prison, and so, probably, would she manage without him. The only thing she hadn't counted on, or at least hadn't fully realised during her reasoned attack on his plan, was how desperately lonely he would be in his cell each night without her sweet face to wake up to each morning.

'How much has been won?' Lizzy snapped impatiently from her buggy, breaking his chain of thought.

Jackie cleared his throat as the hall fell silent once more. 'And so we move on to the claim itself,' he started. Just at that moment, the door to the barn creaked open and in stepped Annie, dressed in a coat and scarf, creeping in as quietly as she could. It was perfect timing, as if she knew he was thinking of her face, and Jackie threw her a smile of such love and warmth and gratitude that she couldn't help but return it.

That was enough for Jackie. His spirits lifted, he decided the time was right to break the news to the village and to finally conclude his speech. Puffing up his chest and beaming at them all, filled with that joyful sense of knowing something wonderful that others are about to discover, he cried: 'The total amount of the jackpot, the total which will be claimed and divided into shares of fifty-two ...' he paused for effect, before his face broke into the most enormous grin, 'is ... six million ... eight hundred ... and ninety-four thousand ... six hundred and twenty pounds.'

There was total silence in the room for several seconds. Breaths were held and hearts stopped as Jackie's words resounded around the rafters, bounced off the walls and

158

reverberated in every eardrum. Pupils dilated, mouths open, the people of Tullymore blinked at the man standing motionless before them, tears of mirth rolling down his cheeks as he stood, watching and waiting.

Then, in one spontaneous gesture, one instant of complete unity, every hand thrust upwards into the air, every mouth opened and every lung filled itself with air, ready to roar its delight and approval at the marvellous news. As the village lay still and tranquil under a pale moonlit sky, the most almighty cheer suddenly rose up from the very rafters of the village barn and soared up, up and away into the night sky, shaking the seagulls from their slumbers and echoing away across the bay like the distant victorious call of some wild animal.

Annie O'Shea was sitting up in bed in her night-dress, pretending to read the newspaper, waiting for her husband.

After witnessing the evening's extraordinary events, she had come home, undressed and sat in front of her dressing table in the lamplight, quietly brushing out her hair and gazing at her own reflection. She had still been uneasy in her heart and had stared hard at the face before her, wondering what the dawn would bring. Laying her brush down, she had climbed into bed to wait for Jackie and reflect on the evening's miracle.

She had gone to the barn in the first place to tell Jackie how much she loved him, regardless of his madcap scheme. She would never have believed the reaction of the people of Tullymore to his suggestion unless she had seen and heard it with her own eyes and ears. But, before Jackie could find her, to thank her for coming, for giving him her support, she had slipped away home again, darting out of the door in the general hubbub and confusion, as the villagers hugged each other and kissed loved ones and danced and wept.

Jackie, who had seen her go and called out her name in vain above the cheering, was prevented from following her by the throng of people pressing in towards him, hands and arms outstretched, wanting to touch him and thank him and ask him how much the win would actually mean for each of them. Distracted momentarily from going after his wife, Jackie basked in the praise, soaked up the thanks and told them that he had worked it out to the last penny. They would each be entitled to £132,588.84 exactly. For married couples such as him and Annie, he pointed out, the total winnings would be £265,177.69, a small fortune by anybody's standards and especially in a place like Tullymore, where an average house cost around £40,000 and a good wage was considered to be £150 a week.

The looks on the faces of the villagers were priceless. They knew then that their moment had come; they were living and breathing that magical instant when their dreams had finally been realised. Pushing forward and ignoring Jackie's attempts to resist, they lifted him high onto their shoulders and carried him around the barn like a much-loved king.

The only one not joining in the celebrations, Lizzy Quinn, drove her buggy to the back of the barn and scowled back at them all with a withering stare. 'Stupid eejits,' she muttered under her breath, but no one noticed her. Her face a picture of malice, she set the driving controls and trundled slowly home.

The celebrations went on for over an hour. It was only after Jackie had banged his head on the rafters for the second time that they let him down, and – with much backslapping and patting of shoulders – allowed him to leave the barn and go home to his wife. His face flushed from the excitement, he hurried in through his front door and, finding the house dark and empty, realised that Annie must have gone to bed. He wondered if she was still angry with him, still threatening to leave him because of what he had done. Climbing the winding wooden stairs, his heart in his mouth, he had entered the bedroom cautiously, expecting to find her in bed asleep, turned over on her side of the mattress, her back to him – as it had been so many times before when she was cross – and was delighted instead to find her sitting up and reading by the light of a small bedside lamp.

Quietly climbing into bed beside her, he lay for a while on his side, studying her familiar profile lovingly and not saying a word. 'What changed your mind?' he asked softly, as he lay next to her, looking up at her fixed expression. He was at peace with himself now that Annie had finally come round to his way of thinking. Her unexpectedly strong resistance to his scheme had bothered him much more than he cared to admit and he had nearly given up on the whole idea on the strength of it.

Annie was doing a very good job of pretending to be angry; he had almost been convinced, but there was something about her body language, the way she had pulled her pillows closer to his, that gave her away. Shaking out the newspaper as if she were irritated, she looked sullen. 'You're no good to me in prison,' she said, glumly, focusing on an article, but not really reading it. Try as she might to be cross with him, she never really was, not deep down inside. She loved him too much for that. It was just that she was such a Christian, so utterly law-abiding all her life, that she couldn't imagine condoning anything remotely unlawful. It was only when she had realised how much Jackie was prepared to risk, personally, so that the whole community could share in poor old Ned's good fortune, that she came to believe that what he was doing was morally right; dividing what was rightfully Ned's among the people who had known and loved him all his life.

The alternative was that all those millions would go back into the kitty, that the company which made a very good living indeed on the back of people's hopes and dreams, would benefit even more substantially, denying the people of Tullymore perhaps their only chance of such great good fortune. She felt, somehow instinctively, deep in her Christian soul, that that would be a greater wrong.

Annie's forehead creased at the realisation that not everyone in Tullymore shared her high sense of morality. Looking beyond the newspaper thoughtfully, she added: 'A hundred and thirty thousand pounds each.' Thinking of the extraordinary reaction of her fellow villagers to the news, she shook her head. 'If they come, they'll be coming for the money,' she said, cynically. 'Not for the spirit of Ned Devine, I'm sure.'

Jackie patted her arm reassuringly. 'And if it's claimed and spent at all, he'll rest in peace.' He was clearly quite convinced that Ned's spirit was still in his head, telling him what to do.

Annie hoped to God that Jackie's head was the only place Ned Devine was; she didn't want to be sharing her bed with any unsettled ghosts – especially not with what she had in mind. Looking down at her husband with a strange expression on her face, her eyebrows arching, she said: 'And if you go to prison, this'll be our last night together for … ten years.' Her eyes gleamed in the lamplight.

Jackie got the message loud and clear and he thanked the Lord for it. His lip curling into a smile, he said softly: 'Then let's not waste it with sleeping.' Annie smiled and slid down the bed in a smooth, well-practised manoeuvre, a twinkle in her eye, as her husband reached behind him to turn off the bedside lamp.

Chapter
Eight

We're on the one road, sharing the one load,
We're on the road to God Knows Where
We're on the one road, maybe the wrong road
But we're together now, who cares.

– 'On the One Road', *a popular Irish anthem*

Jackie awoke and lay in bed listening to Annie's soft breathing and the calm still of the morning. The day was already warm, the sea breeze gently filling the curtains like sails. All in the village was quiet apart from the call of the kittiwakes. How busy they always were, wheeling and circling overhead, looking for food and feeding their young ones. Scavengers of the sky, some people called them; visitors to the coast often complained that they were kept awake at night by the birds' incessant noise, but to people like Jackie, who had grown up man and boy with their distinctive cry forming a permanent background noise, their cries were comforting. They were the sound of home, the sound of Tullymore.

He didn't need to look out of the window to know what was going on outside. The main street would be empty but for a cat softly padding past, or a farm dog down from the hills with its owner, tethered to a gate post somewhere. Tom Flannery would already have delivered the post, the people of the village would be in their dressing gowns and pyjamas, making breakfast and reading the mail, listening to the wireless or watching television. There would almost certainly be not a single indication that anyone in Tullymore was in the slightest bit affected by the momentous events of the previous evening. He wondered, as he often had during the night, what they would eventually decide.

Their initial reaction had certainly been favourable enough, but what would they be thinking now, as they ate their toast and considered the issues in the cold light of day? There would always be those like the greedy Pat Mulligan who would jump at the chance, who would never once question the morality of it and whose only thoughts would be how stupid Jackie O'Shea was for telling the rest of the village and not keeping all the money for himself. But what about the others? What about the young priest, Father Patrick, and old Rennie Finn? Would Mrs Kennedy really be able to go through with it? Jackie wondered how many would falter and search their consciences, as he had, for the answer. It was a mighty decision and one which had undoubtedly kept many others awake all night.

It had to be a unanimous decision or he wouldn't go through with it. If they were all in it together, then that was fine, they would all be facing the same penalty and none would divulge their secret. But if one or two resisted, he knew there would be bitterness and resentment that would split the village and it simply wouldn't work. No matter what promises might be made, he didn't want to live the rest of his life afraid that, one day, some embittered villager who had initially refused his or her share of the money might shop him to the Garda out of spite or jealousy. No, it was all for one and one for all.

Exhausted from his night's exertions and his mental ramblings, Jackie slipped from the covers, leaving Annie dozing peacefully and shuffled out of bed in his pyjamas to get dressed and make breakfast. Still half asleep, he thumped down the stairs wearily, his limbs leaden, his clothes dishevelled. 'Will you bring us a cup of tea?' Annie called sleepily from under the bedclothes, a place she had retreated to the minute he threw open the curtains and let the bright morning sunshine in.

Filling a kettle and lifting the heavy cover from the hot plate of the old stove, Jackie reached up for two mugs from a shelf, and opened the refrigerator door to fetch out a bottle of milk. Disappointed, he found that there was none. Annie had spent so much of the previous day on the rampage after him and Michael that she hadn't had a chance to do the shopping.

'Annie, is there any milk?' Jackie called up to his wife, whom he could hear slowly stirring above him. His voice was thick, like his head.

'You'll have to go to the post office,' she called, indicating Mrs Kennedy's store a few hundred yards down the street. Mumbling his irritation under his breath and picking up some loose change from the kitchen table, Jackie counted it out in his hand and headed wearily for the front door, just as the kettle started to hiss and whistle.

'Oh, Lord,' he moaned, not feeling quite ready to face the day yet, least of all Mrs Kennedy, as he stumbled along the hallway and made for the door. Releasing the latch, he pulled it open and was just about to step into the bright outside when he was met with a sea of faces and a headlong rush of eager bodies.

At least thirty villagers pushed past him and into the hallway, making their way to the kitchen with a cheery: 'We're here!' each one apparently as keen as the others to register their name. Open-mouthed, Jackie was pushed back against the hallway wall as the deluge of people flooded in. He found himself, for once, completely lost for words.

Hearing the unusual early morning commotion, Annie had pulled on her dressing gown quickly and come downstairs, her hair still tousled, her eyes still full of sleep, to find her kitchen and hallway full of silent, hopeful faces. From then on, it was open house. All day they came, a steady queue of villagers leading into their home. They left the door and the garden gate unlatched and, as the queue built up, there was an air of excitement unknown in Tullymore since the end of the Second World War.

While Jackie tried to calm his over-excited visitors and get them into some sort of order, Annie had nipped to the post office to buy milk, whiskey and a hard-backed exercise book in which the villagers could sign their names. On her way back home, she had called in at Michael's and woke him up to enlist his help. Dressing hurriedly, he had arrived with his best friend's wife to find a long line of people snaking its way through Jackie's house and out into the lane. It was a most astonishing sight.

Pig Finn had been one of the first in the queue just after dawn, but had to leave and attend to his pigs when there was still no sign of life at the O'Shea's farmhouse by ten o'clock. Coming back later, he was amazed to see how much the queue had grown, but settled in at the back resignedly, patiently waiting his turn. One by one, the villagers had signed the book as those behind them shunted forward. There was very little talk, apart from a bit of nervous chatter, and each had treated the event with the reverence it deserved.

By the time Pig Finn reached the head of the queue, the system was well-oiled and running smoothly. He knew what to do, he had watched the others before him and he took his place in the specially designated chair, facing Michael, Jackie and Annie across the kitchen table. In front of him, on Annie's best lace tablecloth, were several empty glasses and a bottle of whiskey, and the exercise book with a growing list of signatures. Without a word, he took the pen and scribbled his name in the book. Looking up at the three of them, his lips pursed, he took a small glass of whiskey from Jackie, drained it in one and said: 'Right,' nodding his head affirmatively.

'Right,' answered Michael, nodding back with a smile. Some had wanted to chat, but most had said very little, done the deed and run away. It had been Michael's job to speed those along that wanted to linger, and make those who fled feel better about what they had done.

'Good luck,' Finn said, giving all three of them the thumbs up sign and a wink of his eye. His nervousness evident, he was nonetheless quivering with excitement as well.

'Good luck,' they replied in unison, as he rose to his feet and vacated the chair for the next person in line. Looking from one to the other, Jackie, Michael and Annie grinned smugly. This looked like it was really going to work.

The next in the hot seat was Kitty Moore, dressed in her usual pink, her white hair scraped up into a bun. She stepped forward from the front of the queue, and sat down. 'Hello,' she said, almost shyly.

'Hello, Kitty,' they replied together warmly, flashing her a smile of encouragement.

'Now, Kitty, do you remember who I am?' Michael asked, a wry smile curling the top of his lip. Kitty wasn't that bright and he didn't want her to be letting the side down.

'I do, I do, Michael,' she said, clutching her handbag on the lap of her pink woollen suit. 'You're Ned Devine.'

Jackie watched her say the words and grinned. 'Good girl, yourself,' he said. 'Give her a drink, Annie.' Sitting to her husband's left, a bottle in her hand, a row of tumblers in front of her, Annie half filled one and handed it to Kitty.

'Oh, thank you,' Kitty said, grateful for a chance to calm

her nerves, even if it was awful early to be drinking. Taking a delicate sip and placing the glass gently back on the table, she looked mischievously across at Jackie. 'Now, I'll sign on one condition,' she said.

Jackie grimaced and leaned forwards towards her. 'Well, Kitty, we'd not really counted on conditions,' he started to reason, hoping to God the seamstress wasn't going to be difficult.

'Oh, it's only a very small one, Jackie,' Kitty pleaded, flashing her blue eyes at him and rocking back on her chair with disappointment.

'Go on,' Jackie said, warily. Glancing from side to side, Kitty stood up, leaned across the table and whispered in his ear, her hand muffling her words, as if embarrassed to say what she wanted in front of the rest of the village. As Annie and Michael turned away diplomatically, Jackie listened to Kitty's whispered condition, smiled and nodded his head. 'Of course you can, that's no problem at all,' he replied, a relieved expression on his face as Annie and Michael looked on, perplexed.

'Oh, thank you, Jackie,' Kitty beamed, looking askance at Michael. Picking up the pen, she bent forward and signed her name with a flourish.

'There we are,' Jackie announced to her and to the waiting crowd. 'Number thirty-eight. We're nearing the finishing line.' There was a general ripple of approval.

'Well done, Kitty,' Michael said warmly as Kitty vacated the seat and tottered off in her little pink shoes.

'Thank you, Michael,' she said, with a look that bothered him slightly. 'Bye, bye.'

Leaning forward to speak to Jackie, he whispered curiously: 'Was it a big condition, Jackie?' He had tried to hear but hadn't caught a word.

His friend smiled and shook his head, not even turning to

look at Michael. 'Not at all,' he replied dismissively. 'You're having dinner with her next week.' Michael's mouth fell open, but before he could protest there was a sudden commotion in the hallway outside and Dennis Fitzgerald, dressed in his brown overalls and looking somewhat flustered, pushed his big frame past all those waiting in line and flopped sweatily into the chair in front of the three of them, a worried expression on his face.

Frowning and pointing back at the disgruntled crowd, Jackie said: 'Hey, Dennis, you've just jumped the queue. What is it, man?'

Shaking his head, the big man said: 'Jackie, it won't work.' The room fell suddenly silent, as everyone listened to what he had to say.

Jackie was crestfallen. 'What?' Annie and Michael sat tensely either side of him.

'Well, we're claiming a cheque that can't be cashed, Jackie,' he said, as Jackie's eyes flickered his lack of comprehension. Looking to Michael, Jackie could see he was just as puzzled. It was up to Dennis to explain. 'Sure, Ned doesn't have a bank account,' the publican said, looking at all three of them and watching their eyes upon him as he delivered his bombshell.

Jackie still didn't understand. 'What?' he asked. Michael scratched his head. Only Annie seemed to understand what Dennis was saying and she leaned across the table to pay further heed.

'Now, I, I used to work at the bank,' Dennis reminded them. 'It's not easy cashing such a mighty cheque.' There was an expectant atmosphere throughout the house as he continued. To illustrate his point, Dennis asked: 'Did you think Mrs Kennedy would cash seven million at the post office?'

Aghast, Jackie realised that what Dennis was saying was true. It simply hadn't occurred to him how the money would physically be paid out. He thought of Maeve Kennedy now, warbling a song absent-mindedly to herself while she reorganised the chocolate bars and greetings cards. There was probably no more than fifty pounds in her till at any one time. Very few people in Tullymore had bank accounts, most preferred to keep what little they had hidden in an old sock drawer or under the mattress, rather than trust it to some untrustworthy city slickers from Dublin.

But Dennis Fitzgerald had not gone to Jackie O'Shea's just to spread doom and gloom. Although what he had told them was true, he had a plan and, within minutes of speaking, the relaxed party had turned intense and businesslike as he explained to them what they would have to do. Huddled around the kitchen table, he painted as simple a picture as he could in their minds of what would happen.

'We open a cheque account,' he began, 'in advance. Off shore – maybe Jersey – and deposit fifty pounds,' he explained breathlessly. 'Now, it's a joint account ...'

Wagging his hand at him, his brow furrowed, Jackie interrupted him and pleaded: 'Slow ...'

Dennis hardly slowed at all as he continued: '... in the name of Ned Devine and Jackie O'Shea.' Jackie nodded his understanding. 'Now, I'll pretend to be Ned ...'

Jackie shook his head suddenly, having lost his way again completely. 'No, no, slowly, slowly,' he said, his hand palm down and flapping up and down in front of Dennis's flushed face.

Dennis went on: '... and you, well, you be yourself.' He paused and studied Jackie's concentrated expression. 'Now, the account's open a week ...' he continued. Seeing that Annie seemed to be taking it all in, he turned to her to finish his instructions excitedly. 'Jackie puts Ned's cheque in. He then uses his own signature on the joint account, to share out the winnings.' Pleased with himself, he rocked back in his seat, pulled his chin into his chest, and waited for their congratulations and thanks.

But none was forthcoming. Jackie and Michael seemed frozen to the spot as they stared at him, open-mouthed, completely out of their depth, desperately trying to get to grips with concepts they had never previously had need to understand. Nudged by Annie, Jackie finally swallowed hard and stammered: 'It – it's legal?'

Dennis looked up and beamed at them all, his confidence evident. 'It's as close as you'd want to get, boy,' he said triumphantly. Annie's face broke into a smile and she banged a glass full of whiskey hard down on the table in front of him, slopping some of it in the process. Dennis drained it in one and banged it down equally hard.

Jackie, still confused, turned to Michael and stared at him for a full minute without speaking. Finally, he asked: 'Do you understand it?'

'Not a word,' Michael replied honestly, shrugging his bony shoulders. But seeing the happy expressions on the faces of Annie and Dennis, the two old friends nonetheless breathed a joint sigh of relief.

For the rest of that day, the people of Tullymore went about their usual daily business with no outward sign that it was anything other than a perfectly normal August weekday. Bread was baked, meals prepared, clothing washed and hung out to dry and livestock fed. But, on closer examination, there was an unusually light spring in the step of many who passed down Main Street, and a knowing glance in their eyes. Shoulders were pushed further back, heads held slightly higher and an unspoken tension united them.

At the village post office, Kitty Moore was choosing a packet of biscuits. Picking up her usual fruit shortcakes, she studied the packet and the price. Spotting a box of fancy shortbread on the shelf above that was twice the price but, she knew, quite irresistible, she replaced her usual brand and decided to treat herself. Just as she was about to take it across to the counter to pay, however, she remembered Jackie's warning about having to behave completely normally in case Jim Kelly came back into the village and smelt a rat.

Sighing, she picked up her regular brand and wandered over to Mrs Kennedy with them in her hand. Opening her purse and handing over some small change, Kitty couldn't help but wink at the postmistress as she did so. As the ageing blond took her change, she winked slyly back.

Stepping carefully across slippery rocks way out on the cove at Seal Bay, Father Patrick and young Maurice Tooley picked their way through the clumps of pink thrift and white sea campion to a specific spot, chosen by the boy, and stood watching the waves lapping gently at the granite rocks. Gannets and storm petrels from the nearby breeding colony at Carrickey Point, an inhospitable pinnacle of rock rising out of the Atlantic, flocked and flapped and cried their alarm at the sight of strangers. The young priest picked up some flat grey stones and skimmed them deftly across the surface of the water, as the boy stood next to him, silently contemplating the peaceful scene.

'Sit just there and keep looking at the water,' Maurice instructed, his face pensive.

'Where?' asked the priest, giving up his skimming and mystified as to what the boy was up to.

'Just there,' Maurice pointed to a large flat rock overhanging a deep inlet, before sitting a few feet away, puckering his lips and forcing air through the gap in his two front teeth to make a whistling sound.

'And, er, what am I supposed to be looking for?' Father Patrick asked, pulling on his dog collar out of habit and staring at the water as instructed.

'Just sit there and be quiet,' the boy ordered, before continuing with his low whistling call. They sat companionably for a while like that, Maurice whistling, the young priest mesmerised by the rhythmic motion of the water, but when nothing had happened for several minutes Father Patrick broke the silence and voiced his thoughts with a concerned expression on his face.

'Maurice, do you think Father Mulligan will approve of all this Lotto business when he gets back from Lourdes?' he asked. He had come to like and trust the boy; he felt he was his only true ally in Tullymore. As a man of the cloth, he had been terribly shocked at first by Jackie O'Shea's suggestion that the village conspire together to claim the money. Every fibre of his being told him that it was almost certainly against God's will to defraud the authorities in such a way. But – having given it his most careful consideration, as well as praying earnestly for the souls of the villagers – he had come to see that God probably had very little to do with it.

Where was the harm in claiming Ned's money? He had hardly known the old fisherman, in fact he had only met him twice since he had come to Tullymore, but now that the poor devil's death had been formally announced, his body claimed and embalmed by old Jimmy McGlynn and currently lying in state in his bothy ready for the funeral the next day, the priest felt somehow closer to him than ever before. He had stood over the coffin for an hour that very afternoon, looking into the kind old man's face, trying to imagine what he would have wanted, trying to conjure up his soul.

If he had learned anything of the people of Tullymore in his four weeks living amongst them, it had been that they were very wary of outsiders, suspicious of authority and keen to look after their own. Armed with such limited information, he nonetheless felt sure that, given a choice, the old man would almost certainly have wanted the win claimed and shared among those he knew, rather than filling the coffers of a multi-million pound company or being added to a jackpot which would only benefit another community somewhere else, and leave Tullymore bereft.

Why, an injection of cash like this could be the saving of the place, he reasoned. The village had already shrunk in size in recent memory, the young were all moving away and the future was very uncertain as the old were dying off. But, no matter what he thought, it was not him that was going to be here to see it, he remembered sadly. Father Mulligan would be back any day, and even though Father Patrick would tell him that he had only gone along with the plan and signed the book so that the dilapidated village church would finally be repaired, he still feared his reaction.

Maurice was still considering his answer while he whistled. He summoned up a picture in his mind of old Father Mulligan, the avuncular red-haired pastor and family friend to all in Tullymore. He was a cleric of great compassion, a priest who loved a pint and a crack at Fitzgerald's, a man whose needs in life were simple. 'If you can fill the collection box and mend the church roof, he'll be over the moon,' Maurice said finally, giving his honest opinion.

'Do you think so?' the young priest asked, as surprised as ever at the common-sense approach of his young companion.

'I do,' Maurice answered truthfully, still whistling softly at the waves, his face a picture of contentment. Ever since he could remember, he had felt at one with the sea. It wasn't just that he had grown up with it, it was an innate love of the water, a need to be within sight of it, to smell its spume-filled air and taste the salt on his lips. Old Ned had understood. He had always been very kind to the boy, taking him out in his boat and teaching him the ways of the sea. He would miss him and his cheery singing; he had taught him a few sea shanties and imparted a few fisherman's tricks, one of which Maurice hoped now was about to impress the young priest.

'And what about Tullymore?' Father Patrick pondered aloud, his mind elsewhere. 'I mean, what happens if everyone decides to, you know, to move away and set up somewhere more glamorous with their winnings?' It had been a fear that had bothered him all day; a worry that the money would be a death knell to the village, that Jackie and Michael and Annie and Pig Finn would all abandon the place of their birth for the smarter suburbs of Dublin, or use the cash to emigrate to America or Australia.

Maurice wondered at how little the stranger had really learned of the people of Tullymore in his few weeks amongst them. They might well take a holiday and buy some nice things – central heating, a new car, some clothes, a fancy suite of furniture – but few, if any, would move from the only home they had ever known. Instead, they would gradually settle back into their comfortable routines and spend the rest of their lives light-heartedly vying with each other, bragging about places visited and goods bought, over a few pints of Guinness at the bar. Suppressing a smile at the thought, Maurice said firmly: 'No, the winnings will be spent at Fitzgerald's.'

Raising his eyebrows at the thought as he sat watching the sea, the priest expressed his astonishment. 'A hundred thousand in the pub?' he said. But before Maurice could answer, Father Patrick jumped physically and leapt back as the waves parted and up popped the large, glossy wet head of a grey seal, its liquid black eyes blinking up at him, its wide nostrils flaring.

'Jesus!' the priest exclaimed delightedly, as Maurice grinned with satisfaction, but the priest's outcry startled the animal who dipped beneath the water, leaving only a glistening trail of silver bubbles.

Maurice laughed at his reaction and thought of Fitzgerald's, which had been suspiciously quiet on the outside when they walked past earlier. 'It's probably been spent already,' he added quietly, wise beyond his years.

He was right. The celebrations were already in full swing. Inside the bar, the crush of people demanding drinks, calling out their orders to a flustered Dennis Fitzgerald, hurrying back and forth with pints of draught beer, packets of crisps and glasses of whiskey, was threatening to give the game away. The rowdy singing at the back of the smoky room was in danger of leaking out of the sealed windows and doors, despite Jackie's insistence that they should all behave normally in case the lottery man arrived in the village unexpectedly.

Alone behind the bar as usual, Dennis was desperately trying to keep some order, and to keep tabs on who was buying what and for whom. Pig Finn was pressed up against the front, after elbowing his way through from the back, and was calling out his wish list. 'Vodka tonic, gin and tonic, Bailey's,' he yelled above the din. Dennis heard him but was trying to find some room on the bar, which was almost hidden under the weight of beer and spirit glasses, to put down someone else's order.

'There you go,' he told Finn's neighbour Paddy, as he found space for the drinks, before serving Finn the first of his many drinks.

Finn took them and handed some back over the heads of the heaving crowd. 'Where's Tom's Babycham?' he called, still tickled by the idea that the burly postman drank something as unmanly as the fizzy perry with the baby deer motif.

'All right, all right,' Dennis shouted back at him, unable to keep up. To others yelling their orders, all arms outstretched towards him, he called, in exasperation: 'Would you give me a chance? I've only one pair of hands!'

Finn took his drinks and disappeared before any money had been exchanged. Paddy had done the same. In fact, Dennis couldn't even remember whose round it was. Pulling himself up to his full six feet two inches, he opened his lungs and bellowed: 'Just a minute, hold on, hold on, who's paying for this?' worried that he was losing tabs on who owed him what in the frenzy. But the cacophony continued as nobody paid him a blind bit of notice in the joyful melee.

Reaching behind him and loudly ringing the brass school bell he normally used to signify 'Time, gentlemen, please', he stood, sweat dripping off him, and waiting until the bar was silent. Seeing that he finally had their attention, and with all eyes upon him, he shouted across the room: 'Who's paying for this lot, now?'

Everyone in the packed bar remained silent for a moment, exhibiting their usual reluctance to claim responsibility. But then suddenly, all together as they had done in the barn, the men and women of Tullymore raised their arms in unison in response and shouted: 'I will!' paving the way for a renewed bout of uproarious laughing, patting on backs and even more ordering of drinks.

Dennis Fitzgerald couldn't help but laugh. Rocking back on his heels, his hands on his hips, he shook his head in disbelief. 'I never thought I'd see the day,' he cried, and carried on pouring the pints.

The celebrations were mighty, but they did not spread as far as the hushed O'Shea farmhouse. Inside, the couple were alone in their living room, pensively waiting, as Jackie looked out of the window at the reddening sky.

Annie, sitting in an armchair and twisting a lock of her grey hair round and round her fingers behind her ear, shared her husband's tension but tried to calm him. 'We should give her the day,' she said softly, trying to hide her own increasing distress.

Jackie shook his head, unable to wait a minute longer. Moving away from the window, he said: 'The sun's almost set. I'm calling,' and picked up the yellow telephone sitting on a small side table.

Just as he started dialling, the lounge door opened and they both looked up hopefully. But it was Michael, who entered the room, smelling of beer and cigarette smoke, rubbing his hands. 'Are we done?' he asked. But Jackie ignored him and concentrated on dialling the short four digit number he had been repeating over and over in his head since noon, when the last of the willing villagers had signed the book and left. Unable to get through, he asked: 'Michael, is your phone working?'

'Oh, God no,' his friend replied. 'They're all down since the storm.' It was a regular occurrence in Tullymore, exposed as it was to the elements, its telegraph poles battered and buffeted by winds and rains, whatever the season. One winter they had been without a telephone in the village for over a month. The only one that ever worked was that in the isolated telephone kiosk up on Killian Point, the only telephone for miles.

Jackie put the phone down and looked anxiously across at his wife, who, in turn, looked up at Michael. Seeing his confused expression, she explained, 'We're missing one,' twisting her hair tighter and tighter round her fingers.

Michael's flushed face paled. 'But the village is already celebrating,' he said, still glowing from the warm atmosphere of Fitzgerald's. He hadn't known a party like this in the village since Eamonn Daley's three-day wake all those years before. The bars had run dry, literally, with all the drinking back then, and it took more than a week for everyone to recover. With the party already well underway and Ned's funeral tomorrow, it was already threatening to be a repeat performance, and one which would surpass it in every sense.

He wondered who hadn't signed; whoever it was, was probably down at Fitzgerald's now, too drunk to realise that the sun was sinking and they had yet to sign to unite the community.

Annie faltered. 'It's Lizzy Quinn,' she said, her tone as hushed as if she were invoking the name of the devil himself.

The colour drained further from Michael's face. 'Lizzy Quinn! The witch!' he gasped, realising that she was the last person on earth to be found anywhere near Fitzgerald's. If she hadn't signed, she had a reason, and most likely it was simply to spoil it for the rest of them. Thinking of the others in the bar now, reeling and jigging and toasting each other's happiness with beer and champagne, his throat knotted with a sudden realisation. 'God, if the village finds out,' he whispered, 'she'll burn.'

It was almost dark by the time the small group of villagers had picked their way along the remote coastal path to Drumdolan Cove and Lizzy Quinn's bleak grey house. Jackie had initially wanted to go alone, but Annie and Michael insisted that they come along too. Seen leaving for their unpleasant task, the trio had been followed by a group of curious folk, whose numbers had swelled from the bar once it had been realised what their secret mission was. There were no celebrations now, just shadowy, silent figures standing menacingly in the gloom outside the rusting wrought iron gates which stood at the top of Lizzy's long driveway.

Pat Mulligan, his eyes bloodshot from whiskey, slowly dragged a match across the sandpaper on the side of his matchbox and lit a cigarette. As he did so, the flare from the match lit up his face, which carried an expression like thunder. He stood astride a rock at the front of the large group huddled against the night wind in silence, their mood equally black.

Lizzy's house was as dark and unwelcoming as ever, many of its features obscured by an overgrown garden. A single light glowed in the thick-paned window of a downstairs room. The old woman, still in her outdoor clothes because of the cold, and sitting in her invalid buggy, drove over to the window and peered out to see the villagers silhouetted on the hill. Smiling to herself, she began to sing a childhood song under her breath: 'I don't want to play in your yard, I don't want to play with you ...'

Pushing his way through the group, his hands stuffed morosely in his pockets, Jackie O'Shea halted those wanting to push on through the gates and said: 'All right, that's far enough, we don't want to frighten her.' Looking glumly at the assembled throng and at Annie's small bouquet of flowers picked from her garden at dusk, he asked them: 'Right, what have we got?'

Dennis Fitzgerald stepped up and thrust something forward reluctantly. 'Well, I've her, er, toaster here,' the publican said, 'it's all mended and tested.' He hated to hand it over without payment, he felt as if he had lost a battle, but he hoped it would be for the greater good.

'Good man,' Jackie said, taking it from him and tucking it under his arm.

Mrs Kennedy pushed forward from the back with two tins of Felix. 'And I've got some cat food,' she said, duly proffering her gift.

Jackie nodded. 'Grand,' he said, knowing how her cats were the only creatures on this earth that Lizzy Quinn cared for. With something for her himself in his pocket and taking the other gifts, he invited Annie and Michael to accompany him. They moved forward and opened the creaking gate, preparing themselves mentally to do battle with an evil old woman who was threatening to undo everything they had worked for.

Inside, the cracked and peeling walls bore traces of wealthier times – a few oil paintings hung askew, some stuffed animals in glass cases, an old grandfather clock, its chime long muffled, a grand Adam fireplace, bunged up with old newspapers to stop the draught.

Once ushered into the sparse, cold living room, Michael and Jackie sat side by side in their coats on an old sofa watching Lizzy, who was in her buggy, hands gripping the handlebars, surrounded by a dozen cats who purred and prowled over the dusty furniture and licked filthy plates clean. The whole house reeked of cat urine, a pungent scent familiar to anyone who came near the old woman in the streets of Tullymore. Dressed in her rain hat, scarf and winter coat, Lizzy's expression was deadpan as she looked from the two men to Annie, perched uncomfortably on the edge of an old winged armchair whose springs were broken and had thrust themselves upwards through the fabric, shredded and torn by cat claws.

Breaking the silence, Annie, well wrapped up in her coat to keep warm, asked: 'Will I make you a nice cup of tea, Lizzy?' She attempted a smile, but the old woman had always frightened her and she seemed even more formidable now.

'No!' Lizzy snapped, glaring at her in a way that could turn a soul to stone.

Nodding to the cold, empty grate, stuffed full of rubbish and empty cat food tins, Annie asked kindly: 'Should Jackie get the fire going for you?'

'I'm not cold,' the old woman lied. The fire in that grate hadn't been lit in fifteen years, it was too much trouble and she loathed the expense so she just made do.

Suddenly remembering something he had in his pocket, Jackie reached in and fished it out with a smile. 'I brought you a little treat here, Lizzy, to have with your tea,' he said, presenting her with a packet of biscuits. 'There we go. Some nice coconut creams.' Mrs Kennedy had been quite specific about those being her favourite brand. Holding out the packet, with a smile, he waited for her to take them.

'No, thank you,' Lizzy replied sharply, refusing to take the packet. Giving Jackie a steely glare, she added: 'So, you came to get my name on your paper?'

Annie glanced anxiously at her two companions, willing them to remember her advice to go easy on the old woman and let her do most of the talking. 'Yours is the only one missing, Lizzy,' Annie answered, softly. 'Sure, the whole village is waiting for the news.'

Smiling slyly to herself, the spinster said: 'Give me your list.' Jackie reached into his coat and pulled out the little exercise book that everyone had so willingly signed. Handing it to her a little fearfully in case she tore it in two or did something worse, he waited, they all waited as she studied the scrawled list of fifty-one names. 'And I'm the only one missing, you say?' she asked, squinting at Jackie, spittle firing from her mouth as she spoke.

Michael gave her his most appealing smile. 'You are,' he replied, adding, by way, he hoped, of persuasion: 'Lizzy t'would be good for the village.'

Lizzy put the list down on her lap and looked up. 'Did you know that if you report a fraud to the Lotto you get ten per cent of the winnings?' she said, suddenly, her eyes glinting in the stark light.

Fearful, Jackie asked: 'Have you spoken to the Lotto?' He wouldn't have put it past her. There were probably police surrounding the house now, ready to cart them all away.

Lizzy leaned forward and screwed her face up at him angrily. Hissing, she said: 'I'm not stupid enough to be bought by your coconut creams, Jackie, and I'm not stupid enough to call the Lotto.' Leaning back and crossing her arms across her thin frame, she said: 'But ten per cent is six – hundred – and – eighty – thousand – pounds.' She said the figure slowly, allowing time for her words to sink in.

Annie was the most taken aback, her innately charitable nature genuinely shocked by such a wicked threat. 'Oh, Lizzy,' she gasped. 'How could you bear to live in the village if you did a thing like that?' she asked, aghast.

Michael echoed her thoughts. His face pale, he pointed out: 'The whole lot of us'll be in prison,' a prospect he dreaded more than most.

Lizzy Quinn smirked and slammed the exercise book shut on her lap before handing it back. 'Well, there's your answer,' she said smugly. 'There'd be no one here to be bothered by.' She rocked back in her chair, roughly stroking one of her feral cats. There was silence as they sat speechlessly before her. Seeing that she had their undivided attention at last, she continued: 'You see, I'm after more than a nest egg, Jackie, and as I'm the only one that hasn't signed, I figure there's some bargaining to be done.'

His eyes narrowing, his expression full of contempt, Jackie sat stock still and glared at her. 'You're a right witch, aren't you, Lizzy?' he spat. He had completely forgotten Annie's advice about not losing his temper, but by this time she was past caring.

Completely unfazed by his outburst, Lizzy Quinn settled back into her buggy and set her jaw. 'This is my offer ...' she said, about to set out her terms knowing that she had left them no choice but to consider it, and consider it well.

183

Chapter
Nine

Surely some revelation is at hand;
Surely the Second Coming is at hand ...
A shape with lion body and the head of a man,
A gaze blank and pitiless as the sun ...

– W. B. Yeats, 'The Second Coming'

It was a perfect day for a funeral. After the recent inclement weather, cold nights and stormy skies, the sun was shining, the birds were singing and the light breeze pleasantly refreshing as it whipped in from the sea. All was peaceful and calm as the people of Tullymore locked their doors and windows, shut up shop, put on their Sunday best and prepared to join in prayer and song to bid farewell to Ned Devine, a man whose presence they had all so keenly felt in the past, and would even more so in the future.

The men of the village, dressed in black or grey, gathered at his remote seaside cottage for the traditional wake, raising a glass or two of whiskey to help mourn the recently departed. In the good old days, an Irish wake would last three days and three nights and legendary amounts of alcohol would be consumed. Wilder and wilder stories would be told about the deceased as friends attempted to outdo each other, songs would be sung and fond reminiscences shared. In modern times, the age-old rite of passage usually lasted less than a day and was quite moderate by comparison. Yet the tradition continued and survived in southern Ireland, a last bastion of ancient ceremonial pride in a part of Europe which had long ago given up the custom.

Most of the mourners stood outside Ned's cottage on the little shingle beach at the bottom of the cove, drinking whiskey and reluctant to enter in to somewhere they had rarely been invited when Ned was alive. They stood and watched the sun shimmering on the sea, listened to the puffins chattering on the steep overhanging cliff, and murmured quietly amongst themselves about the latest turn of events. Although they were there to honour Ned, and to thank him for his most remarkable legacy, the name Lizzy Quinn was on everybody's lips as they discussed and debated endlessly what they should do.

Across the bay from Ned's salt-stained window in which a single candle flickered in his memory, white horses rode the waves and the terns circled overhead. It was a view that Ned Devine, his father and his grandfather before him, had looked out upon for more than a hundred years, checking the sea before putting on their oilskins, launching their simple boats and heading out to the grey horizon, their hand-woven nets and home-made buoys on board, and with little more than an innate sense of direction and a nose for the weather to guide them and save them from the storms which regularly lashed the coast.

It was a brutal way to make a living, and one which had claimed the lives of many. Exposed to the elements in all weathers, their callused hands cut and red raw from hauling in the nets, their eyes stinging with salt, Ned and his predecessors would spend all day out at sea, from sunrise or before, often to come home at dusk with little more than a couple of pounds of flounder, whiting, dogfish, mackerel or the odd skate. What they couldn't sell to the housewives of Tullymore, they would pack in ice and send to the fishmongers of Ballyneath, but they couldn't possibly compete with all the high-tech trawlers working out of Dingle with their fish-finding sonar and winch-operated nets, and by the time the merchants had cut and then undercut his prices, there was little enough left for them to live on.

Inside Ned's tiny living room now, his mahogany coffin, its lid leaning up against the wall, took pride of place on the table he had eaten his meals off as Jackie O'Shea, Michael O'Sullivan, Brendy Tooley and Dennis Fitzgerald stood sentry either side, staring down at the dead, weather-beaten face of their old friend, his eyes closed and his mouth unsmiling. The old fisherman looked more at peace than ever before, more serene, nestled in the coffin's white satin lining.

No expense had been spared; the plush coffin had been ordered and brought specially from an undertakers in Ballyneath after a whip-round in the village. Mahogany with polished chrome handles was what had been decided upon, lined with satin, the whole box hand-crafted. He had been bought a new suit too, for as Michael O'Sullivan knew only too well, there was nothing in Ned's wardrobe remotely good enough for such a prestigious and solemn occasion.

Dressed now in the black pinstriped suit, and looking smarter than they had ever seen him in life, Ned's corpse was the focus of attention as his closest friends chatted quietly to one another, each clutching a glass of whiskey against his chest. Dr Moran had done his job well. After some gentle persuasion, and a reminder of how much he stood to gain, he had written out a death certificate, giving Ned's time and date of death a full four days later than reality. There was no harm after all; it was natural causes. What did it matter what the exact date was? £132,000 could buy him an awful lot of reasons to forget. He and old Jimmy McGlynn, the village undertaker, had prepared and embalmed the old fisherman's body and laid him to rest in his coffin.

'And in death, be there some peace,' Jackie recited, meaningfully, his eyes pressed shut. 'An angel will cry with choir and sing, to lift out the spirit, that purity brings. Amen.'

His fellow mourners repeated 'Amen' in sombre unison and silently looked down on poor old Ned, each one struggling with his own feelings of sadness and guilt. They were genuinely sad to lose such a character from their midst; they would undoubtedly miss his voice, his cheerful disposition and his kind-heartedness. But there was plenty of good old Catholic guilt in them, too, as they were forced to accept that – without his death – they would not be able to benefit from his millions. That was, if Lizzy Quinn allowed them to.

Dennis was the first to speak, his face glum. 'So, she'll sign for a million, then?' Jackie had emerged from Lizzy Quinn's house the previous evening and broken the bad news to those who had been waiting outside. Dennis, in particular, was furious that he had given up his hostage – the mended toaster – for nothing.

Visibly riled at the thought of Lizzy Quinn, Jackie was still indignant. 'A million!' he said. 'She'll sign for the same as us or get nothing at all.' He was determined not to be blackmailed by the old witch.

Clearly worried, Brendy asked: 'And what if she calls the Lotto?' It was a question which had vexed him all night and ruined, for him, the early celebrations in Fitzgerald's.

The others looked to their ringleader for an answer. Dennis asked quietly: 'Will we call it off, Jackie?' Much as he didn't want to call it off, if Jackie was as determined as the rest of them not to give in to Lizzy, then it seemed to him that they had no other choice.

Jackie shook his head. 'Ah, don't mind her, boys,' he told them. 'She's trying it on. Don't mind her.' He spoke with conviction, he just needed a little more time to come up with a foolproof plan that would keep her, and everybody else, happy.

One solution he was considering – after speaking at length to Dennis Fitzgerald about foreign investment banks – was telling Lizzy that the village had agreed to her terms so that they could claim the prize and cash the cheque unhindered. Stalling for time, they would then each spirit their money away abroad into Swiss bank accounts, where no one could reach it and no authority touch it, before she could stop them. They would then offer her the original share of £132,000 and not a penny more, pointing out that she could take it or leave it. She would never be entitled to her six hundred odd thousand pound reward if the lottery company couldn't recover the jackpot. Faced with such a *fait accompli*, Jackie believed she would have no choice but to accept. He was playing her at her own wicked game and he hoped to God for her sake that she accepted because if she didn't then she would surely meet an untimely end at the hands of some of the less scrupulous members of the village.

At the sound of an approaching vehicle, the mourners put down their glasses, adjusted their clothing and readied themselves for the task that lay ahead. Jackie pulled open the little front door, as Tom Flannery's green Ford Escort post office van – a ladder still attached to the roof rack from his recent house renovations – was carefully reversed into place, and stopped right by the cottage door. Jumping from the driver's seat, Tom, dressed in his grey post office uniform, opened the double back doors of the van, removed his peaked postman's cap and stood gravely to attention, his cap clamped respectfully to his chest as the coffin was sealed, lifted aloft by the largest and strongest amongst them, and carried out.

A few minutes later, after much undignified heaving and puffing, Tom's van was slowly driven up the hill to St Anthony's. In the back, with the doors flapping open as the vehicle rolled cautiously over potholes and over rough boulders, Jackie and Michael sat either side of Ned's coffin, their feet dangling over the edge, holding it in place to stop it from falling out. For as long as anyone could remember, the post office van had doubled up in this way as a funeral hearse; it was one of the few vehicles in the village, and certainly the only one with the capacity for a six-foot coffin, even if the back doors did have to stay open all the while.

Neither Tom nor his predecessors had ever asked the permission of the Post Office to use their company car to perform this ritual duty, but then they had never felt the need. It was an accepted part of the job as far as they were concerned – the careful transportation and delivery of valuable items to their final destinations. Today Tom was delivering the most valuable of Tullymore's goods to that most final of destinations – the village graveyard.

Following the van were half a dozen villagers, walking briskly behind. The rather incongruous procession rounded the corner of the village and entered Main Street with as much solemnity as they could muster, as the rest of the villagers waited. Nearer the church, the coffin was lovingly lifted out of the back of the van and carried aloft on the broad shoulders of the fittest men of the village – Dennis Fitzgerald, Pat Mulligan, Pig Finn, Dicey Riley and others. Conor Riley, the younger brother of Dicey and one of the unofficial village minstrels, walked a few paces ahead, stepping steadily and carefully in his charcoal grey suit and shiny black shoes as he played a mournful tune on his tin whistle. Falling into line behind the coffin, Jackie O'Shea led the mourners, his wife Annie at his side, her head covered in a grey woollen shawl. Michael O'Sullivan walked abreast with them, and the three were followed by Kitty Moore, Maeve Kennedy and so many others who had known and loved Ned Devine.

Heading slowly up the hill towards St Anthony's Church, past a bright green field full of cows, all eyes were on the coffin, all minds on the man they would miss. The sunlight caught the chrome on the handles and the reflection it made danced on the walls and bushes all around them, as if it was the very spirit of the lively fisherman they had come to mourn. With the church bell tolling solemnly to greet them, all thoughts were on the impending service as they entered the churchyard, all hearts bent on paying Ned his due respect, and all hopes pinned on Lizzy Quinn seeing sense and allowing them to share Ned's legacy unimpeded.

With such mighty issues to consider, it was hardly surprising that no one noticed a silver Ford Mondeo weaving its way aggressively fast down the winding lanes to Tullymore high on the hill behind them. Just as the little wooden door to the church was gently pulled closed behind the last mourner, creaking as it did so, Jim Kelly pulled his hire car to a halt in the main street right outside, got out and looked around.

Once the congregation had settled into the carved wooden pews, and the rustling of clothes and service sheets had ceased, Father Patrick, dressed in his white cassock over purple robe, its broderie anglaise sleeve ornate against the undergarment, a black three-cornered hat perched on his head, walked slowly to the front of the church and took his place at the altar. It was a big moment for him, he knew, a chance to prove himself to these people who had so far been so remote. This was a sermon that mattered, an address about someone they deeply cared for; his words would stay in the

190

hearts and minds of all those gathered to listen, and he desperately wanted to make a good impression.

Having parked up, Jim Kelly slipped his suit jacket on and collected some important paperwork and a briefcase from the back seat of his car. He hoped his business wouldn't take long. He just needed to knock on a few doors, ask a few questions, see Ned Devine and then be on his way, off to meet the helicopter pilot and then on to County Wicklow to tell this week's lucky winner how much they had won. The latest winner was a woman apparently, a widow in her fifties, and she had won £2.4 million.

He hoped she wouldn't be difficult – he had once been virtually sexually assaulted by a County Cork spinster he had gone to see. She had jumped into his arms at the news of how much she had won, kissed him smack on the lips and said to him: 'Now if I ask you to marry me, Jim, you wouldn't refuse me with all me millions, would you?'

At least Ned Devine was a harmless enough fellow, if a little simple and lacking in imagination. Jim Kelly suspected that the shy old fisherman would probably die intestate and fantastically rich, having hardly touched a penny of his millions, or caught up in any way with the £1,000 interest he would earn on his money every day. Still, that was his choice; it was his life. If there was one thing Jim had learned in this job, it was to keep his nose out of other people's business. Closing the car door behind him, he turned to look around at the deserted village and wondered where everyone could be.

The church was as packed as the priest had ever seen it and he felt honoured. There was nothing like a good funeral to bring them in. What a stroke of luck Ned's death had been, to give him this opportunity – on the very eve of his departure – to address them all, and to have them listen to what he had to say, for a change. This was Ned Devine's legacy to Father Patrick. Not the money, not the happiness it might have brought him, but the chance now to reach out to the people of Tullymore, to touch their hearts and move their souls. Feeling more and more kindly to the little fisherman he had never really known, but who had given so much to so many, the young priest was looking forward to saying a few words in his memory. After lighting the two white candles at the altar, he climbed the four steep steps to the wooden pulpit, cleared his throat and waited for the coughing and whispering to stop.

Looking down at all the faces looking up at him expectantly, hopefully, Father Patrick's heart soared. Flashing the villagers a winning smile, he said: 'Please be seated,' and they all sank back into their pews and waited patiently for his words of comfort.

'We are gathered here today,' he began, 'to celebrate the life of Ned Devine.' To his delight, murmurs of 'God bless him' and 'Amen' rose up from the congregation.

In her haste to get to the funeral service, Mrs Kennedy had forgotten to lock the door of the post office, an omission she often made in the crime-free backwater that was Tullymore. Opening the door now and listening to its little bell tinkling, Jim Kelly wandered in and looked around, but there was no one about. Standing at the counter, waiting for attention and receiving none, he peered into the empty back room. 'Hello?' he called, but there was no reply.

Wandering back into the main street, swinging his briefcase idly, twisting and turning on his heels to see if he could catch sight of someone, anyone, he started to feel more than a little uneasy, as if some terrible plague had descended on the village during his absence, vaporising everyone and leaving their homes and businesses abandoned in mid activity. That feeling was further endorsed when he knocked on the front door of a little rose-covered cottage just off the main thoroughfare, stepped back, called hello and looked around in vain. Peering through the letter box, he came face to face with the sad eyes of an old yellow Labrador, sitting waiting for its mistress, its brown nose snuffling at him through the gap. 'Where is everybody?' he asked the dog, but of course it could not give him a satisfactory answer.

'Ned Devine meant something to you all,' Father Patrick said, with great feeling. 'And there ... in his passing ... he has made sure that he has left a little something for you all.'

His gaze caught that of Maurice, peering up at him wide-eyed with encouragement, egging him on. 'You'll be missed,' the boy had told him. 'You've done well.' Feeling awkward now, rapidly running out of things to say about someone he barely knew, the priest hoped Maurice had meant it, and that his expression was one of approval, not pity.

With all eyes upon him, all ears listening to his every word, all hearts turned to God, he launched wholeheartedly into a spirited eulogy of poor dead Ned. 'When we think of Ned's life,' Father Patrick announced, 'when we think of the manner in which he was taken from us, we may find ourselves thinking that he was taken unfairly ...' He went on to talk of the twist of fate, the roll of a dice, or indeed, in Ned's case, a drop of the lottery ball that had claimed him.

Jackie O'Shea, sitting in the front row of the church with Annie at his side, rolled his eyes in disapproval and asked himself if it was a wonder that the Church was losing its flock.

Jim Kelly gave up knocking on the fourth door he had tried and took a few steps back to look upstairs for any sign of life. Finding none, and scratching his head, he peered back down the street to where his car was parked, the only vehicle for miles.

He could hardly believe that he had come all this way, by helicopter and then car, only to find the place deserted. It was like a ghost town, not a soul about, and not even a sign of recent life. If he was a superstitious sort, he might have been spooked. As it was, he was just cross that a working day had been wasted. He would have tried to call, to make an appointment to come, but all the phones were down and he had not been able to get through. Disappointed, he flung his briefcase onto the back seat of the hire car and, sighing with irritation, sat in the driver's seat, tapping the steering wheel crossly and trying to decide what to do next.

Should he wait for a while, or head back to Dublin? That would mean coming back another day, a journey he had little time for in his busy schedule. Stroking the steering wheel absent-mindedly, he was just about to turn the key in the ignition when he checked himself and held his breath. Somewhere, close by, he could hear singing. Unless he was mistaken, it was the strains of a Latin incantation. Looking across Main Street to the small stone church and smiling to himself at his stupidity, he reached for his briefcase and quickly got out of the car. Of course, he chastised himself, everyone was in church.

Father Patrick led the congregation rather shakily through the Latin chants and wished to God Mrs Kennedy would stop trying to lead them all through it as if it were a theatrical chorus. Studying his prayer book in preparation for the rest of the service, he didn't notice the stranger's face peering through the clear glass windows at the back of the church. As the singing ended, he asked everyone to be seated and, sitting down himself, he indicated to Jackie O'Shea that it was now his turn to make the address.

Rising slowly from the front row, his old bones aching after several nights without sleep, Jackie, dressed once more in his best trousers, jacket, shirt and tie, climbed up to the small wooden lectern and stared down on the little community he had known all his life. Waiting for everyone to settle, thinking of how close the community had grown over the years – closer still in the past twenty-four hours – he unfolded the notes from his pocket and prepared to read his carefully prepared eulogy to Ned Devine. It was to be his second important address to the community in as many days, and he wanted this one to be as resonant and as meaningful as the last.

'As we look back on the life of ...' he started, but his words were interrupted by the distinctive creaking of the old church door. Jackie looked up from his notes and watched, in horror, as Jim Kelly entered nervously and slipped into the back of the church, trying to be as unobtrusive as possible.

Catching sight of Jackie and realising that he had interrupted the service, the man from Dublin raised his hand, mouthed 'Sorry', and shuffled respectfully to the back, both hands clasped around the leather handle of his briefcase in front of him.

Jackie O'Shea stared and stared at the stranger in their midst. He was frozen to the spot, his notes visibly trembling in his hand. The villagers, only vaguely aware of the arrival of a latecomer at the back, remained focused on the farmer and completely unaware of the dramatic change in events. Like Jim at the rear of the church, they were waiting for Jackie to continue, but, for only the second time in his life, the old man was almost completely lost for words.

'As, as we look back on the life of ...' he began again, as Annie and Michael stared up at him anxiously and wondered what was wrong. Michael frowned. Had his old friend had second thoughts now that he was having to speak of Ned to them all? Annie, too, was puzzled. She had never known Jackie hesitate at anything in his life. And yet, there was another long pause. The villagers became gradually aware

195

that something was amiss, but they didn't know what. Was Jackie unwell? Had the strains and stresses of the past week been too much for the man? They looked to each other and then back to him, his skin pallid, standing like a statue at the pulpit.

Jim Kelly, standing as inconspicuously as possible next to a large flower arrangement, was also perplexed. He hadn't meant to put the old boy so much off his stride. He wondered what the problem was and if he should leave and wait outside.

Suddenly overwhelmed by the scent of the adjacent flowers, he fought to find a handkerchief and quell a sudden and violent sneeze. It was too late, however. Within a few seconds he trumpeted an enormous sneeze that was so loud and so forceful that it actually blasted several of the petals clean off the flowers. Snuffling and sniffing, Jim was mortified. God, he hated the country.

The people of Tullymore, hearing the massive sneeze echoing round the church and resounding around the rafters, were suddenly and most painfully aware of the late arrival's identity. Turning slowly in their seats to take a look at the stranger, then swivelling back to face Jackie and finally glancing nervously at each other, there was a rising sense of panic in the air as Jim Kelly blew his nose and sneezed again. Jackie, desperately trying to think on his feet, cast an eye over the faces of the congregation hoping for inspiration.

Kitty Moore was clearly worried, her top lip was quivering. Maeve Kennedy – in her best black Italian lace shawl, a legacy from her well-received performance in *Kind Hearts and Coronets* – briefly considered exhuming her once-famous theatrical faint, so as to cause a welcome distraction, and Pig Finn felt like running to the hills. Maurice Tooley leaned over to his mother and whispered into her ear to ask her who the man was. She leaned back and told him, warning him not to give the game away. Maurice, his eyes wide, swivelled round and stared at the stranger as if he had just landed from Mars. Maggie bit her pretty bottom lip and stared up at Jackie like the rest of them. Annie O'Shea, her heart thumping in her chest, felt her husband's pain.

Struck dumb, Jackie's eyes finally rested upon Michael O'Sullivan, his old friend and confidante. Michael's expression was like no one else's. Instead of looking fearful or anxious, it was positive, inspiring and full of encouragement and faith. Jackie nodded his acknowledgement of the support his friend was silently offering him, half-smiled to himself, carefully folded his notes back into his pocket and turned to the congregation. Refreshed and inspired, he started anew.

'Michael O'Sullivan,' he began, his eyes locking with those of the man he was talking about, 'was my great friend ...' Relief and pride flooded into the facing of the smiling villagers who even began – although quickly stopped – a faint ripple of applause. Jackie continued: ' ... but I don't ever remember telling him that.'

As Michael's eyes began to well, and those of Annie beside him, Jackie carried on, his passion aroused, his confidence restored, a smile tugging at the corner of his mouth. 'The words that are spoken at a funeral, are spoken too late for the man that is dead,' he said. Jim Kelly, listening at the back, half-smiled at his words, impressed by his eloquence.

'What a great thing it would be,' Jackie was saying, as all the faces looking up at him smiled, 'to visit your own funeral, to sit at the front and hear what was said, maybe to say a few things yourself.' He stared at his old friend once more and, one by one, the villagers stared across at him also, several eyes moist.

'Michael and I grew old together' Jackie said, his voice catching in his throat, ' ...but at times, when we laughed, we grew younger.' Michael's steel grey eyes nearly spilled over with tears and his Adam's apple bobbed up and down in his throat, as Annie reached across and squeezed his hand.

'If he was here now,' Jackie concluded, his voice rising to a crescendo, 'if he could hear what I say ... I'd congratulate him on being a great man ... and thank him for being a friend.'

The church door burst open, and there was an unseemly rush as the coffin was hurried from the building towards the graveyard, the villagers quickly following. They seemed in unusual haste, Jim Kelly thought as he held back to make his enquiries, talking to a select few about Ned Devine. One by one, those questioned nodded and pointed to Michael as they talked. Kitty Moore, Maeve Kennedy, Dennis Fitzgerald, all concurred in their testimony that the man standing smoking a cigarette next to Jackie O'Shea was, in fact, Ned Devine.

Jackie and Michael were resting on the church wall watching Jim asking his questions, neither one speaking. Breaking the awkward silence at last, Michael said slyly, 'Well, he must have been a great man, this Michael fellow.' His eyes were bright with emotion after the wonderful eulogy he had just listened to.

Jackie shrugged his shoulders, keen to underplay his kind words. 'He had his faults,' he snapped. The last thing he wanted was Michael O'Sullivan going all gooey-eyed on him. He had meant every word he said inside the church, but he didn't want a grisly post mortem now. Inhaling the fresh morning air, he turned to see Jim Kelly approaching.

'Hello there, Ned, are you well?' Jim asked Michael, shaking his hand.

'Er, not bad, Jim, not bad,' Michael nodded, shaking it back.

Turning to Jackie, Jim looked genuinely contrite. 'Jackie,' he said. 'I'm sorry about interrupting like that earlier.' Jackie said little but smiled and shook his head to indicate that it was forgiven and forgotten.

Michael took Jim to one side slightly and said: 'Er, Jackie knows about our little bit of business here, Jim,' he said, referring to the lottery win.

Jim smiled back. 'Ah, good,' he said, nodding. 'Well, I'm glad you've a friend you can confide in now.' Although in his heart of hearts, he wasn't really sure if the lovable rogue Jackie O'Shea was the best person to confide in. Jim couldn't put his finger on it, but there was definitely something slightly shifty about him. He hoped he wouldn't lead Ned astray.

Michael asked: 'And, er, will you be making your enquiries today?'

Jim shook his head and grinned the satisfied grin of a man whose job was done. 'Oh no,' he said. 'There's no need. The village says that you're Ned so that's good enough for me. I can issue you with the cheque today.'

Michael nodded his understanding, puffing on his cigarette furiously. Seeing his face pale slightly and thinking that he might have been too hasty, Jim looked concerned and reached out for Michael's arm. 'Although, are you sure that this is a good time?' he asked, fearing that perhaps he had been a little insensitive talking about money so soon after a funeral.

Michael faltered slightly, but reassured him. 'It is, Jim,' he said. 'As good as any.' He nearly added that this particular funeral day was the best possible day, but he bit his tongue.

Jim's face broke into a dimpled grin once more. 'All right,' he said, keen to be getting on. Asking Michael if there was somewhere quiet they could go to conduct their business in private, he was pleased to hear Michael tell him that he knew just the place.

Fitzgerald's bar was full to overflowing once more. Dicey O'Riley was playing a suitably melancholic tune as his brother Conor kept rhythm on a bodhran and the villagers stood around, murmuring, smoking and quietly drinking. Outside, in the cobbled lane, more people stood around, drinking and talking in respectful tones about dear Ned. There was a sense of great expectancy in the air, nerves were on edge and the funereal songs from the musicians were only adding to the tension.

In the small low-ceilinged back room behind the bar, Jim Kelly and Michael O'Sullivan had been conducting their business behind closed doors for several minutes now. Twenty-eight to be precise, according to Dennis Fitzgerald, who paced restlessly in the middle of the room, checking his watch and waiting for a sign. Finally, the door opened, and the two men emerged smiling, Michael with his jacket off, his braces holding his trousers onto his thin frame.

Pushing their way through the throng towards the low doorway, Michael asked his guest politely: 'You wouldn't like a drink, Jim?' The last thing he wanted was for the man from Dublin to linger, but he felt it would be rude not at least to ask.

'No,' Jim replied, following on behind, anxious to be getting on. He had a rendezvous with the helicopter pilot and he didn't want to miss it.

'No,' Michael repeated, carefully avoiding the piercing stares of his fellow villagers as he picked his way between them.

'I'd best leave you alone now, Ned,' Jim explained, almost at the exit. This job was certainly one in which, with a little encouragment, he could easily become an alcoholic. Drink surrounded him everywhere he went – usually champagne. In any event, the company rules were pretty strict regarding what he could and couldn't accept by way of gifts. One celebration drink was allowed, out of courtesy, but no more, and offers of cash or presents were to be refused at all costs. And there had been many offers. It was amazing how generous people could be when they had just discovered that they had won several million pounds. Why, one old boy had offered him a thousand pounds cash, there and then, as a 'tip' for bringing him the news. It was lucky for the company that Jim Kelly was an honest man.

'Well, that's great, Jim,' Michael replied with feeling as they reached the door. 'Mind your head now.'

'Will do,' Jim said, ducking his six feet two inch frame to get through.

Seeing them leave the bar at last, Dennis Fitzgerald wandered over to the musicians – still playing gloomy funeral songs – and, out of the corner of his mouth, he murmured: 'Tighten up your strings, boys.'

Blinking as they emerged into the bright sunlight outside, Jim and Michael were met by the smiling face of Jackie O'Shea, also in his shirt sleeves and braces, a wicked twinkle in his eye.

Turning to shake his hand for the last time, as another sad refrain wafted out from the bar behind them, Jim said: 'Well, the best of luck, Ned. Give me a call if you need any more advice.'

'Right,' Michael said, his head already spinning with Jim's little pep talk about offshore investments, gilt-edged shares and government bonds. It was that which had taken all the time, the actual signing of the cheque had taken no more than a few seconds.

Pulling Michael away from Jackie slightly, Jim gave him a small word of warning, the same message he gave all his winners. 'And, er, watch your friends, Ned,' he said, half-smiling. 'Don't be spending all your money in one go.'

Michael smiled back and shook his head. 'Oh, no, I wouldn't do that,' he promised.

'Okay,' Jim said, apparently convinced. He turned back to Jackie O'Shea and shook his hand firmly. 'Jackie,' he said, with genuine warmth. 'Good luck to you. Take care.'

Shaking his hand vigorously, a slightly deranged smile on

his face, Jackie answered, a little too enthusiastically: 'Oh, good luck, man.'

'Look after himself, now,' Jim added, nodding towards the man he knew as Ned Devine.

'I will, I will,' Jackie cried, real passion in his voice.

'All right,' Jim said, looking from one to the other for the last time. 'Best of luck.'

Michael, equally euphoric, added: 'Thanks, Jim,' as the man from the city turned and walked slowly away, the eyes of the whole village upon him as he sauntered happily up the cobbled lane, his briefcase swinging in his hand, pleased with his day's work.

As soon as Jim Kelly had disappeared from sight around the corner, and the village had held its breath, waiting to hear the sound of his car's engine fade away, an uncanny silence descended. Jackie and Michael stood squinting into the sun, watching Jim Kelly's car disappear up the lane and over the hill, and the hush crept in to Fitzgerald's bar, filling it, stilling tongues, silencing musical instruments and quashing whispers. The villagers huddled together, gathered around, mute with tension, their attention wholly focused on the open door.

Standing within its low frame, silhouetted against the sunlight, Jackie O'Shea's bear-like bulk appeared and cowed them all into absolute noiselessness. A small piece of paper in his right hand, he moved slowly forward towards them, scattering them in his path, as each person stood back, clearing a way to allow him through. A solemn expression on his face, his eyes blazing, he pushed his way through to the focal point of the bar – the village dart board pinned to the wall to the right of the smoke-blackened fireplace – and raised his big arms.

As everyone stood watching, their breaths still held in abeyance, Jackie O'Shea pulled out a dart and, with a single stabbing motion, used it to nail a freshly-written cheque to the bull's eye. Made out to Ned Devine and dated that very day, 17 August, and signed by James Kelly and other Lottery Commission Officials on behalf of the Irish National Lottery, it was for six million, eight hundred and ninety-four thousand, six hundred and twenty pounds.

The deed done, a tremendous cheer went up and the band struck up a merry jig. As people hugged and kissed, danced and leapt in the air, all hell broke loose. Jackie O'Shea turned to face the villagers, his eyes filled with tears of joy, as Michael and Annie stood in the doorway watching and smiling. Embracing him warmly, congratulating him on his brilliance, the people of Tullymore surrounded the old farmer and thanked him for what he had done.

Basking in the limelight, Jackie nonetheless reminded them through the din that it was Ned Devine they should be thanking, not him; Ned Devine who deserved all their praise. Heading for the bar to buy the first round, he suggested they each toast the man. Dennis Fitzgerald stood grinning behind the bar, his shirt sleeves rolled up, a towel thrown over his shoulder, and prepared himself for a long night of pouring pint after pint after pint.

Chapter
Ten

Fill to me the parting glass,
and drink a health whate'er befalls
Then gently rise and softly call,
Goodnight and joy be to you all.
Of all the comrades that e'er I had,
they're sorry for my going away
And all the sweethearts that e'er I had,
they'd wish me one more day to stay.
Since it fell into my lot,
that I should rise and you should not
I gently rise and softly call,
Goodnight and joy be to you all.

– 'The Parting Glass', *a traditional Irish song*

Jim Kelly's silver Mondeo headed quickly out of Tullymore, winging its occupant home via Wicklow to the fume-filled streets of Dublin where his hay fever rarely, if ever, bothered him. Keen to get home, anxious to see his wife and children, he pressed his foot even harder on the accelerator as he swung the car dangerously round the hairpin bends.

He was genuinely happy for Ned Devine. The man appeared to be as honest as the day was long, and God knows, he must have had a hard life, fishing the seas all his days. He deserved a little happiness and wealth in his twilight years – and nigh on seven million should certainly buy him that, Jim thought with a smile. He wondered if the old rascal would do anything truly risky with the cash – travel the world, marry a supermodel, buy his own yacht – although he had suspected all along that he probably wouldn't. He thought that his eccentric friend, Jackie O'Shea, would probably have more fun with the share that Ned would undoubtedly give him than Ned would himself.

Jim had seen it all before. Time and again he had been invited in to the most mediocre houses, sat in drab living rooms, facing colourless people and telling them the news that most people only ever dreamed of hearing. After an initial flurry of excitement, a brief fluttering of hearts and minds, the winners would often come out with the most unimaginative of answers to the question: 'What do you think you'll do with the money?' Sitting blinking at Jim, struggling to come up with something they really wanted, they would announce that they were going to buy a new caravan, treat themselves to a new suite of leather furniture, remodel the kitchen or go to Europe for a holiday.

Few ever leapt into the air screaming, cracked the champagne and talked of the sort of things he would like to have had the money to do – shopping trips to New York, a cruise to the South Pacific islands on the QE2, a flight on Concorde, an all-expenses-paid safari in the Serengeti, a hot-air balloon holiday over Thailand. He would sit and nod and smile and admire caravan brochures and photographs of the couple's last trip abroad, and wish that they would open their minds a little and allow themselves to go wild.

But he had also come to learn not to judge people too

harshly. Each to his own, the saying goes, and it was necessary to accept that in this job. What some considered the height of luxury and extravagance was, to others, nothing less than common and ordinary. But he suspected that it was the people like Ned, and others with similarly limited horizons, who would – in the long term – be happier with their winnings than those whose expectations were so very much higher.

As Jim rounded the final bend at the top of the hill, he looked back for the last time at the panoramic view that incorporated the little hamlet of Tullymore, and wished Ned Devine and his gentle neighbours nothing but health and happiness.

The celebrations were in full swing at Fitzgerald's. There was dancing, music and drinking. Almost every member of the community was there, celebrating their success, toasting their future and thanking God for Ned Devine. The smoke from pipes, cigarettes and cigars clung to the low-beamed ceiling like a cloud and billowed out through the open door. Kitty Moore, already on her second dram of whiskey, was prancing around nimbly in the middle of the room, her skirt lifted with one hand, as she showed some of the younger girls a folk step she had learned as a child. Michael O'Sullivan sat watching Kitty's shapely legs tapping and skipping in quiet appreciation, a contented smile set deep within his lined face.

Maggie Tooley, her face flushed with the heat and the drink, her eyes on fire, pushed through the crowd, grabbed Pig Finn from behind, spun him round and shouted in his ear to be heard above the din. 'Finn, you're stinking!' she yelled, her lips smiling.

'I'm sorry, Maggs,' Pig said, hanging his head in his customary apology.

'Stinking rich!' Maggie shrieked and fell headlong into his arms, oblivious to his offensive stench as they embraced.

Pushing him off briefly, Maggie grabbed him by the lapels of his best black jacket and said: 'No more pigs,' her brown eyes staring straight into his soul. It was an order, not a request.

Hesitating for a moment and then breaking into an enormous grin that engulfed her with its breadth, Pig replied: 'No more pigs,' and they kissed passionately for the first time in years. Spinning her away from him suddenly along the length of his arm, her long dark hair flying, he started to dance an old Irish reel with her, his eyes twinkling. 'Ah, come for a burl, girl,' he said, adding cheekily: 'You've beautiful calves.'

Pat Mulligan, sitting in a corner, a pint of Guinness in one hand and a meat pasty in the other, stopped eating mid-mouthful and stared at the pair of them frolicking in the middle of the room, his eyes narrowing to slits at the sight. So, Pig Finn had won the contest – and all because of money. Well, he thought to himself angrily, Maggie Tooley was a stupid eejit. Pat had all the money she'd ever needed before the lottery win, and now she was going to end up with a good-for-nothing farm labourer. Pigs or no pigs, Finn was still a peasant worker. She'd soon tire of him and his simpleton ways. No matter, Pat concluded, sipping on his pint once more. He'd find what he wanted in Dublin, where his charms were appreciated. Chances were, he'd sell up now anyway and move there permanently. There was certainly nothing left for him in Tullymore. Downing his pint in one, he decided to drown his sorrows and have another drink.

Finding a brief lull in the celebrations after the initial flurry of ordering, Dennis Fitzgerald poured himself a pint and leaned on the bar facing Jackie O'Shea, Michael O'Sullivan and Brendy Tooley, all in shirt sleeves and braces, all almost lost behind a stack of empty glasses. Jackie was drunkenly enjoying the music, his fingers tapping the edge of the wooden bar in time to the tune, his eyes closed as he revelled in the fiddle playing of young Dicey Riley. God, that man was good. He hoped he'd never leave Tullymore. They'd need a good fiddler now more than ever before, what with all the mighty parties they'd undoubtedly be having in the next few years.

Brendy, maudlin through drink and thoughts of Ned's death, stared morosely into the bottom of his glass. In a pause between choruses, he asked Jackie: 'Any news from the witch?' There was a worried expression etched on his face.

'No, Brendy,' Jackie said, seemingly unconcerned. 'I think we've heard the last from her.' He had decided in the last few hours that Lizzy Quinn would not, after all, go through with her threat. Much as she liked to frighten them all, the idea of living alone in Tullymore would frighten her even more. With all of them in prison, the village would die and she would have no choice but to move away. This was her home, too; she had never known any other and when it came to the crunch Jackie was convinced she would back down and begrudgingly accept the £132,000.

Dennis was not so sure. 'What if she calls the Lotto?' he asked, the thought of prison even less appealing now he could see the cheque pinned to the darts board just a few feet away.

Jackie waved his hand at them. 'She won't call,' he promised. With a twinkle in his eye, he added, grinning: 'Anyway, the phones are down ... What's she going to do, walk to Dublin?' There was silence for a moment as the three men either side of him took in what he was saying. Suddenly seeing the sense of it, they fell against him, laughing riotously at the very thought and raising their glasses in a reverential toast to Telecom Eireann.

Through the haze of the late summer evening, Lizzy Quinn sat at the wheel of her disabled buggy making her way jerkily up towards the second hill on the outskirts of Tullymore, a look of sheer bloody-minded determination on her face. Still dressed in her rain hat, scarf and anorak, her grey woollen tights and moon boots, this was a woman on a mission. If she had to go all the way to Dublin on this infernal machine, she would, she had decided.

Lizzy was completely outraged that the villagers had ignored her demands. With the lapse of time she had realised that the Lottery representative must have fallen for their little ruse. Well, she'd see just how long he would last in his job by the time she was finished calling up the National Lottery company and that award-winning investigative journalist she liked, Sam Smyth from *The Sunday Independent*. He'd soon blow the story wide open.

How dare they ignore her! She had been taken advantage of for way too long by the people of Tullymore. Now she planned on showing them a thing or too. They'd be sorry when the Garda arrived in force and carted them all away in a police van. What did she care if it meant she was left all alone in the village? She might as well have been alone for years anyway, for all they cared about her. And with six hundred thousand pounds reward money in her pocket, she could afford to get in some help. She had it all worked out and she wasn't going to be deterred. Her head down as her machine lurched unsteadily up the steep incline, she cackled at the very thought of Jackie O'Shea's face when they locked the prison gates behind him.

A mile behind her, far beneath the point she had reached, Jim Kelly's silver Ford Mondeo continued to speed upwards along the narrow lane east, lurching him from side to side, as the tyres gripped the tight corners with a squeal. All around him, the heather painted the hills with a patchwork of purples and mauves and whites. The sea was to his right, a treacherous drop away at the bottom of precipitous cliffs, and the higher he climbed, the more spectacular the view across the bay.

He had always enjoyed driving, and he loved the freedom these roads gave him. There was rarely, if ever, another vehicle in his way and he could race along at a fair old speed and pretend he was in the South of France, and that the glinting sea to his right was the Mediterranean. In a few weeks' time he would be on that very road, overlooking the Med, with his wife Helen and his three daughters. The holiday had been booked for weeks; he was treating them to two weeks in the Côte d'Azur, and he couldn't wait. It was the closest he would ever get to living the millionaire lifestyle, and it was only for a fortnight, but it was enough.

Pressing the button that opened the electric window on his driver's door, he inhaled deeply as the wind ruffled his mousy brown hair. Smiling broadly and pressing a compact disc in to the stereo, he waited for the fiddle music to start up and thanked God for a job which gave him so much pleasure and allowed him to spread so much happiness. It was infectious.

After splashing through a high hilltop brook which spluttered and tumbled across the road and down to the cliffs to create a magnificent coastal waterfall, the electric motor on Lizzy Quinn's buggy started to make a strange whining noise, and a hot smell emitted from it as she continued apace. Cursing it under her breath, daring it not to go on, the buggy carried valiantly on up the hill for a few more yards before finally coming to a shuddering standstill, its circuitry soaked and shorting.

Furious, she leapt from it with the agility of a mountain goat and rushed round to the back to examine the gently steaming vehicle. 'Bitch! bitch!' she spat, kicking the buggy violently with her left foot before abandoning it and storming off up the hill like a woman half her age.

She wasn't going to be defeated by the wretched machine.

It could stay there and rot, for all she cared. With all the money she was about to make, she'd buy herself a new one and to hell with it. Scowling miserably, her arms pumping at her side, she marched on to Killian Point, less than half a mile away at the top of the hill, her jaw set firmly, her mind set even firmer.

The heat and the smoke now filled Fitzgerald's Bar like a fog, but no one seemed to mind. Kitty Moore, her cheeks rosy, her eyes bright, clung to Michael O'Sullivan in the middle of the room, watching the dancing and, for once, he seemed to be enjoying her company.

In the middle of the floor, Maggie Tooley was spinning and whirling like a dervish, her skirt flying, her arms outstretched to a dancing Finn, as the music increased in pace and tempo. 'I'm watching you, fella!' Finn joked, as an eighty-six year old fisherman called Joe Sullivan stepped into the middle to give his girl a spin.

'Go on, boys!' someone shouted from the back as Dicey Riley fiddled more and more furiously and his brother Conor, sitting at his side, a burning cigarette stuck between his lips, the smoke closing his eyes, beat frantically on the bodhran, his left hand flicking backwards and forwards so fast over the tight drum skin with the little stick that it was almost a blur.

Father Patrick, his dog collar discarded, his eyes slightly glazed, watched the lustful antics of Maggie and Pig Finn on the dance floor and tried to prise his eyes away. Standing next to him, long given up with women, Dennis Fitzgerald nudged him wryly. The priest blushed and looked away as the thumping Irish music increased to a rousing beat.

Lizzy Quinn, still muttering to herself, her face shiny with perspiration after her spirited climb to the cliff top, reached the isolated green-painted telephone box on the cliff edge and entered purposefully, pulling the door open with a bang and stepping inside, her handbag clutched to her side. Puffing from her exertions and safely ensconced, she slapped the telephone directory open at the page headed Gambling Associations.

Her gnarled and crooked index finger followed the lines down until it stopped at the address and telephone number of the National Lottery in Abbey Street, Dublin. Picking up the receiver with a snigger, and concentrating on the page so hard that her tongue rolled out of the corner of her mouth, she carefully began to dial the seven-digit number.

Jim Kelly entered and cleared the ford further down the hill at such speed that the water sprayed up like a fountain either side of his car, soaking the road and drenching his windscreen. He put the wipers on as soon as he found the correct lever in the unfamiliar vehicle, but not soon enough to see the abandoned disabled buggy he had just passed at the side of the road.

Perhaps he should try the brakes, he thought. It was always a wise precaution after driving through water, and these roads were certainly testing on the braking ability of any vehicle. But before he could put his plan into action, he felt the familiar tingle high up in his sinuses, the tugging of eyelid and nasal muscles, and knew he was about to sneeze. Pulling a handkerchief from his pocket, he tried desperately to steer at the same time as the pollen grains in his nose and throat conspired together to squeeze his eyes shut. Preparing himself for the usual trumpeting outburst, he began the 'Aaah, aah, aaah, aaaah ...' that would eventually end in a resounding: 'Chooo!'

At Fitzgerald's Bar, Dicey O'Riley and his brother had launched into a rumbustious, foot-tapping, harmonious piece of folk music, as the drunken and befuddled villagers stood around in respectful silence, their bodies twitching with the rhythm as they egged them on. Maggie and Finn stood shoulder to shoulder, leaning into each other, nodding their heads in time to the music and holding their breaths as the two men played; Kitty and Michael did likewise. Jackie O'Shea stood in the middle of them all, enthralled. Dennis Fitzgerald, his head shaking in wonder at the talent of the young musicians and the speed of their fingers, felt as if each note was beating on his heart strings. All were transfixed as the music climbed to a climax as Dicey reached and then strained to hold an incredibly high-pitched note, which lingered perilously in the air.

Holding the handkerchief in front of his face, Jim Kelly felt as if his head was on the verge of exploding. This heather was really playing havoc with his hay fever. Gulping in great mouthfuls of air as he started the ascent into his sneeze, he could hardly see where he was going. His eyes streamed water and his nose felt as if it were on fire. Not bothering to slow down to take account of the impending explosion, he maintained the engine's revs as he sped towards a solitary phone box on a sharp curve in the road at the very edge of the cliff.

Inside the telephone box, Lizzy Quinn, her heavily hooded eyes narrowing with concentration, pressed the ear piece into her ear as she finished dialling, and listened attentively as the ringing tone echoed through her head. 'Come on, come on,' she muttered impatiently, keen to get on to the correct authorities and shop the village. The sooner she got through, the sooner she would get her hands on all that money and be rid of the lot of them, she reasoned, as someone at the other end of the line finally picked up the telephone and said: 'Hello?'

Unable to hold the sneeze in any longer, Jim Kelly let it burst out in an almighty 'Aaah – aah – Choo!' the force of which threw his whole body forwards and, for a moment, caused him completely to lose control of his car. Swerving violently to the right, his hands flailing for the steering wheel, he looked up just in time to see the green telephone box just a few feet in front of him. Inside, through the little panes of glass, he saw clearly the horrified face of Lizzy Quinn, who had looked up just in time to see him coming straight for her. Screaming at the top of her voice, she watched in terror as the vehicle travelling in excess of sixty miles per hour, sped towards her on a direct collision course.

Screaming as loud as Lizzy, his mouth wide open, his tonsils oscillating, everything seemed to go in slow motion for Jim as the vehicle and the telephone box moved closer and closer, seconds away from impact.

Grabbing the small leather steering wheel and yanking it dramatically to the left, Jim managed to swerve away from the box at the very last moment, missing it by inches. Glancing back over his shoulder to see what he had just missed, he wondered at his good fortune in avoiding it. Lady Luck really was smiling on him today, he gasped.

Inside the kiosk, an ashen-faced Lizzy Quinn saw the car hurtle past a few centimetres from her and felt its vibration and gasped a huge sigh of relief. Pressing the palms of her hands against the glass to support her legs, which had all but given way beneath her, she found herself completely unable to speak to the woman calling to her down the receiver. 'Hello, hello?'

Jim Kelly was still wildly off course. His tyres screeched and he bumped up the small kerb, heading straight for the flimsy wooden fence that was the only thing between him and oblivion. He violently yanked the steering wheel further round just in time to save himself from going over the cliff edge. Skidding dangerously back onto the wrong side of the road, he opened his mouth and screamed once more when he found himself face to face with the first vehicle he had ever come across on these isolated lanes. He was caught, it seemed, in a never-ending nightmare. The battered blue Ford Transit mini bus came speeding towards him around a blind corner, the Mondeo forcing it to swerve dramatically to avoid collision.

Still fighting for breath and trembling from the shock, Lizzy Quinn heard something in the ear piece as the telephonist at the National Lottery offices in Dublin repeated: 'Hello? Good morning? National Lotto.' Trying to gather herself together, the old woman shakily brought the receiver to her lips and tried to force herself to speak.

The wide-eyed driver of the minibus fought desperately for control of his vehicle after swerving to avoid the silver car. Skidding inexorably towards the telephone box, clinging on to the wheel for dear life and only just managing to avoid going over the cliff edge himself, the driver pulled on the heavy steering wheel to bring the car to the right of the road. As he passed by the box at speed, the vast majority of his lumbering vehicle missed its target, but he was unable to prevent the front offside nose of his bus from clipping the telephone box on the right-hand corner – a collision of such force that it caused the kiosk to break free from its concrete base, launching it high into the air above the precipitous cliff.

Spinning and twirling mid-air in a dramatic pirouette, the booth was breathtakingly suspended in the late afternoon sky before gravity took over and it hurtled head-first down the sheer rock face, sending up a flurry of gulls and terns.

At Fitzgerald's Bar, Dicey Riley had held his high-pitched single note for over a minute, its piercing and pure sound capturing the hearts and minds of all those standing motionless, enthralled. Their breaths held, their eyes wide with wonder at his feat, the people of Tullymore felt as if their very future depended on the outcome of his playing as all eyes focused on the straining string, Dicey's bow vibrating against it in a trembling, quivering motion that matched the fluttering of their hearts.

Finally, and only after considerable and prolonged strain, the note came to a dramatic and sudden end when the string on Dicey's fiddle unexpectedly snapped with a resounding and discordant twang.

It landed with a sickening crump on the tiny shingle shore below, and immediately succumbed to the might of the crashing waves.

Thrilled with his performance, delighted by his bravado, a huge cheer went up for the fiddler, as the villagers of Tullymore put their hands together and cheered, whistled and stamped their applause for the remarkable endurance of the player and a wonderful heart-stopping end to his tune.

Jim Kelly, completely unaware of the accident he had caused behind him, gave himself the sign of the cross in thanks for his life, that of the woman in the phone box and the other driver. Turning off the fiddle music on his CD player, he resolved to take it much easier on the roads from now on. The helicopter pilot would almost certainly wait, and if he didn't Jim would just have to spend a night in a hotel in Ballyneath. Nothing was so important that it was worth dying for.

Reaching for his handkerchief once more and blowing his nose, he slowed right down just in time to cruise out past the little village boundary sign, glad to be away from further danger and heading home.

The St Anthony's Community Club minibus stopped a few dozen yards from where the telephone box had once been and, as the dust settled, the driver's door opened and out stepped a very shaken Father Mulligan, fresh from his pilgrimage to the Grotto de Massabielle, the holy shrine to Bernadette. Leaning against the minibus for support, his knees trembling beneath him, he staggered round the back of the bus. It was plastered with stickers reading: 'Jesus Loves You', 'Honk If You Love Jesus' and 'I Love Lourdes'.

Reaching the cliff edge, a terrifying brink a hundred feet above the sea, and peering down to the shingle far below, he could just see the shattered remnants of the telephone box splintered and spliced on the rocks, being lapped by water. Repositioning his jacket around his plump waist and straightening his thinning hair, he have a huge sigh of relief, looked skyward and made the sign of the cross, grateful at least that the phone box had apparently been empty, and that no one was killed.

By eight o'clock that evening, Fitzgerald's had been thumping non-stop with celebrations as the people of Tullymore got crazier and crazier on a combination of alcohol and delirium. Their boat had come in, the cheque was still pinned to the dart board to prove it, and they could hardly believe their luck. Everyone was drunk, even Mrs Kennedy, whirling and twirling to a reel on the dance floor. Father Mulligan had arrived breathlessly from Lourdes and, on learning of the remarkable events of the previous few days, had joined in the celebrations admirably, sinking the pints after what he had mysteriously described as a 'brush with the devil' on the road into town. He had some good news too for Father Patrick; the church was offering him the chance to stay on in Tullymore for a little longer, and be his deputy. Everyone was delighted, not least young Maurice Tooley, who had taken a real shine to the young priest.

Under a table in the bar now, Maurice was on the floor swigging from a ten-year-old bottle of whiskey and puffing on a large cigar. A hand reached down and unceremoniously pulled him up onto the bench. Pig Finn grabbed the cigar from the boy's mouth but had second thoughts about the whiskey when he saw the quality of it. He poured the boy and himself two small measures before downing his in one gulp. Maurice was impressed and tried the same before coughing and spluttering the whiskey all over the table. Jackie O'Shea watched the two of them from across the room, extremely tipsy, but blissfully happy.

Maurice's mother suddenly joined him, placing her drink on the table next to his, and snuggling up next to him. 'Hello,' he said, smiling at her and putting an arm around her shoulder fondly. He had always had a soft spot for Maggie. He liked to think she was the daughter that he and Annie never had.

'How are you, Jackie?' Maggie asked, leaning into him, the fondness mutual.

'All right, darling,' he replied. Looking across at Maurice who was smoking his cigar once more and snuggled up ever closer to Finn, Jackie added: 'I was just looking at your man there – Al Capone.'

Maggie grinned and nodded, happy to see the two people she loved more than life itself sitting side by side so companionably. Hesitating slightly, she looked suddenly pensive. 'Jackie?' she asked. 'Would you say Maurice needed a father more than seven million pounds?'

Jackie smiled again as he continued to watch Finn playing with the boy. 'I'd say he needed a father more than fifty million,' Jackie said feelingly, his voice slurring.

Maggie nodded her emphatic agreement. 'That's what I thought,' she said, obviously contented.

Jackie sat for a moment before his forehead creased into a concentrated knot. 'But what are you saying?' he asked.

suddenly, his befuddled mind working overtime. 'How would he be entitled to the money?'

Maggie paused a long while before answering. 'Ned does have family, Jackie,' she said slowly, staring at her seven-year-old son.

Jackie followed her gaze to the fair-haired boy and for the very first time spotted the resemblance. That strawberry blond hair, the green-blue eyes, even the gap between the teeth. Both of them had the look of the Viking about them, they were the only ones in the village who had. How could he have been so blind? Shocked, he cried: 'No!' The very idea of Ned Devine bedding the lovely Maggie was quite astonishing to him. The lucky old devil.

Maggie wagged a finger at him, regretting that the drink had finally loosened her tongue. 'You'll not tell a soul now,' she made him promise.

Still astounded, Jackie stuttered: 'M-Maurice is the millionaire?'

Maggie laughed aloud. 'Yeah,' she chuckled. Following Jackie's train of thought, she explained: 'Ned treated me better than any man before.' It was eight years ago, it was just the once, one summer's afternoon after they'd been drinking at a village picnic and he had kindly offered to show her his old fishing books and photographs after she had shown an interest. Wandering back together arm in arm, they had started talking and laughing and she had found herself increasingly drawn to him. By the time he had got her in through the low doorway of his bothy and sang her a lilting song or two in that angelic voice of his, she was smitten. It was she who had made the first move, she who had reached over and kissed his lips, she who had led him purposefully towards the bed. What had followed was a golden afternoon, a few hours of unbridled passion and loving and it was a time she would never forget.

The thought of Ned's tenderness to her in his tiny fisherman's cottage still brought a warm feeling to her heart and a smile to her lips. She was proud that he was Maurice's father, glad that she had known the man, happy to feed on the memory of it for ever. But she knew what the village tittle-tattles would say if they ever found out; she knew Pig Finn would never find it in his heart to understand or forgive her, and she had told Ned firmly that it would never happen again. He was comfortable with that, he had told her. He even joked that now he had been with her, he would die a happy man. He promised never to tell anyone, and she vowed to do the same herself, even when she found out that their lovemaking had accidentally created a child.

It was only then that she had panicked. Terrified of her father's reaction, afraid of what the people of the village would think, she had sunk into a deep despair that had only been broken by the kind attention of Finn, who knew something was wrong but not what, and wanted to help. When the two of them ended up making love a few weeks later, her first thought had been that she was already in enough trouble and shouldn't be so stupid again. Shortly afterwards, she had broken off their affair. But when news got out that she was pregnant, Finn had put two and two together and made three and – fond as she had always been of him – she had never wanted to disabuse him of the fact that he was not Maurice's real father.

Hearing of Ned's death like that – in the village barn, surrounded by all those people, with Jackie O'Shea breaking the news to her so unexpectedly – she had wanted to break down and weep for the man who had meant so much to her, but she couldn't. When Jackie had gone on to tell them that it was Ned's wish that his lottery money be shared between all of them, she had allowed herself a small smile and – remembering the man – had agreed that that was almost certainly what his generous-hearted spirit would have desired.

Jackie's mind was already way ahead of her. He now realised with horror that, by his actions, he had inadvertently deprived this poor single mother and her only child of the money that was rightfully theirs. Through his own personal greed and his stupid interpretation of what Ned had said when he had come to him in a dream, he had robbed her of the cash that rightfully belonged to the boy. Surely that wouldn't have been what Ned really wanted? Surely the old fisherman would want his only living relative to inherit the lot? Sitting upright and speaking forcefully, Jackie said suddenly: 'You must take it all, Maggie. Take it all. Put it away for yourself and the boy.'

But Maggie shook her head. 'No, no,' she said firmly. 'Maurice can do without it. Besides, Finn would know he wasn't the father,' she added, her eyes glowing with love as she looked at the swineherd ruffling her son's hair. 'I can do without the millions,' she said, a smile twisting her mouth, 'but I can't afford to lose Finn.' Grabbing her glass and patting Jackie's arm, grateful nonetheless for his generous gesture, she said briskly: 'Sure, a hundred and thirty thousand each is plenty.' In fact, by her calculations, once she had married Finn – as she fully expected to do – she and Maurice and he would have a nest egg of nearly £400,000 between them.

Raising her glass and leaning in to Jackie, who raised his own, she gave the Gaelic toast for good health. 'Slàinte,' she said, beaming at him.

'Slàinte,' Jackie repeated, smiling back.

As the hours slowly passed and the people of Tullymore wandered home drunkenly to their beds, a peace descended over the village. With the stars still twinkling in the last

221

remnants of the clear night sky, a final group staggered from the bar, singing one of Ned Devine's favourite shanties before joining their womenfolk.

Dawn loomed pink and golden, threatening to bring bright shafts of sunshine to sensitive eyes and sore heads. High on the hill above the village, a group of four weary men and a young boy were staggering to the top to watch the sun rise. Legs were tired, but spirits were high, as Jackie O'Shea, Michael O'Sullivan, Tom the postman and Dennis Fitzgerald neared the summit. Each man was carrying a bottle or glass. Maurice slumped sleepily on Dennis's broad shoulders.

When they had first set off from Fitzgerald's an hour earlier, their number had been ten. Worn out by the exertions of the night – many villagers had been dancing a jig for three hours solid before the old farmer had suggested they go climb the hill – one by one, the younger men had faltered at the back, their legs giving way as they collapsed to the ground exhausted and fell into a deep slumber where they lay. Swigging from the bottle, Jackie had ploughed on through the dripping trees and heather, ignoring their dwindling numbers. 'Come on, now,' he encouraged. 'We're almost at the top. We can sleep it off later like the rest of them.' Only Michael and big Dennis kept up, with Jackie close behind. Tom, whose legs were used to walking these hills, maintained the rear.

Finally reaching the top, a craggy tor known locally as Ballybere Head, the men stopped and looked out across the sea, swathed as it was in a mystical mauve mist.

Inhaling deeply, filling his lungs with the crystal clear sea air, Jackie O'Shea stood tall and proud, looking back down at the place of his birth and the home of his heart, and across the smooth waters of the bay to the most glorious sunrise which was just about to begin. The soft pink sky of dawn had faded, the mist was clearing and shafts of gold and red fractured the haze, filling the sky with a golden light that danced in their eyes. Jackie's spirit raged as he stood, his fist clenched in victory, his animated expression firing each one of them with enthusiasm as they gradually caught their breath, looked up and drank in the breathtaking scene. Each man stood silently for a moment, basking in the glow and grateful for the moment.

Filling his glass and passing the bottle of finest malt whiskey around the little group, Jackie said: 'Do we all have a drink?'

Michael took the bottle from him and poured some whiskey into his own glass which he then passed up to the boy – still sitting astride Dennis's shoulders – with the words: 'Here, Maurice, take a drink ... and remember the man.'

Lifting his glass skyward, and squinting into the brilliant red sun that was just emerging as a dazzling light on the horizon, Jackie stood square into the breeze coming in off the sea and allowed it to buffer his clothes. His voice tremulous with emotion, he called on his fellow men to pay their respects. 'Then raise your spirits to the sky,' he said, his hand way above his head, his eyes momentarily closing. 'Raise them to Ned Devine,' he said. 'God bless you, Ned, and may we be forever in your debt.'

The three men standing behind him each stood just as proudly and held up their own glasses to the heavens in salute. 'To Ned Devine,' Michael echoed, raising the bottle, his eyes misting over.

'To Ned,' the other two men chanted in unison, before taking a large swig and closing their eyes in sweet remembrance.

Maurice Tooley, the very future of Tullymore, the only living relative of the man whose life and death they were acknowledging, wiped the sleep from his eyes and ignored his pounding headache to raise his own glass to the heavens.

'To Ned,' he said, addressing his toast to a man he fondly remembered, and knowing instinctively that it was a name he would somehow never forget.